DOUSED

the white warrior series: book four

Nichelle Rae

The White Warrior Series

Book I: Only a Glow
Book II: The Blaze Ignites
Book III: Steady Burn
Book IV: Doused
Book V: Embers Under the Ash (Coming Soon)
Book VII: Fire of the World (Coming Soon)

Other Books by Nichelle Rae

Frost Burn
Lights Fall

PROLOGUE

"We can't get near him, your majesty," the Salynn standing beside me offered, wisely keeping his distance from me. "He has some sort of powerful shield around him. None of us can penetrate it."

I kept my gaze on the king. He was a tall, barrel-chested human man. He was intimidating in many regards, with thick steel gray hair cut to the nape of his neck, and a kempt beard of the same color. He sat on his throne, looking down at me with intelligent and curious blue eyes. He was wrapped in so many layers of red and gray royal robes that I began to wonder if he was actually as thickly built as he looked.

As he gazed at me with seeming kindness, I actually thought for a moment I could respect the man. But he was still king of the realm I loathed. This land had banished my parents and cut off their hair centuries ago for speaking highly of the White Warrior. If it hadn't been for two rebellious Wizards who also had thought highly of the White Warrior, my parents would have died and I never would have gotten the gift of two ancient Wizards— something unheard of in this modern age of weak and watered down magic.

I wished I could be somewhere else, but I was here for Azrel, standing here, demanding to be heard, even though I wanted to run in the opposite direction. I wouldn't fail her. She needed an army desperately and Godel's military was massive! Three million strong in the land alone, though I wasn't dumb enough to think that would all join our cause. Some would rather die than trust the White Warrior again. Still, Godel made for some very intimidating numbers.

The king raised his nose to the air and scratched his neck, keeping his eyes fixed on me. "What are you saying, Siado? That you and your best cannot take one boy?" But I knew he wasn't truly interested in capturing me—not that he could if he tried. I sighed softly, realizing the king just wanted to see what I could do. "Take him," the king ordered. Curiosity came over his face as he watched and waited.

Siado approached me wearily and slowly. They had already tried to apprehend me outside the mountain, a venture that hadn't worked out very well for them. The king's eyes became intense as he watched. When the thirty of them got within four feet of me, there was a loud snap, as sharp and loud as a boulder snapping in two. All of them flew through the air until the walls of the throne room stopped them, hard.

I crossed my arms, keeping my eyes on the king. He didn't flinch, nor did he show any concern as Siado and his men picked themselves up off the floor. His eyebrows went up, though, as he looked at me. "Apparently you *cannot* apprehend one boy." He stood from his throne, hiking up his robes, and made his way down the short staircase toward the floor. "Tell me, has he given voice to his demands?"

"No, my Lord," Siado responded with a slight groan as he rubbed the back of his head.

"Well then, boy," the king said, coming toward me, "What can the people of Godel do for you?" He paused a distance away and narrowed his eyes as he looked at my hair, seeing my red Sallybreath flowers for the first time. "A boy who seems to be one of us, but whom I have never set eyes upon."

"I am *not* one of you!" I barked back.

"But you have red Sallybreath flowers. Those are the Godel color, yes?"

"I am not one of you," I said lower.

The king nodded once. "Very well then. Clearly you are not a threat. One as powerful as you could kill my men, and kill me for that matter, at any moment. Yet you have not. So what is it you would like? And may I have your name as well?"

"My name is Addredoc and I would speak to you, King, in private. I have sensitive matters to discuss with you."

Siado stepped forward. "I must advise against this, your majesty. This boy cannot be trusted."

The king had yet to take his eyes off me. "Nonsense, Siado. He is a Redian. I will speak with him privately." The king held open his palm to a small door to the right of the throne room. "Shall we?" I nodded and we both headed toward it.

I entered first and walked to the right toward the very back of the oval-shaped room so the king could enter without feeling the effects of my shield. He closed the door and with a wave of my hand, I took my shield off and put it on the door. The king took a seat at the head of the long oval table and I took the seat diagonally to him.

"Well then, dear boy. My name is King Irban. What is it I can do for you?"

I sighed. "Do you want the sugar-coated version?"

He eyed me quietly for a moment. "That bad, aye?" I merely nodded. "Very well," he said and sat back in his chair. "Give it to me straight, young Addredoc."

I interlaced my fingers on top of the table and leaned forward. "Have you deployed any scouts beyond your boarders recently that might give you *a hint* as to what is happening in Casdanarus?"

"No. All of the men I can spare are on our eastern and western borders protecting my land from the savages in the Ruin of West Godel, and the ever-looming threat of Shadow in the Black Mountains."

"You're still at war with the Ruin?" I asked, confused.

Irban shrugged. "I suppose those posts are more like sentry duty now. No one has been seen on either border for quite some time. But that might be because my military is in place. It is an effective deterrent."

I looked down at the table and rubbed my forehead with my fingertips before meeting the king's eyes again. "I understand your concern in the east and west, but I guarantee you those militants are just getting fat and bored. I need you to call them in."

Irban looked at me evenly. "And why would I do that?"

"Because I need them to go to war."

"War?" the king said, showing surprise and concern for the first time. "What has happened?"

I was quiet for a brief moment. There was no telling how this man was going to react to the news. His reaction could bode very unpleasantly for me and for him, because if he panicked, I had already resolved to cast a spell on him to fire him up for war. It wasn't something I wanted to do, but it was something I'd need to do if this didn't go well.

"Hathum has returned," I finally said, and watched him closely through a narrowed gaze. The king's eyes went wide with fear for a moment, but also seemed to ignite with a warrior's fire at the same time from deep within. Next would come the real reaction I was interested in. "And so has the White Warrior."

The king hesitated a moment and then quickly got up from his chair and went to the opposite wall of the room, standing with his back to me. I trembled as I watched him. I had a spell ready for an unfavorable reaction to that news, too.

The king placed one hand on his hip and stroked his beard with the other as he stared at the blank wall. "The White Warrior, you say?"

My eyes narrowed. "I also said 'Hathum'—or did you miss that part?"

"No no, I heard it," the king replied, and then stayed quiet for a long stretch.

I finally sighed. "Look, I don't know what your views are on the White Warrior, but she's the only one that can stop Hathum, and you know it. If you know any of your history—"

"She?!" The king cried and spun around. He stared at me, wide-eyed. "The White Warrior is a woman?"

I narrowed my eyes dangerously. I was keenly aware that I was losing the support of this king and thus losing Godel. "She's also a human without her crown and all of her powers."

Irban threw his head back and laughed so heartily that his belly shook. He bent over the table and pounded his fist on the tabletop in hysterics. "Oh son," he said, taking a few deep breaths and wiping tears from his eyes. "Thank you," he gasped. "Oh thank you, dear boy. I have not had a laugh like that in many years."

I pressed my lips together and gave him an even gaze. "I'm not joking." I began to realize that I might actually have to use force to get Godel to cooperate. I could do it. I *would* do it for Azrel's sake. She needed them and I wouldn't fail her.

"What? I am sorry, what did you say?"

"Tell me, king," I said, glaring up at him, "how would you define a warrior, a soldier?"

He looked at me for a moment as if he didn't understand the question. He flinched a little and blinked a couple times trying to comprehend it. "Well, a soldier is both strong mentally and physically. He is able to hold his own bravely on a battlefield."

"Is that all?"

"Well, yes."

I stood from my chair and, even though I made no sudden moves, the king shrunk away from me slightly. "Allow me to show you the kind of warrior this woman is."

"I do not think—"

I threw him against the back wall with a force of my magic. He looked at me with only a little fear as I walked up to him. "Maybe this will convince you that she is worthy of the title of the White Warrior."

From my palm came a rapidly swirling stream of red magic that I sent towards his face. I showed the man everything I knew and had seen of Azrel's life. I went straight down the chronological line, starting with the twenty years of her warrior training with her father, to her horrible abuse and torture in The Pitt, to the past three months of her journey and the already overwhelming odds that she had faced and overcome.

When I finally pulled my magic out of Irban, there were tears running down his cheeks. He met my eyes with a deep sympathy and compassion. "That woman, she is a *human* woman?"

I nodded.

"And she has endured that much already?"

"And survived," I stated matter-of-factly.

The king looked away from me and wiped his tears with the sleeve of his robe. I backed away a few steps and let what he had just seen sink in. "Addredoc," he said carefully after a few moments, "my people are not fond of the White Warrior."

"I know," I said, "but I doubt they're fond of the Shadow Gods either."

Irban sighed and gripped the back of a chair leaning heavily onto his arms. He remained quietly in thought before he looked up at me. "I need to protect my kingdom from the east and the west."

The defeat started to sink in. Where else might I go to gather Azrel an army? I could not, *I would not*, go back to her empty handed. Maybe I could cross the sea to the south? I was unfamiliar with those lands, or what their views of the White Warrior were, but it might be worth a shot.

"Addredoc," Irban said, breaking me out of thought, "I need to know that you can protect my land on the east and west, and crush any rebellion or uprising from my people when I tell them we are going to war with the White Warrior." My chest swelled with pride and excitement, suffocating my fear of failure. Irban saw my reaction and gave me a small smile. "Are you powerful enough to do all of that, young Addredoc?"

I held my head high. "Yes, your majesty. I am."

————

PART TWO: LISSWILLA

As I climbed the steep green hill, I ran my finger absently over the hooked scar on my face, the constant reminder of my people's defeat 10,000 years ago. It had always been a terrible shame and burden for me—until Rabryn had given me a new way to look at it. Now I could actually view it as a mark of pride because my land, Triple Peaks, had outlasted the Shadow Gods long enough for its people to receive the slavery scar on our faces. We had been the very last stronghold to resist in all of Casdanarus.

When I reached the top of the hill, I smiled at the magnificent land sprawled out below me. The tree coverage was so thick from above that you couldn't see the white cobblestone roadways or sidewalks beneath it. Here and there the massive buildings, some rising up thirty stories, rose above the tree line and filled the horizon. We called them skyscrapers because of the way they reached for the clouds. The various metals and the glass windows of the tall buildings shone brightly in the sun, and I immediately felt at home once again.

I was excited and nervous to see my friends again. I hadn't been gone all that long, twelve years—a drop in the ocean compared to the 3,000 that I actually lived here after the war ended. My friends, however—even my best friends—didn't know I wasn't an elf. The black mask I always wore over the bottom half of my face hid not only my scar, but also my unpointed ears. When, a long time ago, my friends had asked why I wore the mask, I'd told them it was to hide a birth deformity. They'd accepted that and never asked me to remove it. It had just become a part of who I was, or who they knew me as.

I took in a deep breath as I made my way down the hill toward the trees and thought about where I should begin to recruit Azrel an army. I doubted I could start with King Geollyn. I had no influence with that man; in fact, he didn't even know I existed. He had a kingdom to run. I would need help, and I would need numbers to get his attention. I had to start small.

Ekar Bar. I grinned. That's where I would start. It was my and my friends' favorite spot to have an ale or wine. The sun was going down here in the far north, so that's where I would find them all.

At I entered the canopy, I found myself gazing at the bustling city of Ryddal. People were going to and fro, walking hastily along the white cobblestone sidewalks to run errands or shop. Horse-drawn wagons rumbled down the streets. A good number of lady elves in their best dress were shopping, ducking in and out of stores with large windows that displayed their merchandise. All the elves on the streets greeted each other respectfully. It was all so different from Casdanarus, and wonderfully familiar to my heart.

I walked for about four blocks and crossed a side street before I reached a small building on the corner. Eagerly pushing open the glass door, I was greeted by the familiar sound of a bell ringing, which brought a wide grin to my face. My eyes swept over the crowded, but brightly lit bar, and I already saw a half a dozen faces I knew well.

My eyes locked with a pair of large brown eyes, and my heart skipped a beat. It was Saellyra, my first love. Her eyes got wide when she saw me, and my heart softened. She was still lovely, with thick, curly, shoulder-length brown hair and fair peach skin that made her eyes look even darker than they were. She wore a long pink dress that came gracefully off her shoulders and thin white shoes on her feet.

Without averting her eyes from me, she slapped the back of someone's shoulder sitting next to her. I knew exactly who it was, even just by looking at the back of his head. He had short, closely cut black hair, except for the front, which fell long and straight over his forehead to the top of his eyes. In the endless millennia I'd known him, that elf had never once changed his hair. His memorable ears had a more prominent point at the tips than most. He looked at Saellyra and then, seeing her expression, spun to look over his shoulder. His blue eyes went wide when he saw me.

I smiled, though he wouldn't be able to see that behind my mask. "Hello Anatus," I said. I looked at the beautiful elvish woman next to him. "Saellyra."

A smile slowly crept across Anatus' features before he quickly stood up from the bar stool. "Lisswilla!" he cried and came toward me.

He embraced me tightly, and I laughed and returned the embrace, slapping his back. Soon the entire bar was looking at us and coming up to greet me and welcome me home. It took about twenty minutes to say hello to everyone. Twelve years was barely a blink in the eyes of immortal elves, but they still acted as if I'd been gone for an eternity.

"Oh man!" Anatus said, exasperated, slapping my shoulder and guiding me to a bar stool beside him. "It is so good to see you. How are things in the south?"

I sighed. Might as well get right down to business. "Not so great, actually," I replied.

"Uh oh," he said, getting serious.

"That's why I'm back." I looked at him and Saellyra and other close friends surrounding me. "I need your help."

"What's wrong? What's happened?" Saellyra asked. Her voice, even worried, sounded so sweet.

I sighed again. "Hathum's back and he's gaining strength quickly." I glanced over all the eyes that now looked around at each other in worry. "He's already overrun Dwellingpath."

"What?" Morsby exclaimed. He was a tall, thin elf with orange hair that was styled into short tight curls against his head, and he always wore a well-aged brown leather jacket. "When did he manage that? *How* did he manage that?"

"Dwellingpath has been in disarray for decades," I replied. "I'm sure it was easy enough for Hathum to worm his way into their good graces–probably by promising them power and glory and so on."

"So this happened recently?" Anatus asked. I noticed him shifting gears from the happy-go-lucky elf I knew to the warrior I had seen him be only once before. His blue eyes got darker, more stern and serious, and his posture got stiff.

"Within the last twenty years, we figure. Hathum likely made his move soon after Socrat, the last heir to the throne, was killed."

"What about the younger prince?" Anatus asked.

I shook my head. "Ortheldo wants nothing to do with that throne. He left when he was ten years old and never looked back."

Anatus downed the rest of his wine in one gulp. "So what do you need from us?"

"Support." I sighed and let myself deflate a little with the overwhelming odds. "A lot of support. Hathum has about six million soldiers strong since he took Dwellingpath, not to mention an untold number of Shadow creatures. The White Warrior has nothing. She needs an army."

"A woman!" Saellyra cried, her eyes bright with excitement. "The White Warrior is a woman?"

I nodded. "She is, and she needs Alkgwathien's soldiers."

Anatus shook his head and put his mug down. "The king will never go for it."

I nodded, "I know. That's why I'm hoping we can rally Alkgwathien and get as much support for the war as we can before we go to the king."

Anatus met my eyes. "Well, I'm with you, but a hell of a lot of good that will do you."

I clapped him on the shoulder. "It's a start."

"I'm with you too," Saellyra said, nodding.

"Me too," Morsby added, and soon everyone in the bar was nodding at me.

"This is going to take a while," Anatus warned. "Alkgwathien is a big land."

"I know. But I'm ready for the run if you are."

Anatus nodded once with steely confidence. "Hell yes. I was getting bored anyway."

"And fat, too!" Morsby cried, and everyone in the bar laughed.

Anatus playfully threw a napkin at Morsby's face, bouncing it off his forehead. Then, right there in the bar, all of us brainstormed about how to go about mounting this campaign. We needed to gather support of the entire land, while somehow keeping it from the king. This was certainly going to be a challenge.

PART THREE: REESE

"You can't be serious, your majesty!" I didn't care how much anger and disrespect trickled through my tone. I was so angry— and, honestly, afraid—that I was shaking. "You didn't seem to object to her killing the subjects in your realm when she actually did it! As I recall, you thanked her for purging the Shadow beings from your land."

"What was I supposed to do?" he responded abruptly. "Condemn her while she was still in my halls? What would have stopped her from slicing me open? I wasn't going to challenge the White Warrior to her face!"

"But she cleansed your mountain of Shadow!"

"She killed forty of my people. In case it has escaped your notice, there are not many Rocksheloc Humounts left. Most of them are human and will die off someday. My very race is in danger, Reese! I cannot let the murder of forty of them stand. She could have crippled them and we could have put them in our dungeons and then—"

"And then what?" I interrupted. "Breed them like animals so your race doesn't die out?"

The king's round, pale face got extremely red and he stood up from his throne. "I do not have to justify myself to the likes of you! I am your king! I will not tolerate backtalk from someone so below me!"

I couldn't help the dark smirk that came to my face, "Below you? You really have an inflated sense of your importance, don't you?"

The king's eye bulged and his face got so red I thought it might pop. "I beg your pardon?"

I glared at him. "I'm pretty sure *I'm* the one fighting directly beside the White Warrior. Not you. If anyone should have an inflated sense of importance, it's me. I'm her protector. What are you?" I sneered. "The king of a quickly dying race. The leader of a kingdom with no income, no trade, and no export. You are old, and cowardly, and as hollowed out and dead as this mountain is, Elraramir!"

I could see the man trembling with rage. "As far as I'm concerned," he said slowly, rising from his throne, "you are no longer a member of this kin."

His words stabbed me like a knife, but I wouldn't give him the satisfaction of knowing it. "As far as I'm concerned, I don't *want* to be a member of this kin any longer."

The king was still shaking. "You have until tomorrow to get out."

"I'll be gone tonight," I fired back and then left the throne room with every pair of eyes on the balcony watching me leave.

The entire land had been summoned for this meeting and now I was leaving without any of Rocksheloc's soldiers. Granted, it wasn't an enormous loss. There were only about a hundred total that would have been able to go, but it would have been nice to have a few familiar faces with me in battle. Plus, riding through Crox Path trying to recruit soldiers would have probably gone more smoothly if I already had a small following when I arrived. I could only hope Narcatertus would be willing to come if I just showed up as Azrel.

I went into my chambers and gathered everything I cared about. I mostly grabbed weapons and letters from my aunt, who had been one of Azrel's father's protectors. She'd predicted, when I was just a babe, that I would be chosen as one of the new White Warrior's protectors. My father had prepared me as a warrior for the role. He'd also taught me advanced shape shifting. Every magic user in Rocksheloc could transform his or her appearance into other people, but only special people could become animals. I was the only one left who could do both.

I loved my cat form, though I didn't particularly like the taste of blood when tearing throats out. The black blood of Shadow creatures was nasty too! But it was a burden I was willing to bear for such a powerful fighting form.

"I'm sorry," I suddenly heard a gentle voice say behind me.

I spun around and my good friend, Pidash, standing in the doorway to my room. I sighed and looked back down at my packing. "It's not your fault. Fear is a powerful thing."

I heard his soft footsteps come closer. His curly black hair just barely touched his shoulders, and his sensitive, emerald green eyes were sad. "Why did you have to talk to our king like that? He wouldn't have sent you away."

I sighed and stared at the wall in front of me in annoyance while I tried to reign in my patience and failed. "Why don't you go lecture someone else about how wrong I am? I'm sure they'd love to hear it and probably agree with you wholeheartedly."

He flinched at my tone and then bowed his head and started to leave my room. He was such a shy soul, one of the reasons I had taken him under my wing when he was young. Even looking at the kid cross-eyed would break his tender heart.

I sighed. "Wait, Pidash. I'm sorry." He stopped and turned

back toward me, unable to meet my eyes. I walked up to him and rested my hands on his shoulders. "Hey," I said gently. He slowly looked up. His eyes were filled with tears. "I'm sorry." He pressed the sleeve of his purple robe to his eyes. I rested my hand on the side of his head. "I'm not angry at you. I'm angry at Elraramir. The White Warrior needs as much help as she can get right now, and he's angry because she fulfilled her purpose by purging Shadow tainted people from here."

Pidash nodded. "I understand."

"I know you do." I sighed, "Look, I have to go." I smiled encouragingly at him. "I have work to do."

Pidash nodded and I went back to my bed to finish packing. He was so quiet that I thought he left.

"Reese," I heard him say softly, after a few minutes, "will you take one last walk with me in the garden before you leave? Just to say goodbye?"

I looked back at him and smiled. "Sure. I'll be out there in a couple hours."

He smiled hopefully and left my room. I sighed and sat heavily on my bed. I had been counting on my kin's abilities to change their physical appearance into other people to gather Azrel an army. I was just realizing now I had counted on it too much. I wasn't completely sure I could do this alone. I was afraid of making Azrel look pathetic and desperate if I strolled up to a massive village and asked them to join me without any following whatsoever. Granted, Azrel *was* rather desperate for an army right now, but looking desperate wasn't a great way to go about recruiting one.

I suddenly felt incredibly alone here in Rocksheloc, my homeland. I sighed heavily and thought about my friends that I missed. Addredoc, Rabryn, Ortheldo, and I even missed Lisswilla and Yarin. I especially missed Azrel. What was I doing here? I should be with my friends! I sighed, but I had a job to do.

Addredoc. He had the worse task of all of us for certain. I suddenly was overtaken by a longing for my friend; the rejection here likely intensifying it. Even though we'd only been separated a day, I missed them. I reached for that sliver of Azrel's magic that she left us so we could communicate with each other. I touched it with my own energy and thought about Addredoc. It only took a second before I felt his presence with me.

Reese?

Hey, Addredoc. I'm sorry to bother you so soon. I know it's barely been a day since we parted.

It's okay. He faked sniffed. *I miss you, too.*

I grinned and let his presence fill the emptiness that Rocksheloc had just left me with. *Wow, it's good to hear from you.*

Having trouble in your area of the world, too? he asked.

I felt slightly comforted that he was having issues as well, but he was in a much bigger and more dangerous place than I was. *Oh no. What's wrong on your end?*

Not much, he replied. *I'm just walking up to the throne room to meet with the king, uninvited, and being attacked on all sides.*

What? Do you need me there? Teleport me, and I'll help you!

No, no. I'm fine, Reese. I have a shield around me. If anyone comes within four feet of me, they get violently thrown backwards thirty feet. He paused. *Oh, here comes another one. Wait for it.* Then Addredoc burst out laughing. *And there he goes!* I threw my head back and laughed. *You think they'd learn their lesson the first dozen times they get flung backwards.*

You'd think, I agreed still chuckling.

So what's wrong on your end?

I sighed. *Rocksheloc isn't going to help.* I bowed my head. *And I just got banished for asking.*

What? Oh crap, Reese. I'm so sorry.

I'm not really concerned about getting banished. I'm concerned I won't have my kin's transforming abilities. I need a Rabryn, an Ortheldo, an Acalith. I sighed. *Now I have to just go alone in Azrel's form and hope I can recruit some people.*

That might not go very well, he said regrettably.

Tell me about it.

Well listen, just take one step at a time. Worry about people not joining you when they actually don't. You never know what could happen.

I smiled. *Thank you my friend.*

Of course. Listen, I have to go. I'm heading into the throne room. Contact me again if you need me, okay?

I will. Be careful.

You too.

I released the magical link with him and it settled into the back of my brain, where it would wait until I needed it next. I propped my elbows up on my thighs, interlaced my fingers, and rested my chin on top of them. He was right. I couldn't worry about people not joining me until they didn't. I got off my bed and finished packing my things. Queen Sauryavia had supplied us very well before Addredoc teleported me, Lisswilla, and Yarin into our various corners of the world, so I didn't need much for the journey. When I had gathered what I could carry, I headed out towards the garden to meet Pidash and say goodbye.

The sun was setting as I stepped outside, and the sky was dark enough that I could see the stars start to come out. I found Pidash sitting on a bench along the stone path with a few white butterflies flying around him. One sat on the tip of his finger, slowly flexing its wings while he gently stroked its back with his free hand. The scene made me smile. Pidash was so gentle and soft that even butterflies trusted him. As soon as I neared, all the butterflies flew off at once. I smiled as I watched them go.

Pidash stood up, a rather broad smile on his face as I approached. Odd. I'd never seen him smile so wide. I'd never seen what excitement looked like in someone so reserved.

"Reese," he said softly, "you've been a wonderful friend to me since we met, and I've never really had the chance, or the opportunity, to thank you and repay you in kind." He took a deep breath. "Until now."

I couldn't help the anticipation that bubbled up inside of me as he headed around the corner of the garden toward the stables. As we approached the stable doors, my eyes went wide when I saw every single being, even the few dozen women and the only two Blue-Violet Salynn children that existed, packed and mounted up on every horse we owned. Rocksheloc mountain was completely emptied out, save for the king.

A single rider eased a horse forward. When the dusk light fell on his face, I realized it was Haliser, the younger brother of Fali, the Salynn who had tried to kill Azrel when she first stopped by here. He was holding the reins to my horse which was also packed and ready. I couldn't stop looking around in awe as he handed my reins down to me.

"We're not going to sit here idly while Shadow tries to enslave the world again," he said matter-of-factly.

I took my reins, half dazed at the wonderful, familiar, and courageous faces of my people. With a shy smile, Pidash went into the stables and mounted his own horse.

"You did this?" I asked in a breath.

He nodded and smiled at me. "We have work to do, Reese."

I grinned like an idiot as I mounted my horse. I glanced behind me at all 260 people, my kin, that were left in this mountain. They were the only Blue-Violentians left in the entire world. If anything happened to them, especially the children, my entire race would die out. But it was something they were willing to risk to join me and the White Warrior for war.

I couldn't even speak as I gazed around the stables at them one more time. Then, I nodded with incredible conviction. "We've all got work to do." With that I kicked my horse up to full speed.

All of my people followed behind, the sound of horses' hooves like wonderful thunder in my ears as we headed west to Narcatertus. I prayed that this sound reached Elraramir's ears in this moment, and he would know that he was alone and that he had lost.

PART FOUR: YARIN

I held up my hand, stopping the large host of horses behind me, and dismounted. Immediately the whispers began.

"I think he's got another already."

"My, he is talented, isn't he?"

"Have you ever heard of such a thing?"

"It has to be something magical."

"But he's not a magic user."

I had to clench my teeth in frustration so I wouldn't bite anyone's head off. "Shh!" I commanded without looking back at them.

We had been on the road together for over a week and I'd told them, time and time again, to stay silent when I got off my horse. I sighed and bowed my head. My original Gleo'gwyns knew the ropes. These new ones just needed time to learn, and my patience—something I was finding difficult to give them. The only thing keeping me from barking out the rules and orders every time they missed a step was because of the fine riders they were. Not a word of complaint came from a single one of them as I drove them mercilessly across Casdanarus.

I just had to keep reminding myself what it was like to break in my first Gleo'gwyn troops. I'd been labeled a self-righteous tyrant by them for the first year or so, but they had eventually understood what I required from them and had accepted it.

When my riders went silent, I closed my eyes and blocked out every sound except the wind. It only took a moment for her to tell me where I would find the next disaster and thus my next recruits for Azrel's army. I didn't have magic anymore, not since the Shadow forces cut off my hair eons ago, but I'd had enough time since then to train myself to hear nature when it spoke. It would have been impossible for a human, but for a former Gold Flower Salynn, it was hardly an issue. Nature was its own force with its own energy, and I'd learned quickly that it didn't speak if it didn't want to.

The wind and I had formed great partnership over the years. She was the most compassionate of all the elements and wanted me and my Gleo'gwyns to save people. As soon as she had learned that I could hear her, she began speaking to me eagerly, letting me know if she needed me to go somewhere, and I became a fast servant of hers.

When the wind told me where I was needed next, I turned and mounted my horse again. "Full gallop!" Given the distance the wind needed me to go, I calculated instantly we would need to ride at a full gallop for three hours and forty-eight minutes.

As soon as we set out, I heard faster galloping coming up behind me. I knew exactly who it was before she even appeared at my side. "Obelya," I said without looking at her.

"How is it you always know just where to go?"

I glanced over at her. With her long straight blonde hair that flew behind her and her big turquoise eyes that matched her armor, no one would guess she was a Fayithjen whose animal half was a falcon. Like all the other Fayithjens, she kept to her human form so we would look like a unified group instead of a mismatched crew of different species. Obelya's questions hadn't ceased since we left Fayithjen. It was flattering but annoying, especially when she asked me questions about Azrel or my past. I didn't know

Azrel that well, but I knew the White Warrior; at least I had when Azrel's father was the White Warrior. Azrel was a fantastic new mystery to me. I tried to explain to Obelya that my and Azrel's history was incredibly brief, which stopped the questions for a bit. But then she turned her questioning to my own past instead—and I wasn't about to discuss that with anyone.

"I just hear voices in the wind," was all I told her each time she asked when I stopped to get directions from the wind.

"You always say that," she complained.

"It's the only way I know how to describe it."

She was quiet a moment. "So what's waiting for us?"

"A village fire."

"How long?"

"Just under four hours."

She went quiet for a moment. "You're a man of few words, Yarin," she finally said.

Something in her tone made turn to look at her.

"You can't stay this cryptic forever if you want to keep your riders," she said. Her voice was firm, but there was sympathy in her expression. "They're not going to trust someone they don't know for very long." She shrugged. "Might not be a bad idea to work on your public relation skills." With that, she fell back from my side into my pack of riders.

I just wanted to do my job, and I wanted them to do theirs without caring who I was. There wasn't any time right now for establishing trust and camaraderie. We needed to gather the White Warrior an army. We had work to do!

But she was right, of course. Mine was a foolish longing. No one could trust a leader they didn't know. I deeply missed having my original Gleo'gwyns at my side, the ones with whom I'd spent years and years and who already knew me and trusted me.

I sighed. I missed Azrel and her current companions, too. A few of us knew each other well enough from the meetings the White Warrior used to hold in Azrel's mind, but we had very little experience with each other in the physical world. Though I had a communication link with three of them, I hadn't heard from a single one this week. Surely by now they had something to report. I wanted to reach for one of them through the magical link of Azrel's, but hesitated because I didn't want to disturb them. They could be busy, or in a battle for all I knew.

I felt like we should have communicated by now though, so I probed for the pureness of Azrel's magic in my mind. The energy of it seeped throughout my entire head like a bowl filling with warm, delicious wine. I sighed at the calming, comfortable feeling. So this is what pure Goodness felt like.

Yarin? I heard Reese suddenly say in my head.

I smiled. *Hi, Reese.*

Hey buddy! We were wondering if you were still with us.

So you've been in touch with the others? They're all right?

Well, "all right" is a bit of a strong term.

Oh no. What's happened?

Eh, we've all had a rough time of it. Here, let's get Lisswilla and Addredoc in on this. We can all update each other. I think it's overdue. I'll get Addredoc; you get Lisswilla. The Light Gods forbid we have them contact each other.

I threw my head back and laughed, which made Reese chuckle. The animosity between Addredoc and Lisswilla was hilarious. I'd seen enough of it in the meetings, where they bickered over the dumbest things.

I reached deeper into the piece of Azrel magic until I felt Lisswilla, the handsome, exotic Alkgwathien. At the same time, I felt Addredoc's presence slide into the magical link and then all three of them were with me.

Well, hello friends, Lisswilla said, *and Addredoc.*

Oh please. Grow up, would you? Addredoc shot back.

I knew Reese was barely contacting his laughter right now. I was biting the inside of my cheek already.

I'm not the one that needs to grow up. You're the one that thinks you're better than everyone with your stupid gifts of two Ancient Wizards!

I never said I was better than everyone...just you!

You know what—

Children, children, Reese interjected. *Can we at least pretend to be mature adults here? Yarin is joining us for the first time.*

Both of them went quiet for a moment. I smiled wider than I had smiled in over two months.

Sorry, Addredoc muttered.

Sorry, Lisswilla added.

Thank you. Now, Yarin would like an update from all of us to see how we're doing. Addredoc, let's start with you, since you have the worst news.

Damn, I muttered. *What's wrong?*

Addredoc sighed. *Well the good news is, I got the king of Godel's support to join Azrel's army.*

That's great! Godel's army was huge! It was the biggest in Casdanarus besides Dwellingpath, which was already fighting for Hathum.

Yeah, well, two problems followed that.

Wonderful.

First, most of Irban's military were on the eastern and western borders as glorified security guards. Over the years they got incredibly slow, some incredibly fat. They barely remember how to use a sword since they didn't do any military drills or anything while they were on sentry duty on those borders. So I've got to completely retrain them and get them back into soldier shape. Addredoc paused a moment and sighed. *That is, I've got to retrain the soldiers that want to join Azrel's army at all.*

I grimaced. *I take it you've had difficulties in that area.*

To say the least. Civil war has broken out.

What? I cried.

Yeah.

You're serious? With a Shadow war at hand, they're fighting amongst themselves?

Tell me about it. It's deadly, too.

Son of a bitch! I cried. *Are you all right? How are you dealing with it?*

I'm doing the best I can to squelch it, but more and more militia are popping up all over the mountains, taking out Godel soldiers by the hundreds. Right now the loss isn't too devastating because Godel's military is three million strong, but if this civil war lasts too long, I'm going to start worrying about the numbers. Not to mention, I had to put a powerful magical barrier on the eastern and western borders of the mountains to protect Godel from the Black Mountains and the Ruin of West Godel, too.

What? There's nothing left in those places anymore.

Try telling the king that. He won't listen to me on that matter.

*And...*I actually flinched...*you're okay on strength? I mean,* *you're fighting a civil war, protecting a massive mountain range on two fronts, and trying to retrain an army of three million?*

I'm good for now, but if this civil war isn't put to bed in the next six months, I'm going to start having issues.

Like you don't now, Lisswilla muttered.

What? Screw you, Lisswilla! Addredoc cried.

I didn't...wait! Addredoc I didn't mean that as an attack on you. I'm—Lisswilla sighed—*I'm just worried about you.*

Oh.

Look, do you need me there? I can help and take some of the burden off you.

Addredoc sighed. *No, I'm okay for now. Ask me again in six months, and I'll let you know.*

I shook my head in disbelief at Addredoc's magical abilities. He was doing three incredibly draining things simultaneously and could keep doing them for the next six months without needing help. That much demand would probably kill Azrel within three days! Damn it, that girl needed her crown!

How are things with you, Lisswilla? Addredoc asked in the first friendly tone I'd ever heard him use toward Lisswilla.

I've gathered a bit more support from the Alkgwathiens, but not enough to take our request to the king yet. We're still holding meetings in secret, in private homes. We might be about a month away from doing public rallies, if I can get enough support behind me in that time. Most of the elves want to fight. They're bored. Besides, they remember what slavery was like under Hathum's Nameless One. Just about all of the elves here were original victims of It.

But they want to come? I asked. *That's good.*

It is. I'm just worried about playing the part of deserter or betrayer if the king won't release us to go fight in Casdanarus. With those labels threatening the elves, I could lose half of my following. Elves are honorable people, and those kinds of brands are enough to make even the bravest and most zealous warrior stay put.

Damn, I muttered. I couldn't believe the odds stacked against these two. It was unbelievably daunting. *Reese, tell me you're faring better then these two chuckleheads.*

That made them all laugh, which was the goal. I now felt

incredibly guilty about whining that my followers wanted to know their leader. That was ridiculous compared to what Lisswilla, and especially Addredoc, were facing.

Yeah, I'm doing much better because we all know I'm smarter than the whole lot of you put together.

All of us burst out laughing.

You wish! Addredoc said.

Admit it! Reese said, still laughing.

Never! Lisswilla added, and I could hear the smile in his voice.

I swear my Gleo'gwyns are thinking I've lost my mind. They're watching me burst into laughter at the air! All of us just laughed harder. *So you're all right, Reese?* I asked once it died down.

Yeah, I'm good. I'm in Azrel's form right now, riding to various villages in the Mongerst Mountains and gathering people up. Not as many as I would like, but at each village I gain a solid seventy five to two hundred people, and I've only hit about ten villages so far. I got an impressive 15,000 from Narcatertus.

What? I cried, relaxing at this first bit of good news— tremendous news, really.

Heck yeah, brother! They pretty much emptied that place out for Azrel.

You're serious? You have 15,000 soldiers right now?

Actually, I have about 18,000. But—his tone dropped to a slightly sad one—*these aren't soldiers, Yarin. They're farmers, miners, and innkeepers.*

Well hell, don't balk at that! Those are able bodies that can fight!

I know, but they barely know what they're doing. They have families and homes and...I don't know. It's just hard. Their courage is unbelievably admirable, though.

You can say that again. Don't worry about them not knowing what they're doing. We can train them so they can defend themselves in battle.

I've already started to train them. Each night we stop, my people from Rocksheloc do weapons training with them for a few hours before we go to sleep.

I was quiet a moment while I let that sick in. *Reese,* I said with conviction, *you are awesome.*

His tone brightened a little. *Yeah, I know.*

I grinned, and Addredoc and Lisswilla laughed.

So how are you doing, Yarin? Addredoc asked.

I took in a deep breath. *I'm not bad. My mission is much more scattered and broad, so I've only gathered about fifty people that I've run into in the wild. I haven't hit any villages yet, but I'm on my way to one now. I might get a good number here. The village is on fire, so there won't be much holding them to a charred homeland. I'm going to have to slow my pace to a regular, non-Gleo'gwyn trek soon, though, as I gather more people. Most will be on foot, and that makes travel slower. I've been lucky to get fifty riders with horses that can keep up so far, but that will change. I'm not certain how many people I'll be able to actually gather with this method, but I'm doing the best I can.*

Hey Yarin, Reese suddenly said, *I think if Azrel needs to send me to White Veilvin in Rabryn's form, you and I should meet up first.*

Why? I asked, surprised at the sudden request.

You just know the place better than I do. I know I'm going to need help negotiating that land, especially trying to act like their king, and you grew up there.

I nodded. *All right. Addredoc, do you think you'll be okay to teleport me and my followers to Reese when the time comes?*

I should be able to, I hope. Too soon to tell.

All right, we'll be in touch then, I told him.

All right. Listen, I have to go, Addredoc said. *I just got reports of another militia attack.*

I have to go as well, Lisswilla added. *I've arrived at another house where I'll try to siphon some support.*

And I've got another village in my sights, Reese added. *It was great to hear from you guys. Be careful, all of you, and keep in touch.*

You too, I added.

I felt all three of them leave the magical link one by one. I sighed heavily as the magic settled into the place at the back of my mind where I'd pulled it from. I suddenly felt very cold and alone. The usually kind wind seemed to seep under my armor and bite my skin. I was happy to have heard from them, but now I was even more worried about them. I shook my head and worried about

Addredoc being in Godel alone. I felt like I should be there with him, but I knew he could handle it for now though he was burdened with so much. Azrel certainly had made the right choice in sending him there. He wouldn't fail her. He'd die first.

My mind drifted to Azrel, and I sighed. "Good luck, brave girl," I whispered aloud, hoping the wind would carry my voice to her. "We're working hard for you. Take care of yourself, so you can lead this army we're bringing you."

ONE

Clink! Clank! Grunt! Argh! Clink!

Clink! Clank! Grunt! Argh! Clink!

I sighed softly and opened my eyes to look at the back of Ortheldo's head. He lay curled up on the ground in his cloak and blankets, trying to protect himself from the pelt of cold rain. He could pass for being asleep, but I knew better.

"At it again, are they?" I muttered.

"Yup," he replied flatly without looking back at me.

I sighed and turned onto my back, looking up into the black sky and blinking out the fat rain drops that fell into my eyes.

Clink! Clank! Grunt! Argh! Clink!

Clink! Clank! Grunt! Argh! Clink!

I listened silently to the sounds that had become familiar over the past two weeks—two hours, every night, before they finally went to sleep. At first Azrel went out alone to work out and practice, but by the second night, Acalith had joined her. Now the noise was doubly loud.

Clink! Clank! Grunt! Argh! Clink!

Clink! Clank! Grunt! Argh! Clink!

"Don't they care that it's raining?" Moifulyar mumbled, lying down across from me, also curled up tightly in his cloaks and blankets. I liked Moifulyar and was glad for his company. He didn't say too much, but his presence was a comfort.

"No, they don't," I replied, looking back up at the black sky. Water fell into my eyes again and I blinked it away.

Clink! Clank! Grunt! Argh! Clink!

Clink! Clank! Grunt! Argh! Clink!

I smiled broadly, stuck my tongue in my cheek, and cast another glance at each of them. "Want to watch?"

On cue, all of us jumped up from our sleeping spots and quickly went toward the clearing of the woods. We were only too eager to watch the two most beautiful women in Casdanarus fight each other in the rain. We went to the edge of the brush and crouched down.

In the middle of the small clearing, they danced together, barefoot, in a tangle of swift moves and strong blocks, each holding a sword in one hand and a smaller knife in the other. They wore short pants and sleeveless shirts tied up to reveal their sleek muscular stomachs. Their hair was tied up in sopping knots. The rainwater on their skin shone in the moonlight, giving them both an otherworldly glow.

Clink! Clank! Their swords crashed together.

Grunt! Acalith tried to send a deadly blow to Azrel.

Argh! Azrel blocked it with little effort.

Clink! The dance continued.

The sounds went on echoing through the night while the three of us watched, transfixed by every move the women made. I gasped when Acalith used some beginning techniques of Azrel's empty-handed fighting style. I glanced over at Ortheldo and saw his eyes go wide, too.

"Good!" Azrel cried, and the practice stopped, both women breathing heavily from exertion. After giving Acalith some directions in a low voice, Azrel demonstrated some moves. That fighting style was sacred to Azrel, yet she was sharing it. Though Acalith looked clumsy and shaky with the techniques, I could see on her face that she was determined to master them. Afterwards, still barefoot, they disappeared into the woods for a run.

When they were out of sight, the three of us silently headed back to our sleeping gear. I doubted we would get much sleep in the rain, but we had to try. We were on the brink of Tabway Pass, a dangerous gateway that led to the even more dangerous Spar Ridges woods. The kingdom was beyond that. Since nothing was ever easy, Azrel figured that the necklace's owner could be found in the most dangerous and hard to reach place in Casdanarus aside from Dwellingpath.

Spar Ridges was the second largest Humount kingdom in Casdanarus, second only to Godel. Its denizens were unique, however, in that while they didn't live inside their mountains, the mountains completely surrounded them, putting them in total isolation. No one got in, and no one ever came out—until Acalith.

The entire land was a mystery even to Ortheldo and Azrel, but Acalith gave them all the useful information she had. She kept quiet, though, about the time she lived there and the details of how she got out. All we knew was that Tabway Pass was the way into the woods that surrounded Spar Ridges, and that the woods were incredibly dangerous. Ancient creatures, many immune to modern-day magic, called the woods of Spar Ridges home.

Beyond the woods, actually getting into the kingdom of Spar Ridges would be treacherous because that land, more than any other realm in Casdanarus, hated the White Warrior. No one was going to be Azrel's friend there.

With Spar Ridges, and Acalith, on my mind, I curled up in my soaking wet sleeping gear. I did my best to cover my head and face, but it was still miserable. Hours passed. I heard Azrel and Acalith return and settle into their sopping beds and heard their breathing go steady as they fell asleep. I finally passed out from exhaustion a little while after that, too tired to feel the rain any longer.

———

I awoke to a dismal gray morning, the smell of food, and the sound of gentle feminine laughter. I slowly turned my head back to see Azrel and Acalith cooking a large breakfast from the abundant supply that Queen Sauryavia had given us. Both women were fully dressed and looked like they'd been awake for hours. I resisted the urge to roll my eyes as I turned over, putting my back to them again. How could they be the last ones to sleep and the first ones up, and in a good mood nonetheless?

"Good morning, little brother," Azrel said cheerfully to the back of my head.

"Yeah? What's so good about it?"

Azrel chuckled and then knelt behind me and hugged me as I lay on the ground, still soaked from last night. She kissed my cheek numerous times, making me turn my eyes up to her with suspicion.

"What's gotten into you today?"

She smiled down at me. "I heard from Addredoc last night."

I sat up quickly. "What? What's going on? How are they?" Even Ortheldo and Moifulyar were suddenly wide awake and sitting up in their beds. We hadn't heard from them in two weeks, since we'd parted in Fayithjen Forest.

Azrel sighed. "Well, Addredoc's not doing so great, but everyone else is okay."

"Why? What's going on in Godel?" Ortheldo asked.

Azrel met his eyes. "Civil war broke out in the mountain."

"What?" I cried as my heart leapt up into my throat.

"Damn it," Ortheldo replied, running his hand through his wet hair.

I was suddenly terrified for my friend. Godel was massive, and he was there all alone. It didn't make sense! Addredoc must have told them about Shadows return to the realm, yet they thought it would be a good idea to fight amongst themselves? Stupid, stubborn Humounts. I knew Azrel must feel terrible that hatred for the White Warrior would run so deep as to cause a civil war break out. And yet, she seemed cheery despite that.

"Addredoc swore he was okay for now," she went on, "but if the war doesn't settle in a few months, he's going to need some serious help."

Azrel went into detail about how everyone else was fairing and how much magical strain was on Addredoc at the moment.

"And he can expel and hold that much magic for six months?" I asked, both awed and horrified.

Azrel shrugged. "That's what he said."

I shook my head. "Look, maybe we should head there first? It sounds like he really needs some help."

Azrel shook her head. "Rabryn I need to rid myself of this necklace burden first. Then we can do whatever we want, and go wherever we need to go. But the gem is still dying. The orange light has dimmed further. You can barely see it glow anymore."

"This damn necklace," I muttered to myself, shaking my head. My friend was in trouble, and we were on a wild goose chase we couldn't avoid.

"Tell me about it. But look"—Azrel smiled again— "Addredoc is very powerful, and he said he can hold it for six months, so I'm going to give him the time he needs. I have faith in him."

I sighed heavily. "I guess we don't have a choice in that matter."

She looked at me and gave me a helpless shrug. "Unfortunately not. But come on"—she patted my knee and turned to go back to the fire Acalith was attending—"breakfast is ready."

Moifulyar, Ortheldo and I changed into dry clothes and went to the fire to eat. Ortheldo sat right next to Azrel, putting his arm around her kissing the side of her head, and she snuggled up tightly against him. I was glad they had finally buried their issues. I looked at Acalith in that moment, only to find her already looking at me; now Acalith and I were the ones with an issue. She quickly looked away and down at her breakfast, pretending she'd been looking at her plate all along. I sighed and shook my head before taking a plate of food.

As we ate, I brooded over what Acalith was keeping from us about her time in Spar Ridges. I had to get it out of her. If there was some danger to Azrel, or even to Acalith, in that place, I needed to know.

I looked at Acalith again and, probably feeling the heat of my stare, she looked back at me. I raised an eyebrow, indicating a warning to her that I knew she wasn't telling me something. She averted her eyes quickly and continued eating her breakfast. I felt my lip twitch as that mistrust toward her started to take root, the same way it had when she left Galad Kas without Ortheldo and me. I'd buried that issue back in Fayithjen, but it was surfacing again.

Azrel was the first to finish and began to break camp. As she started to pack, Lightning, back in his normal tan hide and black main form of Forfirith, came trotting up.

"Good morning all!" he said cheerfully.

We all greeted him as Azrel began to pack him up. I was glad he could still talk in his normal form. He was funny, and Azrel loved talking to him. It gave her a sense of peace and joy that I rarely saw in her otherwise.

"Let's get going everyone. We're burning daylight," Azrel said.

All of us finished our breakfast and began to pack our horses up. I doused the fire and mounted, and we started through the woods at a gentle trot since it was fairly open and friendly looking. As the day wore on, however, and we neared Tabway Pass, the woods seemed to gradually die. More and more naked branches hung over our heads, though it was nearly summer time. Though the wind blew more freely without leaves on the trees, it was moist and thick and uncomfortable to breathe in.

As night fell, the forest gave way to more swampy terrain. A thick mist began to creep around the horses' legs, staying low to the sparse and soggy ground. Gray tree stumps stuck out of the earth like the bony fingers of dead, half-buried beasts. Death itself seemed to linger here all around us.

Soon, a rotten smell nearly made me retch, and it only got worse as we went on. Moifulyar and I had the hardest time of it because our senses were so much more heightened than those of the others. The back of my and Moifulyar's throats burned and our eyes watered. Taking extra material from our packs, we wrapped it around our faces to keep our noses and mouths covered, cutting holes in the material to hook our ears into and keep the makeshift masks up securely.

"You babies," Acalith said, "the smell isn't that bad." She smiled back at us teasingly.

Her smile was like the remains of the sunlight that refused to reach us here in the dead, gray place. The sight of it made me smile in return. "You try on a Salynn's heightened senses in this place, *and then* tell me we're babies."

She chuckled and faced forward again. Stuck staring at the perfect blonde ringlets of her hair, I sighed. It was good to see her smile, but I still wondered what she was hiding. I wanted to trust her. Azrel trusted her, and Azrel would know whether Acalith was trustworthy. But there was something about her I couldn't shake. Why the secrecy?

As I looked at the back of Acalith's head, I saw Azrel look over her shoulder for the fiftieth time today and probably the five hundredth time since we left Fayithjen. When I'd asked her about it a week ago, she'd told me that she'd felt a pair of eyes on us and she wasn't sure if they were friendly or not.

I sped up my horse a little, passing Acalith and Ortheldo, and pulled up next to my sister. "See anything this time?" I teased.

She looked at me and smiled with a little embarrassment. "No."

"What a surprise."

She drove her fist into my shoulder. "Shut up, you!" We both laughed quietly. "I really wish I could tell if whatever is following us means us any harm."

"So do I," I admitted, looking over my shoulder in hopes to see something she may have missed. I saw nothing, though.

"Don't worry, Rabryn," Moifulyar said from the back of the pack. "The girls will protect us."

All of us laughed quietly again. The image of their intense practice session last night flashed in my mind, and my smile widened. They certain could. I had no doubt.

"Were you three watching us again last night?" Azrel asked, eyeing each of us suspiciously, trying not to smile.

"To tell the truth, or to not tell the truth?" Ortheldo piped in, looking up and pretending to ponder it.

"You guys need to get a hobby," Acalith said, and all of us chuckled again. I thought I even saw Forfirith laughing. We couldn't be too loud this close to Tabway Pass, for reasons Acalith wouldn't go into, so we kept our laughter quiet.

We rode well into nightfall in complete silence. The foreboding of this area, in a way, commanded quiet. We were still a day away from Tabway Pass, and I was not looking forward to camping out in this wretched smell, which was already seeping through my mask. Plus the place was creepy. My heart sank when Azrel called for a halt, and I looked over at Moifulyar. He rolled his eyes and shook his head; we knew neither of us was going to get any sleep tonight.

We ate a light and silent supper until Azrel whispered, "Rabryn, I don't want you taking a watch tonight."

I flinched. "What? Why?"

"You either," Azrel said to Acalith.

Acalith's brows dropped. "Me?"

"Don't argue with me," Azrel said, shooting us each a stern look before looking at Moifulyar. "Moifulyar, will you take third watch?"

Moifulyar glanced at me for approval, and I nodded. He looked back at Azrel. "Yes, of course."

"Ortheldo, you take first. I'll take second," she said in a tone of finality.

He nodded at her. When I met his eyes, he shrugged. When I looked back at Azrel, I realized she was staring hard in the distance that we'd already put behind us.

We cleaned up dinner, and all of us but Ortheldo lay down in our sleeping gear. After grabbing his weapons, he stepped around the fire so he could bend down and give Azrel a quick kiss goodnight. I watched him walk down the path in darkness until the mist swallowed him.

I slept fitfully until the morning dawned, gray and dismal like yesterday. Mist still floated around the dead rotting tree stumps and clung to our damp clothes. The rancid smell hadn't improved any; in fact, I thought it was getting worse. My clothes were starting to smell of it. I couldn't breathe through my nose anymore or I would risk puking. I breathed through only my mouth, and I could still taste it in my throat. I'd be only too happy to put this place behind us.

We had a short breakfast and broke camp quickly, Azrel looking no more at ease this morning than she had last night. At one point I saw her pull Acalith aside and speak to her privately. As I packed up, I magically turned up my hearing to listen.

"No matter what, I want you sticking close to me or Rabryn," she said.

"Azrel, tell me what's going on," Acalith insisted. "Is something coming after me? Or Rabryn?"

Azrel sighed. "I'm not sure. Just stay near me or Rabryn. Do you understand?"

Acalith let out a frustrated breath. "Yes, I understand."

"Thank you," Azrel sighed.

Regardless of that little chit-chat, we were on the move quickly. As we rode, Azrel looked over her shoulder constantly. Though before leaving camp we'd agreed we weren't going to talk at all, I couldn't stand this. I pulled Eleclya up next to Forfirith, summoned a swirling gold light into my eyes, and lightly backhanded Azrel's shoulder to get her attention. When she looked at me, my magic went into her so I could hear her thoughts.

Forgot I could do this, didn't you?

She chuckled. *I did forget.*

Tell me what's happening. You seem more anxious today.

She sighed. *Last night, when I went to go get firewood, I felt the eyes close by, but they weren't on me—they were on all of you at camp. Whatever it is isn't after me.*

That's surprising.

No kidding. So I used a tiny speck of magic and put myself behind the eyes.

Azrel! You said you weren't going to use your magic. Hathum can find you all that much easier when you do. You know he hones in on your power.

But he's going to hone in on me eventually anyway, either from the pureness of the magic inside of me, or from the necklace.

Well, don't help him along!

I had to. I can't ignore someone, or something, trailing us.

I sighed in frustration. *What happened when you put yourself behind the eyes?*

Well, they were mostly watching you.

Me? I asked surprised.

Azrel nodded. *I was relieved at first, because the presence seemed friendly—that is, until it began watching you and Acalith at the fire pit.* She met my eyes. *It was very hostile then.*

I felt my face twist with surprise and confusion. *That's weird. Why us?*

Azrel looked out ahead of her again. *I don't know. But that's why I didn't want either of you taking a watch alone last night. I didn't know which one of you the presence hated more, or if it hated the both of you. I'm still not sure, but I figure the hatred came when Acalith joined you, so that's who the presence has a problem with.*

I looked over my shoulder at the path behind us, hoping again to catch a glimpse of what seemed to be threatening Acalith.

Don't bother, Azrel said lightly. I looked at her and saw her smiling at me. *I already looked a thousand times.* I grinned at her. *Now will you please get out of my head? You know that creeps me out.*

I gave her a broader smile and nodded. *Thanks for telling me.*

She smirked. *You say that like I had a choice in the matter.*

I chuckled lightly, pulled my magic out of her, and then fell to the back of the pack once again. I deliberately put myself behind Acalith and I looked over my shoulder yet again, but didn't see anything. If this thing wanted Acalith, it was going to have to go through me first.

TWO

AZREL

Night had fallen again, and I had been dreading this part of our journey—Vefur Swamp. What an unlovely place to visit just before getting into Tabway Pass which, in of itself, would have tons more fun waiting for us. Steam rose up from the shallow water to join with the thickening mist around us, and the wretched smell nearly made me dizzy. I was surprised Rabryn and Moifulyar hadn't passed out yet. It was the kind of horrid, rancid smell that overwhelmed your senses and swam around in your skull.

The gray tree stumps gave way to a vast open clearing in front of us. I looked over the swamp, feeling slightly weary. The thick, brown, filthy water was five miles wide and surrounded by patches and small hills, of soft mossy, wet ground. Though it should only be knee deep at most so I didn't have to fear drowning, I still hated water.

Ahead of us, at the back end of the clearing of the swamp, was a huge cliff face—Tabway Pass. It served as a massive and, in some ways, magical front gate to Spar Ridges. Beyond that, Spar Ridges woods was like a front yard with a few thousand attack dogs in the form of magic-resistant Shadow creatures. Vefur Swamp was their combined moat and "Keep Out" sign. Spar Ridges took their isolation very seriously.

It was three hours into the night when we reached the cliff faces of Tabway. My brows drew together as I dismounted and looked up at the three-hundred-foot rock faces that stretched far out to either side. I walked along the length, dragging my hand lightly over the stone and pondering. I had no idea how to get in.

I sighed softly as I looked up at the ragged cliff face again. There was only one way to figure this out. It was time for a little freestyle rock climbing.

While everyone else was in front of me, examining the cliff faces and trying to figure out a way in, I put my hair up into a messy knot and took off my boots. My scarred toes would be enough protection from the rocks during the climb. I grabbed some long strips of cloth from my pack and bandaged myself up to my wrists to absorb the sweat.

When everything was wrapped and secure, I looked at Forfirith. "Care to give me a boost?" I whispered.

He nodded and ducked his head low. I placed one foot on top of his head and pressed my palms against the cliff side. Forfirith lifted his head high, lifting me. I kept my balance by pushing against the cliff face and moving my hands in a crawling movement until I was as high as Forfirith's neck could stretch. I brought my free foot forward and settled it tightly into a crevice. Then, I grasped two crevices with my hands, and I was able to take my foot off Forfirith's head and wedge it into another.

A few minutes went by before I heard Rabryn whisper harshly from below, "Azrel! What the hell are you doing?"

Acalith elbowed my brother in the side. "Use your magic if you want to talk. We have to stay quiet!" she whispered just as harshly.

I looked down and saw the tail end of Rabryn's swirling magic in his eyes. *Azrel! What the hell are you doing?*

I continued to climb. *What does it look like?*

It looks like you've lost your mind! You don't even have shoes on!

I chuckled. *I don't need them.*

It's been a long time since you've done that, I suddenly heard Ortheldo say in my head. Apparently Rabryn had started a party line. *You might be rusty. Be careful.*

Always. I looked down and smiled at him and then met Acalith's eyes. *Want to come?*

She grinned up at me and began to pull back her curly blonde hair.

There should be some extra cloth strips in my pack, I told her.

Don't need them, she declared as she began her climb from the bottom of the cliff face, also barefoot.

I raised my brow and hoped she knew what she was doing. I was stunned when just a few moments later she was right next to me. I'd had a thirty foot lead on her!

Impressive, I told her.

Thank you, Azrel. She didn't pass me, though I'm sure she could have. She just stayed next to me and we climbed together.

We stayed quiet, mostly concentrating on the climb—where

to place feet and hands and the pushing and pulling up. Ortheldo, Rabryn, and Moifulyar, however, shared some quiet conversation below. Mostly, they expressed their worry for Addredoc, Lisswilla, Reese and Yarin, and their nervousness about what might happen once we got into the Spar Ridges woods. It was a good two hours before I saw the top of the cliffs within reach.

What are we looking for up here, Azrel? Acalith asked.

A way in, perhaps, I replied. *I mostly wanted to gauge the landscape from above to figure out some strategies of moving through it. It's going to be a two day travel through here before we get to the woods, and I want to make sure we don't walk in blind.*

I was dripping with sweat from every pore of my body when I finally pulled myself over the edge at the top. Red-faced and exhausted, I suddenly felt bitter because I would have to climb back *down.* I suppressed a groan as I slowly got to my feet.

As I looked out in front of me, I was consumed by awe. Even at night, the view could not have been more spectacular. From up here, Tabway Pass didn't look so intimidating; it didn't look dead, or ruinous, or bare. It was beautiful. The Pass was a massive canyon far below, bathed in glorious silver moonlight. Stone pinnacles and platforms of every shape and size lined the outside perimeter of the unsymmetrical crevasse below. Far in the distance, I could just make out a thin, dense shadow against the horizon that would likely be Spar Ridges' woods.

Rabryn, I said in awe, *you need to see this. Use my eyes.*

What? What's wrong?

Just do it.

I felt the heat of Rabryn's magic in my head increase. *Oh wow!*

Can you show the others? I don't think it would be fair to deprive any of you this spectacle.

I soon heard similar reactions from Ortheldo and Moifulyar as they gazed upon the sight through my eyes. Smiling like an idiot, I looked at Acalith next to me...and my joy quickly melted into horror.

What the...?! Rabryn cried. Ortheldo and Moifulyar both gasped.

Acalith's green eyes were glowing!

She had been looking at me with a soft smile, but it quickly faded at my reaction. *What? What's wrong?*

I couldn't even answer her. Her eyes slowly and steadily glowed brighter and brighter. I cowered back a step.

Suddenly those eyes widened. *Are my eyes glowing?*

I could only nod my head. An instant later, Acalith tackled me to the ground and wrestled me behind a nearby rock formation. Before I could protest, she was behind me, her hand covering my mouth.

Azrel stop! she begged as I struggled against her. *Stop it! Don't move! Don't make a sound! Don't even breathe if you can help it,* she said urgently in my head.

She kept me in a tight hold as we waited on the ground behind some rocks. Finding that some part of myself trusted her, I held still and waited.

Suddenly, I heard it—a steady rhythmic beating in the distance. I could only describe it as rock hitting against rock. I searched the cliffs that I could see as the sound seemed to get closer and louder. A few moments later, a giant Stone Troll came into sight on a ledge below us in the distance. My eyes went wide. The thing was two hundred feet tall. I watched in terror as the mammoth creature approached, the tip of its head reaching the ledge we were on, and I felt myself begin to tremble. Acalith, however, stayed steady and calm.

Hold your breath, she said in my head, and I felt her chest stop moving against my back. I did as she said.

With one stride, the creature that had seemed so far off a moment ago was right next to us. It was slow moving, so we waited. I watched as it lifted a massive leg and brought it forward. With three more strides, it passed us below, and was far enough away to where I felt Acalith start to breathe again. She still didn't move for another minute to two, not until I couldn't hear the rhythmic sound of its walking any longer. Only then did she release me. I moved away, staying in a low crouch as I turned to face her. Her eyes were still glowing green, but the light seemed to have softened considerably.

Ever since I'd first set sight on those strange eyes of hers back in Oaksher Village, after Ibalissa had driven a knife into my back, I knew they'd had a strange quality to them. They were uncommonly bright and intense, but never had I actually seen them glow.

She slumped against the rock that we'd hidden behind. *That was entirely too close.*

I gave her a look of warning. *You've got some explaining to do, sister.*

Acalith sighed and stood up. *I'm surprised you don't know,* she said. Both of us turned and headed towards the cliff's ledge to start the trek back down the rock face. *It's a warning system all Spar Ridgians are born with. Tabway Pass is officially the border of Spar Ridges, though it has long been overrun by those Stone Trolls.* Sitting down and dropping one of her legs over the side, she looked back at me. *When we're in our realm, and danger is near, our eyes glow green.* She found a foothold, turned, and began to lower herself over the side of the cliff. I reached my foot down to a crevice, dreading the climb down but occupying myself with her words. *As danger gets closer to us, the glow gets brighter. It's been that way since the war ended.*

Why didn't you ever tell us?

I thought you knew.

Why hadn't I known this? Clearly, Ortheldo didn't know either, he'd sounded just as surprised as I'd been. Glowing green Spar Ridgian eyes was not something my father had taught us about.

Anyway, that's why no one is allowed to travel alone around Spar Ridges. There is a special security detail, people trained in combat, that is assigned to patrol the kingdom in pairs. Their function is strictly to escort people that need to go somewhere and have no one with them. Every person needs to be walked. No one travels alone.

That sounds incredibly invasive! I cried.

Oh, it is! she exclaimed. *On a bright side, if you have a neighbor or a friend to walk you to where you need to go, you're fine. There's no need for an escort. As long as you have a pair of eyes you can look at to see if any danger is near.*

I thought Spar Ridges was powerfully protected from the Shadow creatures of the woods. Why is that kind of invasive security required?

It is powerfully protected. It would have *to be for them to survive here as long as they have. There hasn't been a Shadow creature breech in Spar Ridges for over 3,000 years. Hence why I find the escort practice incredibly outdated and downright disturbing. I'm pretty certain they just kept it active in order to keep an eye on the Spar Ridgian people—reason number one why I jumped at the chance to get out of there.* I looked down at her and saw her shaking her head. *I probably would have killed myself if the White Warrior hadn't called me to duty.*

My heart ached at trying to imagine strong and self-assured Acalith being so desperate to get away from here that she would consider killing herself. *I'm so sorry, Acalith.*

She paused in her climb and smiled up at me. *What are you sorry for? You're the one who saved my life by giving me an excuse to get away.*

I grinned before continuing my climb down. *I'm guessing those Stone Trolls are the reason we have to be so quiet around here.*

Yes. They can't see very well, but they can hear humans breathing from a full stride off. I'm actually surprised it didn't hear our heartbeats when it was right next to us. They were racing so fast.

Are Stone Trolls the only thing in the pass?

Yes. They're dumb and have only about a sixty-second memory, so they stay calmly in the pass, circling the canyon like fish in a tank. If they hear you, though, they become more like rabid sharks.

Stay calm and keep quiet and we should get through the pass, right?

We should.

I nodded. *All right then.*

We reached the bottom of the cliffs a short time later, sweat dripping off the ends of our hair and soaking the backs of our shirts. Both of us collapsed on our butts against the cliffs, panting heavily. The boys were on us quickly with water and cold cloths.

"Rabryn," I panted and pointed to my head. I couldn't even give voice to asking him to take his magic off me, but he knew. He grinned at me as the swirling gold light appeared in his eyes and I felt his magic pull away. I sighed. "Well, the good news is we saw some beautiful scenery," I said softly. "Bad news is I didn't see a way into the Pass." I shook my head. "I don't know how to get in."

"All right," Ortheldo said, crouching down in front of me and patting my forehead with the wet cloth. "Then what do we know about the history of Tabway Pass? Acalith, feel free to chime in any time. You should know it better than we do."

I sighed and rubbed my forehead with my fingertips. "It used to be a tunnel."

"Right. Keep going."

I looked at him suspiciously. "Have you figured out a way in?"

He smiled mischievously and patted my face with the cloth again. "Not entirely. Keep going."

I rested the back of my head against the rock. "Well, it was used as trading tunnels for hundreds of years." I looked up in thought. "When war broke out, it was used as a refuge for the Light God's people. The Nameless One collapsed the roof, turning the tunnel into the canyon that it is now."

"So, the refugees would need a way to get in and out of the tunnels without the Shadow soldier's detection." He smiled at me. "How did they get in, Azrel?"

I thought about it a moment, until it occurred to me and I smiled. "Underground."

He grinned and nodded.

Thoughts were turning over in my head. "So we're not looking for a door in the rock face of the Pass. It was probably one farther away to keep the Pass safe from Shadow soldier detection." I looked around the Vefur Swamp and sighed. "Well, that's not much easier. We still have to find an obscure door somewhere around this hideous swamp."

Ortheldo tilted his head to the side and smiled. "Azrel, you've forgotten that you have a little brother who can talk to nature."

My face brightened and I looked up at Rabryn, whose face brightened at the same time. "Yes!" he softly exclaimed, and then he was immediately down on his knees.

I saw his hands start to glow with his gold magic. He pressed his palms into the ground, and the most deathly blank look came over his face. He seemed to be staring intently at nothing. He stayed completely still for a few moments before he finally blinked, lifted his palms, and looked at me with a big smile. "Let's go."

I grinned, and both Acalith and I got up. We quickly put our boots back on, and all of us headed to our right along the cliff face. "What did nature tell you?" I asked eagerly.

"She didn't tell me anything. She showed me where the door was."

I grinned. "My brother is awesome," I said to no one in particular. Rabryn smiled at me over his shoulder.

We walked for about an hour before Rabryn stopped at a small, unassuming mound of mossy earth that was practically the middle of the swamp. There was nothing special about it. It looked like every other mound of earth in this place. His hand started to glow gold again, and he pressed his palm against the moss. I watched as the plants rolled away, unveiling a small but incredibly thick metal door. It was only about four square feet in size so we'd have to duck to get in, but it was no doubt the door to Tabway.

I crouched down and took hold of the handle. I pulled, but nothing happened. Confused, I got down on my knees and pulled again, and still nothing happened. I bent closer to the door, examining it. My heart sank when I found a small key hole in the metal.

"It's locked." I looked up at Rabryn. "Do you think the earth can release the lock so we can get in?"

Rabryn's hand glowed again, and he pressed his palm to the ground. After a moment, he shook his head and straightened. "No, she can't. The door isn't alive, so she has no will over it to make it open."

I sighed and sat back on my heels. "Now what?"

The key, the White Warrior suddenly said in my head.

"Yes, I know we need a key. That's the problem. We have no key."

Yes you do. Then she was gone.

My brows dropped. She'd been silent for over two weeks, ever since I told her that the reason we were still two separate people may be more her fault than mine. I wasn't sure if she was mad at me or what her problem was, but I hated to admit it was rather nice to hear her voice again.

"What did she say?" Ortheldo asked.

"She said we have the key," I replied.

My face brightened when I recalled the parting gift that the king of Rocksheloc Mountain had given me; it was a key. I couldn't believe I was only just remembering it, but he'd told me it once opened the ancient tunnels of Spar Ridges. I had been in a desperate hurry when leaving Rocksheloc, though, so I hadn't paid much attention to the parting.

I stood up quickly, went to my horse, and started digging through my packs.

"Azrel? Do we have the key?" Ortheldo asked.

I didn't answer and kept sifting through my things until I felt the cold metal of the small, unimpressive brass key. I pulled it out and presented it to my party. "We do."

All of them smiled as I knelt down on the ground again and slipped the key into the keyhole. It fit perfectly. I turned it, and with a heavy metal clang, the door unlocked. I pulled on the handle again and the door opened all the way. I sighed with satisfaction but then looked at my horse and my heart sank. This was the part we had to take on foot. Not only would the horses not fit through the door, but we couldn't chance their hooves clopping too loudly over the barren rock in Tabway Pass and drawing the Stone Trolls' attention.

"Hey," Forfirith said, "this isn't goodbye forever. We'll meet again on the other side of Spar Ridges."

I petted his cheeks and kissed his forehead. "I know, but that's two weeks away—a week in and a week out."

"Eh, it will fly by in no time. You'll see." I smiled. "You'd better get your stuff."

I nodded and went around to his side, as did everyone else to their horses. We gathered our packs, which were going to be a huge burden to begin with. They were so full and heavy, but we needed everything we could carry. The Pass was two days travel on foot, and going through Spar Ridges woods would take another five days. There was no guarantee that Spar Ridges would even resupply us when we got there, so we had to take that much extra to get us another seven days out the other side.

I said goodbye to my horse and he led the other horses away to go the long way around Spar Ridges. I wasn't looking forward to going through one of the darkest realms of Light in Casdanarus, but the White Warrior wouldn't tell me who the damn necklace's owner was until I did.

I sighed and hiked my heavy pack up higher onto my back. I looked at my friends. "Shall we?"

Rabryn picked up some long, dead sticks, and with one swipe of his hand, they blazed to life with his gold magic, lighting our way in the tunnel. We each took one and headed down the stairs in front of us. Ortheldo closed the door behind him.

THREE

"Why are you playing with her?" Glondra asked in a tone I really wasn't in the mood for.

I spun to face her with a look that made her cower back a step. I couldn't wait until she was gone, something that would occur soon. "I have my reasons," I replied, silencing her. I turned back and continued to gather the precious and rare materials for the drastic move that was about to take place in this war.

"Hathum," she said carefully behind me, "I want you to succeed. You may not be powerful enough magically yet, but with the size of your force you could wipe out Casdanarus. Why aren't you?"

I didn't respond as I concentrated on plucking a very fragile jar off the shelf in front of me. I slowly and deliberately put it on the floor with both hands.

Glondra sighed, "You know I hate to admit it, but I honestly don't mean to question you out of disrespect. I just wish you would tell me what you were thinking. Let me serve you, brother. I want to help."

She really was desperate for information if she wasn't mouthing off to me like she usually did. I looked over my shoulder at her. "I have no qualms about enlisting your service when I need it," I said. "I just don't need it right now."

She caught sight of the jar on the floor, and a mischievous smile spread across her face. "You're doing it?" she asked eagerly. "It's happening?" Suddenly Thaybo appeared in front of me next to Glondra, sensing her excitement at the ingredients I was gathering. They both exchanged mischievous smiles before looking back at me.

I turned my back to them and continued gathering ingredients in the Wizard pantry of the great Black Mountains. This place held the rarest magic ingredients in the world. I would know, because I was the one who had acquired the collection.

"The Shadow Gods used Their limited power to resurrect these three vessels because we were the only magic users in the history of creation who could contain Their power." I met Glondra's and Thaybo's eager eyes. "Now it's time to Surrender these vessels back to Them."

Thaybo smirked. "Well it's about damn time," he said, pleased.

Both of them gathered to pick up the ingredients I had pulled from the shelf while I carefully took the edges of the black clay pot. I started to make my way slowly up the stone steps with both of them following close behind. At the top, on the long abandoned main floor of the Black Mountain kingdom, was a gaping hole in the wall of the mountain that allowed full view of the neighboring realm of Godel. The only boundary between the two mountain ranges was Blood River, named so because of the red color it turned when the first war with the White Warrior ended. Blood from friend and foe had been washed into it during a catastrophic rainstorm that had cleansed every battlefield on the face of Casdanarus.

I felt my eyebrow twitch as I gazed at the towering peaks across the river. There was a powerful presence around Godel. Something ancient was protecting the realm now. Not that it really mattered. Once I completed the Surrender, there would be no power on earth, ancient or otherwise, that could keep the Shadow out of those mountains.

I started heading down another stairway that lead to the crypts of the Black Mountains. "Is everything ready for the march to Godel?" I asked, my voice echoing dully off the stone walls.

"Our forces are already on their way," Thaybo replied.

"Good. The Surrender will leave us useless for at least a week while these vessels heal. The army is on their own after that."

The stairs ended in a vast gray stone room with twelve arched hallways, four on each wall. Stone columns stood everywhere, and it had low stone ceiling. My head nearly brushed the roof as I walked straight across to one of the arched tunnels directly in front of me. Inside that crypt was a grave I had unearthed from the stone not yesterday—Ghee.

Ghee had been the first ruler of the Black Mountains, a Salynn Humount Queen from eons ago who had established the Black Mountains as a place of sanctuary and worship for the Shadow Gods and Their followers. She'd lived for countless millenniums and was on the tail end of dying, being called "home" she'd referred to it, when I had been able to meet her. During that meeting, she'd given me a powerful magical ingredient for this very Surrender. Somehow she knew it was coming and she knew I would be a vessel, even though I had barely come into my black Wizard powers back then.

I set the fragile pot down carefully at the foot of her skeleton, which was barely more than dust, and slowly opened it. Wisps of her black Salynn magic gently swirled around the rim like tiny light sprites. Lighting my hand up with black fire, I slowly reached into the pot. The wisps of energy converged onto my hand until I was able to reach the very bottom. I gripped what was inside and slowly pulled it out. It was a long, fully intact strand of blonde hair with healthy, living black Sallybreath flowers still present on it. Ghee's hair. She had cut off the strand in my presence when I met her, leaving a piece of her life force and her magic with it to keep it alive until this day.

The "Life of a Dead Ruler" was the rarest and most difficult ingredient to get for the Surrender spell. It required steps beforehand that involved necromancy and bringing a ruler back to life in an animated, but not alive, form, and then trying to convince him or her to sacrifice himself or herself. It was all a very difficult and long process, but one I could avoid because right in my palm I had some of Ghee's life that she'd willingly handed over, and even had preserved.

I walked around the corpse and rested the strand of hair gently across her ribcage. Then, taking the other ingredients, I started building the spell. I pulled out a long, thin knife and began to chant incantations, cutting myself and drawing sigils all over the crypt in my blood—on the floor, on the walls, and on the bones.

Suddenly, the entire earth started to tremble—gently at first, but with increasing force, until everything shook so violently that my surroundings were a complete blur. I clenched my teeth and grinned menacingly, knowing the Light Gods would feel this quaking in their bones! They would know then. *They would know* that I was calling the full power of the Shadow Gods to myself and my companions, and the Light Gods were powerless to stop me. Before, I'd had a piece of Them, my Shadow Gods' black fire, but just a piece. Now, however, this was something more.

An unexpected white light formed above me. I looked up to see a section of the stone ceiling had vanished, and the sky just above me opened up, going from blue to white. The Light Gods were standing there, looking down at me from their lofty perch in the Sky Sanctuary, and I smirked at Them.

"Your precious White Warrior never had to face these odds, now did he?"

They cast worried glances at each other, which sent a wave of exhilaration through me. Clenching my teeth, I looked down so I could slice the skin of my forearm wide open. My blood sprayed all over the corpse and I bled heavily onto the pyre of spells and ingredients in her ribs. Maniacal chuckling began to bubble up in my chest as thick black smoke began to fill the crypt. The laughing gradually got louder and louder until I could barely control myself and barely breathe. The Light Gods were watching Their defeat right before Their eyes.

My companions also began bleeding onto the fire, and we called all three Shadow Gods to ourselves, surrendering our bodies to Them so They could walk the earth in the flesh for the first time ever.

I glanced up at the Light Gods again as I felt the end of myself at hand. "Enjoy your defeat," I said to Them. "It's been long in coming." I threw my head back and laughed hysterically.

In that moment, a tidal wave of black fire erupted from the ground with the force of a volcano, blasting through the top of the Black Mountains. I was gleeful as I heard screams of terror come from every single Light magic user in the known land, even beyond Casdanarus. Their terrified screams filled my ears as much as the roars and cheers of victory that arose from my Shadow soldiers and creatures. I laughed hard as I lifted my bleeding arms over my head and the oceanic tidal wave of black fire seeped into my wounds, as well as those of my two companions.

I felt the merge of myself and my Shadow God, and a storm of ancient thoughts, knowledge and existence swirled through me like a hurricane. I felt him inside me, and soon I wasn't sure where he started and I ended. I had relished this moment, dreamed about it, and now it had arrived. Once the black fire was absorbed, my body fell to the crypt floor. There I stayed and let the pain of the fusion fill our vessels.

My vessel was that of Hathum, my strongest magical warrior that ever existed. It wasn't often I was proud of a minion of mine, but Hathum had done exceptionally well, better than anyone before him. He'd died long ago from energy loss of creating the Nameless One. That creation was so powerful it had taken all of Hathum's magic and his life force, too. Although the creation was defeated, thus destroying me, I'd resurrected Hathum's body as soon as I had regained a fraction of my power, and had waited for this moment.

Being so weak after being destroyed in the form of the Nameless One, there was nothing I could do but rest and recharge. Over the past three thousand years, I had done what I could with the small amount of power I had, but it wasn't much. It was Hathum who had done most of my bidding. He was faithful like no minion of mine ever had been.

Now, all hell was going to break loose—because I was about to rip it open.

FOUR

It had been silent and easy through Tabway Pass for nearly two full days. It was actually really beautiful walking through the canyon. Rock colors and formations that I could never imagine surrounded me wherever I looked. Though the Stone Trolls were a constant threat that kept me on edge, we stayed silent by communicating through Rabryn's magic link in our heads. We were just about eight hours from Spar Ridges' woods when I began to relax.

I had just started to prepare myself for those woods when something out of the blue felt terribly wrong. I stopped in my tracks and began to look around the pass in a mad panic. Something huge was happening. Something! Something! But where? I met my brother's eyes and saw him and Moifulyar looking around in the same manner. It felt like the sky was about to fall on my head, but I couldn't see anything! I spun around looking for something, *anything* that could cause this horrible, dreaded sensation.

What's wrong? Ortheldo asked casually.

How could he not feel that!

Azrel... Rabryn said breathlessly.

Suddenly the entire earth started shaking. It was gradual at first, and somehow I knew it wasn't just beneath me. I could feel it everywhere! Then it became so violent that my brain felt like it was bouncing off the sides of my skull. The shaking threw all of us down hard. It was so turbulent that I could feel my body vibrating against the stone ground.

As I forced myself to my hands and knees, I suddenly got the strange sensation of being solid and whole, but at the same time my entire consciousness seemed to shatter and spread out to the very ends of the earth! I could see and feel the entire world shaking as if I were in every single place at the same time. I saw people, Light and Shadow alike. The Shadow soldiers and creatures were shouting and cheering as if they were at a victory rally, and millions upon millions of people were screaming in terror at some invisible enemy I couldn't see.

I crushed my hands over my ears to try to block them all out, but it was useless! My head throbbed and ached from feeling like it had just exploded. I could see people and creatures beyond the oceans and into lands I'd never seen or heard of. Yet I was still somehow still intact, here, in the same place, Tabway Pass.

My eyes started hurting and my vision blurred. There was nothing I could do but endure the horror of whatever was happening across the globe. My nose started to bleed. The screams! They were everywhere! I could hear them *all!*

Azrel! Azrel! Addredoc was suddenly yelling in my head as well. *Something happened!*

I couldn't take the noise or the stretching of my brain! I squeezed my eyes shut, hoping it would stop, hoping to shut out what I was seeing everywhere. I pressed my hands against my ears harder, but nothing blocked it out. I finally couldn't squelch the long scream of pain that erupted from my throat.

Then it was silent. The shaking stopped. The screams stopped. Even Addredoc was silent. I was in one piece. I couldn't see or feel the terror all over the planet anymore.

I collapsed onto my side and then rolled onto my back, half from relief and half from exhaustion. I was trembling and panting and my ears were ringing loudly. My entire body felt heavy, so I just lay limply on the ground trying to slow my breathing.

Ortheldo's face appeared above me. He was yelling something, but his voice sounded like it was coming from a mile underwater. That was when I felt a gentler, more rhythmic tremor in the earth. I forced some feeble strength into my arms and sat up propped on my elbows. Looking past Ortheldo, I caught sight of Acalith behind him; her eyes were glowing so bright green that I could see it in the daylight.

My eyes went wide. "Oh no." The Stone Trolls. My scream. They must have heard it.

I shakily got to my knees, using Ortheldo's shoulder for support and balance. My whole body was still trembling as I looked at my brother. He was sitting on the ground against a nearby rock formation with his eyes half closed, and he was panting. Moifulyar was kneeling beside him in the same shape.

I quickly made my way to them and cupped Rabryn's face in

my hands. "Are you all right?" They'd clearly been affected by whatever that was, yet Ortheldo and Acalith had not.

He was nodding. "What...what was that, Azrel?"

I shook my head and ran my thumb under his nose when a drop of blood seeped out. "I don't know. What did it feel like to you?"

Rabryn shook his head. "Just fear. Terror. It rose up in me from out of nowhere, like something was deeply wrong, but nothing was around; then the earth started to shake."

My brows dropped. "But it was just you?"

Rabryn looked at me confused. "What? What do you mean?"

I sighed and bowed my head before looking back up at him. "You couldn't feel everyone's terror? Or see the Shadow regimes cheering?"

"What? No." His eyes filled with deep concern as he leaned toward me. "Why? Is that what you felt?"

I shook my head and pressed the heels of my hands into my eyes. "I can't explain it."

A distant moaning sound came to my ears. I got to my feet and glanced around the Pass. Suddenly I saw them, only a mile off—at least eight enormous Stone Trolls coming straight toward us. Before I could gather my thoughts, one of the trolls reached out to its side and yanked a huge chunk of rock off the top of a stone pillar. My eyes went wide as I watched its arm arch back and hurl the gigantic boulder at us.

All of us jumped out of the way as it smashed into the barren ground nearby and exploded into splinters. I heard everyone cried out in pain as shards hit us. We scattered instantly, hiding behind various rock formations. Ducking behind a small plateau of rock, I suddenly realized I couldn't move my left arm. When I looked down, I saw a long, thin shard of stone embedded in the outside of my shoulder. Gritting my teeth, I gripped the shard with my right hand and yanked it out, screaming as it dislodged. The blood flow was heavy as I pressed on the wound trying to stop the bleeding. This was bad, really bad.

I peeked around the formation I was hiding behind and saw at least a dozen Stone Trolls against the horizon now. Several boulders slammed into the ground near me. The loud snap of stones filled the entire canyon. Pressing my palms to my ears did little to muffle it. After two days of utter silence, I now felt like I was going deaf from the eruption of all the loud, terrible sounds.

"Addredoc!" I screamed out loud, as well as into the magical link, as another barrage of boulders cracked into the ground nearby.

I couldn't overtly use my magic; I *wouldn't* overtly use my magic! Not until I found out what just happened with that earthquake. I could *not* risk being found by Hathum now, because whatever had just happened was bad news for me. I didn't know what it was, but I didn't want to give Hathum any way to find me. Hathum could *not* hone in on me by any means!

Azrel! Addredoc screamed over another thunderous snap and explosion of boulders breaking into a thousand pieces. *What the hell is happening? Something terrorized most of the magic users here, but there was nothing! Then black fire erupted from the Black Mountains, taller than the mountain itself! Then there was an earthquake!*

I know! I cried. *The whole thing was global. I felt the terror and heard the screams all over the world.*

What?

Never mind! We're under attack from Stone Trolls!

What!

Another boulder was flung at us. It exploded closer, and I heard another few cries of pain come from my companions as they were hit by shards of it. The constant barrage of stone was successfully pinning us all in our places. I peeked around my hiding place again and saw the Stone Trolls were only about ten strides away.

I need to use your magic to destroy them! I can't use mine. Not until I find out what that earthquake was. If Hathum caused that, if he's powerful enough to do that, he will obliterate me if he finds me now!

All right, I'll be there in a second.

No! You stay and protect Godel. That black fire came from next door to you. They need you. Just feed me your power. Can you do that from this distance?

Yes. How many are there?

At least a dozen.

Damn it!

Addredoc, I said, trying to stay calm. *You might have to clear out the people of Godel. Keep an eye on the Black Mountains, and if you even* think *Hathum is coming your way, get them the hell out of there. Bring whomever you can to me. Some soldiers are better than none. Leave the ones that have rejected me.*

You got it.

My entire body started heating up as Addredoc poured his incredible power into me though that magical link. Another barrage of boulders hit the ground around us. Rock exploded everywhere! The boulders landed in front of us, behind, and on both sides, sending up shards in every direction. I threw my arm up on front of my face trying to protect myself from them, only to have my forearm impaled with small slivers.

At one point I found myself glaring up at the sky towards the Light Gods, my heart racing with more anger toward them than any other emotion. "Any time You want to give me my full powers and my crown, I'll take them. But please, take your sweet time. It's not like the world is ending or anything."

I peeked around the rock again to see three more boulders being flung at us. There was absolutely nowhere, and no way to run. The Trolls were only five strides away. *Don't drain yourself, Addredoc!* I cried, feeling hot enough to combust.

Please. I'm fine.

Another boulder exploded near me, and I screamed as my head snapped to the side and flash of white hot pain shot from the front of my skull all the way down my back.

Azrel!

I paused a moment, taking inventory of the damage. I wasn't blind. My head was hot and throbbing. It must have just missed my eyes and sliced open my forehead. My arm was starting to bleed through my fingers, but I was still breathing.

I'm fine, I replied as I blinked away the blood that was trying to drip into my eye. I slowly got into a low couch and peeked around the rock formation again. My eyes went wide. *They're only two strides away, Addredoc!*

Then go!

I pulled Addredoc's magic into my hands until red fire erupted in my palms. I actually flinched when I realized it was fire. Wizards couldn't conjure fire in their magic, only heat and light separately. They could do smoke, too, if need be, or maybe jagged lightning, but never fire. Only I had the power to conjure fire…only I and Hathum.

I gave Addredoc a sensation of slight wonder and a bit of suspicion mixed with awe before I jumped out from behind the rock and threw my hands out in front of me. I sent up a wall of red fire three hundred feet high toward the Stone Trolls! They were so close I could make out details of the bottoms of their feet that were now frozen in midstride. All twelve monsters bellowed loudly as tiny jagged red lights zigzagged all over their bodies. It only lasted a moment before, in a thunderous explosion so loud it shook the ground, they were destroyed.

I immediately felt the weakness seep in and dropped to a knee. I only had enough time to wonder why I was weak when I had used Addredoc's magic, not my own. Then the rock ground came up to meet my face and everything went black.

FIVE

ACALITH

It turned out that Spar Ridges woods was a humid, horrid terrain. Our clothes were soaked from both the moisture in the air and our own sweat. They clung uncomfortably to us like a miserable second skin. Not to mention that the thick leafy foliage was a continuous obstacle that we had to cut, duck under, step over, or move aside. Even though I'd grown up in Spar Ridges, I'd never been here, nor had I ever been to Tabway Pass before yesterday.

Azrel was ahead of the pack right now, having rested and been carried by Ortheldo, until we reached the edge of the woods. Upon waking, Rabryn had healed her wounds and after eating something, we entered this ridiculous terrain.

Azrel still remained exhausted and terrified in more ways than one. She didn't realize how much she actually wore her emotions on her sleeve, at least enough for me to take notice of. She was trying to figure out what that earthquake was, why she had fainted in Tabway Pass, and why Addredoc was able to conjure fire, while at the same time worrying about him, since he wasn't answering her in their communication link. None of that really concerned me as much as the fact that today she was still looking over her shoulder at our covered trail, just like she'd been doing for the past two and a half weeks. I thought for sure whatever was following us, which apparently had a problem with me, would have been lost when we entered Tabway. I guess that had been too much to hope for. On top of all of that, Azrel was trying to keep her guard up as we trudged miserably through these dangerous, wet woods.

This entire area was infamously known for the amount Shadow creatures it harbored, most of them so old that they were all but immune to modern-day magic. I didn't understand it. Did Shadow creatures *enjoy* extreme wet heat or something? Maybe these woods were the same climate of the Abyss from where they spawned, so they felt most comfortable here.

Everyone took notice quickly that my eyes continuously glowed green. While we weren't under attack, the soft steady glow just went to show that we were under constant threat. The cause for worry now was to see if they brightened, which would mean danger was on its way.

We didn't talk much. Well, Azrel didn't talk much. I looked at her now as she walked in front of the group. She looked positively weighed down with sagging shoulders and limp, damp hair. I imagined, as she stared at the ground, that she was constantly trying to reach Addredoc.

It didn't help that I couldn't magically transport her to Spar Ridges. Neither could Rabryn or Moifulyar. Azrel believed the White Warrior wanted her to walk it to learn more "lessons" before she would give up the name of the necklace's owner. The sooner we got rid of that necklace, the better, but Azrel was right in not allowing magical aid. The White Warrior told me and Moifulyar personally not provide it on this journey. She hadn't told me why, but then again, she never explained herself. Though I questioned her, I wouldn't disobey her. Who was I supposed to be loyal to, though? Azrel or The White Warrior? But my problems were minimal. Azrel had the real gnarly looking pile of mess in front of her.

I picked up my pace to walk beside her. "How are you doing?"

She didn't even lift her head to look at me. "Fine."

"Liar."

She glanced up and gave me a small smile of appreciation before casting her eyes back down. "Okay, I'm not fine."

"Have you heard from Addredoc yet?"

She shook her head. "I keep trying to reach him."

We walked silently for a few moments. I sighed when she looked over her shoulder yet again. "Still being followed?"

Azrel nodded in response as she faced forward with her head down again. "I'm pretty certain now that it has a problem with you, though, not Rabryn."

"How comforting."

She met my eyes. "I'm not going to let anything happen to you."

I gave her a small smirk. "I'm the one that protects you, remember? Not the other way around." She gave me a small, tired smile before facing forward again.

We trudged on in silence until the sun went down. That night, Azrel set up watches and actually gave me the second one. I was surprised because she hadn't given me a watch on my own since before we entered Tabway Pass. I had an idea of what Azrel was thinking and it was just fine with me. She was probably just as sick of looking over her shoulder as the rest of us were.

I didn't sleep very well because my mind wouldn't stop running. So by the time Ortheldo came to get me for my watch, I was already up gathering my weapons. I cast a quick glance at Rabryn asleep on the ground and gave a forlorn sigh. I thought I was quick about it, but when I met Ortheldo's eyes, he was looking at me sympathetically.

"Still trying to deny you're in love with him, I see."

I couldn't discuss this with him. I just shook my head and walked past him to go take my watch.

"You can't keep it up forever," he said after me, making me look back over my shoulder. He still had a sympathetic look on his face. "It will eat you alive, and you know it."

There was a pause. I knew he was right because it was already eating me alive.

He took a few steps, closing the distance between us, and put his hand on my shoulder. "You have to tell him who you are." I looked away, only to have him gently push at my shoulder until I looked back at him. He stooped, bringing his strange eyes right in front of mine. "He'd rather hear it from you before we get to Spar Ridges than hear it from some stranger there who recognizes you."

I hiked the quiver of arrows higher onto my shoulder. "We still have a week before we get there. I'd rather enjoy what little time I have left with him before he knows."

Ortheldo nodded and straightened, dropping his hand off my shoulder. "Just tell him before we get there is all I'm saying. Trust me. It will be better that way for both of you."

I nodded before I walked away. I found a rock that gave me full view of the camp while keeping me hidden from sight. I sat down heavily and continued to indulge my racing mind that refused to let me rest. I was dreading the return to Spar Ridges. It was the single most brutal land when it came to hatred for the White Warrior. Azrel had decided since the earthquake that she was not going to use her magic, and that gave me some comfort about her not being discovered. But if I was discovered, we would probably be spending more time in Spar Ridges then we liked, which only allowed more time for Azrel to be found out. I could not let that happen while we were there. She *had* to stay hidden. After that earthquake, it was vital that she stay off Hathum's magical radar. The Gods only knew what had triggered something that massive and widespread. Ortheldo and I hadn't felt it, but Azrel, Rabryn and Moifulyar's descriptions were terrifying.

I looked up at the sky and thought about praying to the Light Gods with a slim hope They might actually answer me. I shook my head, then, and looked down instead. Faith. I wasn't much for it, but I had to trust the Light Gods. They wouldn't let the world end. If They wanted that, They would never have created the White Warrior in the first place to save it. They would have just let it die under the Shadow Gods' rule. They gave a damn about the world. They had to! But what were They doing?

I interlaced my fingers and rested them behind my neck as I stared at the ground. My mind went to this mysterious presence following us. My lip twitched with reined-in rage. The last thing in the world Azrel needed right now was some nuisance on our tail. It had to go...which was probably the reason she'd set me up on a watch tonight. She'd wanted me to draw it out, or perhaps take it out. I was happy with either.

I felt eyes rest on me. My brows drew together and my lip twitched again as I brought my head up. They were behind me. I stood up slowly from the rock and turned around to face the darkness. None of us were in the mood to be hunted by this thing any longer.

Clenching my teeth, I quickly drew my sword out and gripped it in a fist. "All right!" I called into the darkness. "You want me? Come on!" I glared into the silent night, waiting. The moments dragged for eternity, but I knew it hadn't left. I could still feel it watching me. "What are you waiting for?" I yelled. "Let's get this show on the road!"

I heard a low growl. It was closer than I thought it would be. Suddenly, a moonbeam passed over the creature's eyes, making them flash blue, and the shadow of a massive wolf took shape as it slowly came through the trees. I thought it was a Welptack at first, but it wasn't a deformed ugly beast. It looked like a normal wild wolf with silver gray hair, only it was nearly the size of a horse. Even on all fours, it stood as tall as my shoulders.

When it came fully into the moonlight, my eyes widened. "Ceco?" I breathed, recognizing her. She was the wolf guard from Fayithjen Forest, a Born Wizard, and she was one of Azrel's protectors under my command! "Ceco, what the hell are you..."

She lunged at me. I managed to spin away, so she jumped past me. Barely before I regained my composure, she lunged at me again, forcing me to spin out of the way a second time. I brought my sword up and around and felt a satisfying chunk of skin get sliced from her shoulder. I faced her, taking a battle stance. She faced me with her head bowed low, teeth bared, and lips trembling.

I didn't want to hurt her, but she wasn't giving me any choice. She lunged again, sailing straight toward my head. I dropped my sword and took a fist full of fur in my hands from her chest and stomach and, using her own momentum, slammed her headfirst into the ground behind me. I heard bone crack. I picked up my sword again and ran at her. I kicked her as hard as I could in the ribs, slamming her against a rock behind her once, twice, three times and hearing bone crack each time.

She tried to get up, but she was too slow, so I kicked her hard right underneath her chin with the toe of my boot. I was hoping that would subdue her enough before she forced me to kill her, but before I could even take a firm battle stance again, she was at me faster than I thought she was capable of.

I brought my sword across her chest in an attempt to defend myself, but I moved too soon and felt her powerful jaws clamp down on my forearm. I screamed more in shock than pain as my sword clattered to the ground. Desperately, I started slamming my fist into her eye over and over again. She didn't back down or let go. In fact, I felt her bite down even harder while I brutalized her eye. She seemed to barely even feel it, while I felt every single one of her wet teeth sink deeper into my skin. Blood poured from my wound, dripping off her chin and onto the ground. I tried to reach around behind me for my hunting blade, but she clamped down harder on my arm and my bone snapped.

I screamed in pain this time and dropped down to a knee. It felt like she had ripped my arm completely off. I tried to punch her in the eye again with my free arm, but it still barely fazed her, even though her eye looked more like ground mutton now than an eyeball. The entire side of her face was a puffy, bloody mess.

As the world started to get fuzzy, Azrel's grim face appeared before me as she wrapped both of her arms tightly around Ceco's throat. Only a few moments passed before the wolf's good eye began to roll into the back of her head and the grip on my arm loosened. When Ceco finally passed out on the ground, Azrel was the one that caught me before I did as well. She gently laid me on my back and started screaming something at Rabryn that I couldn't really hear.

Oh no. I'd lost too much blood.

Rabryn, Ortheldo and Moifulyar suddenly came running up. Rabryn dropped to his knees by my side. Damn. I didn't want to die like this. It was too soon. I somehow felt like I was failing Azrel by dying right now. I looked up at her, vaguely trying to voice my apologies, but I wasn't sure my mouth was working.

My gaze then shifted to Rabryn. As I looked into his blue eyes, I thought I began to say something to him as well, but I wasn't completely sure. I started having to take in breaths in jerky pants just to get some air. Then a very relaxed, calm feeling started to settle in all around me. Rabryn was shaking his head at me. I staved off death for a little bit longer just so I could look at his face for a few more seconds.

Yes. If I was going to go, this was a good way to leave, looking into Rabryn's eyes. I don't think I blinked even once as the darkness took me.

———

I was surprised when I felt the sun suddenly warming my face. I was sure I'd been dead. But upon opening my eyes, the daylight burned a hole in that concern. I flinched, closing my eyes quickly again as I took an inventory of my situation. I quickly realized that I was being carried. Oh how embarrassing! The Deralilya, being carried through the forest as if she were a newborn.

I struggled against the person holding me. "What? Are you...Put me down!"

The person desperately held on to me as if they thought I was too weak to stand on my own, but the truth was I never felt stronger. I felt ready to take on an entire army of Gorkors! I wasn't even groggy or weak. Eventually my struggling became too much and my feet were placed onto the ground. I stumbled away and realized it had been Rabryn carrying me.

I sighed heavily and pulled down the bottom of my shirt as I composed myself. I was about to say something rude about how I wasn't a weakling, when I suddenly realized I was using both of my arms. My eyes widened a bit as I held up my right forearm. Pulling up my sleeve I saw smooth, healed skin. There wasn't even a scar left, never mind any chewed up flesh and bone.

I smiled at Rabryn. "I guess you got to me in time, huh?"

With a grateful smile, he stepped forward and pulled me into a tight, warm hug. I let myself enjoy it for a moment, long enough for him to whisper in my ear, "I don't know what I would have done."

I wanted to stay in his arms forever, even more so as he buried his face into my hair and sighed. But all this was just a painful reminder that we couldn't be together. I sighed and pulled away from him, giving him an awkward smile in response to his confusion. I couldn't bear the hurt I saw in his eyes so I turned away, only to find myself face to face with Ceco.

I gasped and spun around faster then I'd ever moved in my life, yanked Rabryn's sword out of his belt, and took a battle stance before her. It took a moment to take in the scene before me. Ceco wasn't a threat. Azrel had her sword against Ceco's throat and was riding her! She even had all of our packs strapped onto her back like a pack mule.

Azrel looked over her shoulder. "Moifulyar, take over."

"Yes, Azrel."

With that, Azrel slid off Ceco, dismounting her. She kept her sword against the wolf's throat until Moifulyar had mounted and taken out his blade to replace her sword. "Let's go, wolf," Moifulyar said. He pulled one of Ceco's ears to the side as if it were horse reigns and turned her. Ceco tried to glance back at me, but as soon as she did, Moifulyar's sword came down in front of her eyes, blocking her view. She turned and began to make her way through the woods again.

Azrel quickly came toward me and embraced me tightly. I found myself eager to accept it, and I embraced her as well. "I was so afraid we'd lost you," she said softly into my hair.

I couldn't help smiling. "Who me? It's going to take more than a dog bite to get rid of me."

Azrel laughed and held onto me for a moment longer before

pulling away and looking at me with concern. "How do you feel?"

I shrugged. "Honestly, I've never felt better. Your brother gave me some super juice or something when he healed me. How long have I been out?"

"Only a few hours."

"Long enough for the sun to come up," Rabryn said behind me.

I looked at him over my shoulder and held his sword out to him. "Thanks for saving my life."

He looked at me begrudgingly and then snatched his sword from my hand. "Don't mention it," he said coldly and started to walk away. I gazed after him longingly and sighed. I'd hurt him. I *was* hurting him.

"All right!" Azrel suddenly yelled so loudly that I jumped and Rabryn stopped in his tracks. "That's enough!" She looked at me. "What is going on? What are you not telling us about your time in Spar Ridges, Acalith?"

I looked away from her to Rabryn. He looked back at me with weary expectation. I didn't want to tell them. I particularly didn't want Azrel to know. I didn't want her to see me as weak or undermine my prowess as a warrior. I didn't want her to have to worry about me doing my job properly of protecting her. Of *all* the times she could have pushed this issue, it had to be now, after my pathetic display with Ceco last night. Couldn't she have waited so I could build up her confidence in me again?

"Acalith!" she yelled in such a sharp tone that I jumped a little again. Her teeth were clenched and she was glaring at me. "Look, I know you've fallen in love with my brother."

My eyes widened, as did Rabryn's, the expression of disbelief on his face mirroring my own. How could she have known?

"I read eyes like a book, remember?" she responded. "Don't worry," she went on a little softer. "He's in love with you, too."

My heart leapt up into my throat and I made a conscious effort to not look at Rabryn at the moment. I wasn't sure I could handle the way he might be looking at me.

"Whatever secret you're keeping, it's hurting him." Azrel shook her head. "And I don't tolerate harm coming to my brother—emotional or physical or anything in between. Not if I can do something about it." Her voice and eyes got a bit softer as she took a step toward me. "I also know that whatever you're hiding is hurting you as well. So what it is?"

I bit my lip. I couldn't bring myself to say it. But she looked in my eyes, and when she saw the answer there, her expression dropped. All I could do was bow my head in shame.

"Hey, what's taking so long?" Ortheldo said, appearing on the path in front of us. "Why are you…" His voice trailed off when he took in the scene in front of him. Me, my head bowed under Azrel's astonished gaze, and Rabryn still looking confused, his eyes pleading for an answer.

I turned my eyes up to Azrel to see if her expression had changed at all, but it hadn't. I wanted to say something, but I didn't want to snap something that would provoke her to start in on me. I glanced at Ortheldo, who was looking at me with a sympathetic gaze, and I silently begged for his help. He could calm her down. I was afraid to move or even swallow too hard, and my lungs burned for more air than I was allowing from the short swallow breaths I was taking.

Ortheldo finally stepped up next to Azrel, putting his arm around her waist and pressing his face into her hair to whisper something in her ear. Azrel stood there staring at me a moment longer before reluctantly allowing Ortheldo to guide her away. I stood motionless and quiet under Rabryn's eyes until I couldn't hear Ortheldo and Azrel's footsteps any longer. Then I blew out a breath and my entire body sagged in relief and dread. I stood there a moment, letting my nerves settle before attempting to take a step.

When I looked up again, Rabryn was walking up to me purposefully. "What is it?"

I sighed and closed my eyes in defeat and tried to walk around him. I was not prepared to discuss this with him.

He quickly moved to stand in front of me stopping me and looked at me intensely. "Acalith."

I rolled my eyes. "Rabryn, look, I can't deal with you right now. In case you missed it, Azrel sort of just revealed something I'm not entirely comfortable with thinking about right now. I need time to compose and adjust."

He gave me his stubborn look, and I knew I wasn't going to get away with not telling him. "Fine. You can compose and adjust *after* you tell me why you're in love with me but closing yourself off from me."

"Gods almighty, Rabryn!" I cried, slapping both of my hands over my face. "Love! Ugh. I can't deal with this. You were never supposed to know!" I looked at him. "How can you talk about it so casually?"

"Don't try to change the subject," he said, narrowing his eyes at me. It amazed me how he could look so upset but so kind at the same time. He always looked kind, no matter what sort of battle he was facing. His big blue eyes always looked soft and inviting. "What are you not telling me?"

I glared at him as hatefully as I could in hopes he would back off, but he didn't. He just gave me the stubborn look again. Resigned, I sighed. "You're the king of White Veilvin, right?"

He rolled his eyes away briefly, still not completely comfortable with that matter. "Yeah," he said looking back at me.

I glared at him, "Well, congratulations. Now you're not allowed to even *be* with anyone outside of your own race." I swallowed heavily. "Least of all, the Princess of Spar Ridges." His eyes went wide. "Unless you want to start a war between our lands."

He looked at me, silently horrified. I crossed my arms and cleared my throat, trying to ease the pain and the awkwardness. "So I figured I would spare us both the pain of attempting to start a romantic relationship. Only to end it later in order to avoid war between your land"—I swallowed heavily—"and mine."

He was quiet for a long time before he glanced down and nodded. "So you closed yourself off from me," he said with understanding.

I nodded. "There is some serious bad blood between our realms. Your people, especially, would never let their king become involved with someone outside of White Veilvin." I gave him a sarcastic grin. "Can't have the likes of me polluting your royal line, Rabryn."

Rabryn met my eyes suddenly with such fierce defiance that I didn't even have time to take a breath before he swept in, wrapped an arm tightly around my back, and pulled me against him in a long, firm kiss. I would have gasped if I could. I nearly pulled away and slapped him, but then his other hand gently rested on my cheek with his fingertips just touching the edge of my hair, and I absolutely didn't have the strength to resist him. He held me tightly, which was a good thing because my knees went weak. He pulled away and my heart nearly failed when I saw how deeply he was looking into my eyes. He kissed my lips gently once more before he softly caressed my cheek.

"Rabryn," I said breathlessly. "Your people will kill you or, at the very least, disown you if you take this path. My people will, too."

He didn't look away from my eyes once as he smirked. "Do I look like someone who cares about the rules? Have you met my sister?" I found myself smiling as he shrugged a shoulder. "They want to disown me, let them. I didn't want this crown in the first place."

"But it's your father's crown too."

"My father is dead. Besides"—he shook his head with conviction—"I know my dad, and he would want me to have love over a piece of metal and a position anyway." He smiled down at me. "So please"—he slowly leaned his face toward mine again and glanced at my lips—"stop shutting me out."

I actually smiled and let myself be happy for an instant as his lips came to meet mine again. Maybe it wouldn't work, maybe war couldn't be avoided, but if anyone could deal with it, it was he and his sister. That was, if Azrel even approved of me being with her brother.

I knew that if Azrel had an issue with it—and it was likely she did, based on her reaction a moment ago—Rabryn would not choose me over his sister. Never in a million eons would that happen, and I wouldn't want it to.

I reluctantly pulled away from Rabryn. "I think Azrel will have a problem with this."

His brows dropped. "Why?"

"You saw just now. She couldn't even say anything to me."

Rabryn smiled. "Azrel's not mad that you're the Princess of Spar Ridges. She's mad that you didn't tell her right away."

"You think?" I asked, letting myself feel hope.

"I *know*. Why did you keep it a secret from her anyway?"

I sighed and pulled away from him, but reached down and took his hand as we started walking to catch up with the others. "I didn't want my being a pampered princess to make her question my ability to protect her. I wanted her to have complete confidence in me. I know her views of royalty, and they are less than positive to say the least."

"That was actually probably a good call on your part," he conceded. I smiled at him. He smiled back and then put his arm around my waist and kissed my cheek. "Azrel will be fine soon enough. She cares more about my happiness than her pride, so if being with you makes me happy, she'll be okay."

I allowed myself to rest my head on his shoulder. We walked for a few moments in silence and I tried to fight the negative thoughts coming to my mind about being with Rabryn and what could happen. Soon the silence needed filling. "So did the psycho pup explain why she attacked me last night?"

Rabryn shook his head. "No, but I know why, I think."

"You know she's supposed to be under my command, right?"

Rabryn pressed his lips together in annoyance and nodded. "Yeah, that's why Azrel didn't kill her, only choked her out."

I shook my head. "Why did she attack me?"

"Because she thinks she's in love with me."

I snapped my head to the side and looked at him, "What?" I moved to stand in front of him, stopping our walking. "She what?"

Rabryn reached his finger into his collar and pulled out the red beaded heart necklace I'd never seen him take off. "She lost her mother and father at a young age. Her father, Norka, was a very good friend of mine."

I nodded. "Ortheldo told me about Norka."

"Ceco gave Norka this necklace when she was a little girl. When Norka died, he gave it to me. She saw me wearing it when they stripped us down in the Fayithjen dungeons. So she sees me as a last link to her father because he and I were close enough for him to give this to me." He tucked the necklace back under his collar. "So she wants to be close to me, in essence, thinking it's like being close to her father." He shrugged. "She could tell I was in love with you, so you immediately became a threat to her." Rabryn shook his head sadly. "She's a little crazy because of the trauma she endured so young, so she took her anger, hatred, lost, and bitterness out on you. If you were in the way, she couldn't be close to me."

I shook my head as I turned and started walking again.

"Weirdo."

Rabryn gently took my elbow keeping me in front of him. "Take it easy on her. She hasn't exactly had an easy or normal life. She's just a little strange." He glanced out into the woods where our party had gone. "When you see her next, though, check her shield and see if she should even be around. If not, kick her to the curb. But if her shield is intact"—he gave a resigned shrug—"she's a Born Wizard. Rare and you know it. She could still be able to protect Azrel, and it's probably not a bad idea to have another Born Wizard around."

I smirked at him. "You're a Born Wizard. That's weird."

He narrowed his eyes in a playful look of annoyance and anger. "You're telling me!"

He and I started laughing, but his laughter was cut off by a mix of a choke and a gasp. He was suddenly pale and looking past me with a look of utter terror. I spun around and my heart leapt up into my throat, causing me to make the same gasping choking noise. A very distinguished shadow stood in the trees in front of us. My weapons! They were with the others! Realizing this, Rabryn pushed me behind him and drew his sword.

"Damn! The daylight makes the glow in your eyes hard to notice!" Rabryn said, frustrated. Finding this humorous, the creature before us started laughing, or so it seemed. There was a low rumble coming from it that sounded like a laugh. "What is that?"

I narrowed my eyes and knew immediately the kind of trouble we were in. Rabryn's sword and magic were useless, and his arrows were nowhere to be found; most likely he'd packed them on Ceco. "It's a Balyanas. That's not the only one, though. Three of them roam these woods, and they always hunt together."

"So I take it the odds are not in our favor?"

"Not at all."

"Great."

"Don't bother with magic."

"Immune?" Rabryn asked, sounding slightly panicked for the first time.

"Yeah."

The beast examined us coolly. "I'm not sure if it's bravery or stupidity, finding you alone in this area," the beast said. Its voice was raspy and rather high pitched. "Either way, you will make a fine meal." I saw a flash of its tiny teeth when it smirked slightly. "You have no arrows."

"But *we* do," a voice suddenly said from behind the creature. It was Azrel's voice. The creature's eyes went wide. "Move," Azrel ordered.

The creature's expression fell to one of annoyance, and it begrudgingly stalked forward from the shadow of the trees, as did the other two creatures on either side of us. Each one of them had a member of our party at its back, with arrows aimed and bows drawn. The creatures were about the size of bears with horrible, beady black eyes. They only had two small slits for nostrils and a slightly larger slit in the middle of their face for a mouth that was filled with tiny sharp teeth. They were nothing more than masses of gray, wet looking lumps. They had two deformed appendages that could somewhat pass as arms, and four stumpy legs that made you wonder how they could hold up the bulky mass of its upper body. The entire beast jiggled when it moved, its lumps shaking as if they had a life of their own.

Azrel's magic was probably the only thing that would work on them, but she was too worried about Hathum finding her after that earthquake to use it. "Up against the tree and face me," Azrel said, and she, Ortheldo and Moifulyar all lined the beasts up against a thicket of trees.

Without a formal command, they all released their arrows, pinning the creatures against the trees through the arms. All the Balyanas roared in pain. Drawing another arrow each, they fired again, pinning the creatures in each of their legs. Gray blood sprayed out of the wounds. Drawing a third arrow each, the three of them pinned the creatures one last time for good measure.

Azrel looked at everyone. "Go! Those arrows will melt soon enough."

Rabryn and I turned and headed into the woods. We didn't even get ten paces before we heard a loud roar. Spinning around, we saw one of the Balyanas forcefully yank its shoulder from the tree, dislodging the arrow. It immediately was able to dislodge the rest of the arrows and ran straight towards Ortheldo. Ortheldo fired two arrows from his bow while Moifulyar shot two from his. They barely fazed the beast as it still barreled toward them.

It was too close to them!

I yanked Rabryn's sword from his belt again and ran. I watched as Azrel grabbed Ortheldo's shirt collar and pull him behind her so she was right in the path of the creature. I passed her and in one leap, I was standing on one of the lumps on its belly and pushed up, which gave me the height I needed to slice right through its blobby neck. The sword cut more smoothly and cleanly then anything I'd ever cut into before, since there were no bones to hit; gray liquid sprayed out of the injury, soaking my arm.

I fell hard to the ground and screamed as my skin started to bubble and blister and smoke. It even made a horrible hissing noise that I knew I would never forget until the end of my days. I would have preferred chewing my own arm off to feeling this burning pain.

That was why only arrows could be used on these things—their blood was acid.

I sucked in loud gasps of air as I lay there on the ground. I thought I heard a battle going on, but the pain! The burn seemed to reach right down to my bones. Darkness took me. The last emotion I could recall wasn't fear; it was the embarrassment of having nearly died twice in the same damn day. Pathetic.

———

Waking up this time was far more unpleasant. My arm burned and throbbed so badly that I couldn't contain the small cry of pain that crept up into my chest and throat. I felt the burning in every inch of my body like I had been tossed into a bonfire. It hurt to move, so I didn't. Tears erupted in my eyes, but I refused to let them fall. I'd made enough of a fool of myself recently to allow them to drip down my face.

I wearily looked around at my immediate surroundings. I was in the bed of a small and hastily constructed wooden cart and the sun was setting. A darkness hung in the woods that made my insides cringe. I hated this place. It felt wretched and evil, like something was lurking in every dark corner my eyes passed over. Shadows seemed to hang in the air as abundantly as what we breathed. Looking around, I noticed the ground was getting softer. The deep tracks the cart left in the terrain behind us indicated that the bog was close by. It was still hot as hell, and my clothes and hair were soaked with sweat. I knew I must be utterly filthy.

"One's awake," an unfamiliar, harsh female voice said.

As the movement of the cart slowed, I looked in the direction of the voice and saw a woman standing just alongside it. My eyes widened when I saw she was in filthy black traveling garb from head to foot; it was the uniform of the Spar Ridgian mercenaries.

The mercenaries of Spar Ridges were people that lived in these mountains and woods for months at a time to monitor them—to keep an eye on the population of evil creatures and report any growth or decline. Once upon a time, citizens of Spar Ridges used to line up in droves to have the honor of coming into these woods and protecting the land. By the time I came of age for my coronation, though, people were forced into this job by my father's command. Mercenaries had to be incredibly skilled and, if possible, have magical abilities so they could at least heal themselves if they had any run-ins with magically immune creatures. They were also supposed to kill intruders like us.

The female had a wide square jaw and, from what I could see under her black hood, thin, light brown hair streaked with silver. Her face was relatively youthful save for some thin lines around her mouth and eyes. Her lips were a light pinkish gray color and they looked dry and chapped. Looking around, I saw another unfamiliar mercenary on the other side of the cart. It was a younger man with the same light brown hair resting on his forehead, the rest hidden under the black hood. He had a long, square face and a mouth that looked too big.

I met the female's eyes again and she looked at me hatefully. Having been very sheltered as the princess, I didn't know her, and hoped she didn't know me; but both of their eyes glowed softly from under their black hoods like I'm sure mine still were. If they didn't know I was the princess, they sure knew I was from here at the very least, and they were likely confused seeing me trying to get back into the land that no one ever left.

Azrel's beautiful, bright face suddenly filled my vision when she jumped up into the cart from over the side. Her blue eyes were wide and eager for a moment and then relief flooded her entire expression. She knelt in front of me and leaned in, being careful to avoid touching my burned arm. I caught a glimpse of it just before she embraced me, and I had to squeeze my eyes shut when I saw the black charred and raw blistered skin. I even saw some exposed red muscle and few spots of ivory bone. I noticed it shimmered slightly, like it was wet, before I pressed my face into Azrel's shoulder.

"They had a salve that stopped the burning and numbed the pain as much as possible," Azrel said before pulling away.

When I glanced around the cart and caught sight of the entire bed for the first time, it felt like someone was squeezing my lungs too tightly. Rabryn, Ortheldo and Moifulyar were all severely injured and sprawled across the small cart bed, unconscious. I brought my healthy hand up in front of my mouth to hold in a scream. They looked dead. With those injuries, and the pain they must be, in I almost wished, for their own sake, that they were.

I looked up at Azrel. "Are they alive?"

She swallowed. "Barely."

One side of Ortheldo's entire neck and shoulder was burned so black that it looked like his skin was peeling off in hard, black chunks. Moifulyar had a broken shoulder that was wrapped tightly in a makeshift sling, and one side of his entire face was red with blisters and charred areas. Rabryn's hands were burned black, with red raw muscle showing through and a couple spots of exposed bone. He had a wide cut on his forehead, too, that stretched from the middle of his hairline all the way to his left ear.

With my hand still over my mouth holding in the screams, I looked into Azrel's eyes and realized she was in a grave mental panic. She desperately wanted to heal all of us, but the magnitude of that earthquake and what it could mean was keeping her from doing so. She could not use her magic and be discovered by Hathum right now, even at the risk of all of us. She was wrestling with this to the point that I saw her sanity stretching into near madness.

I swallowed down the screams of fear and worry that wanted to erupt from my throat. I couldn't lose it. Azrel needed me right now. I took a deep breath before lowering my hand from my face. "It's okay," I said softly to her and rested my hand on her shoulder. Azrel chewed her bottom lip and desperately looked into my eyes for the comfort I was trying to offer her. I nodded gently, trying to keep her calm. "You're doing the right thing. It's okay."

Still not looking completely convinced, she gave a short nod. "Yeah," she choked out on the verge of tears.

"Don't cry," I said with an edge of urgency. These mercenaries could *not* see her white tears! "It's okay."

She nodded again and, after a moment, bowed her head and pressed her fingers into her eyes, hiding the tears that wanted to spring forth. She looked back at me with a little more calmness in her expression and nodded with resolve. She had nothing on her mind right now but that terrifying, global earthquake. It was smothering her.

I glanced outside the cart again to our two escorts. "Azrel," I said cautiously, "do you know who these people are?"

She nodded. "I do. But they're taking us to their barracks to get better medicine for all of you."

My eyes narrowed. "Why haven't they killed us?"

"Oh, they tried," Azrel said matter-of-factly. "How do you think Rabryn got that head wound and Moifulyar that broken shoulder?"

My brows dropped. "What happened?"

Azrel swallowed. "One of the other Balyanas got free after you killed the first one. We all fought it." Azrel nodded her chin towards the mercenaries. "These two came out of nowhere with bows, turned it into a pin cushion, and then attacked us. Rabryn got an arrow across the forehead. The only reason it didn't go through his temple is because Moifulyar tackled him to the ground, breaking his shoulder in the process. They landed in a pool of Balyanas blood, which is why Rabryn's hands and Moifulyar's face are burned." She nodded at Ortheldo. "He got a full spray of it when an arrow pierced a creature in the throat." Her eyes shifted dangerously to the two black clad newcomers. "They tried to attack me but, well"—she shrugged and met my eyes again—"you know how *that* usually goes for folks who make the attempt."

I almost smiled.

"When they realized how highly skilled I was," Azrel continued quickly, "they decided it was in their best interest to help me rather than fight me. They gave me the salve for your burns, helped me build this rugged cart, attached it to Ceco, and have been acting as my personal escorts all day."

I looked at the mercenaries outside of the cart again, and suddenly saw their eyes dancing with menacing glee. Crap. They did recognize me. I quickly looked away with my head down and shook my head.

"Acalith? What's wrong?" Azrel asked.

"Humph," the boy said, "What's wrong is that…"

"Was I talking to you?" Azrel snapped and glared at him. He quickly fell silent, and his eyes even lost their glee under her gaze. Azrel took a moment before looking back at me. "What's wrong?"

I sighed, taking one last glance at the two mercenaries before looking at Azrel. There was no use hiding it now. "Do you remember, when we first met, how I had to keep coming and going so often?"

I put an intense message in my eyes telling Azrel, "Be careful what words you use." As the White Warrior's Deralilya, her lead protector, the position came with the magical ability to travel instantly, so I could always be at the White Warrior's side the second I was needed. It was the only magical ability I had. These people couldn't know I was the Deralilya, or that Azrel was the White Warrior. Let them ponder amongst themselves what I meant.

I gave her a moment to read my eyes, and she nodded. "Yes, I remember."

I swallowed. "The only way I was able to stay with you consistently was to stage my own death in Spar Ridges."

"What?"

I gave her an uncomfortable look. "My murder, to be more specific."

Azrel's eyes bulged. "Murder?"

I sighed as a flash of burning pain shot up my arm to my temple. "Look, I'll tell you on the way. Let's keep moving so we can get to that medicine."

Azrel debated it briefly, glanced down at my wrinkled, black charred arm, and nodded. "All right." With that, she hopped over the side of the cart to the ground and disappeared from view. A moment later, the cart was moving forward again. "How did you manage to fake your own death?"

I sighed and tried to settle as comfortably in the back of the small cart as best I could, which wasn't comfortable at all. "I had help from two dear friends of mine, two of the very few Salynn Humounts that live here. I pretended to want to court Augatlos, though he was married to Vorenia. We met in secret a lot and planned my murder so I could get away. Augatlos and Vorenia wanted to get out of Spar Ridges anyway, and being fugitives for my murder was a good enough cover for them."

I just happened to catch a glimpse of the boy outside of the cart at that moment, and though his eyes stared straight ahead, I saw a fire of wrath erupt in them that made me blanch. I even attempted to reach for my sword with my left hand. Luckily, it was right next to my leg. I griped the hilt tightly and kept a close eye on the two mercenaries. Something wasn't right with this whole scenario.

I heard Azrel sigh, "So what's going to happen if you're seen?"

"I have no idea," I replied honestly, though I was distracted now by that wrath in the boy's eyes. "What is your name?" I asked him.

He barely glanced at me. "Onofreo."

I looked at the woman on the other side, who I realized was glaring at me with the same fiery wrath. I kept my face as impassive as I could through the pain I was in. I couldn't let them intimidate me. "And you?"

She looked at the path ahead. "Yaljasa."

"I'm glad to meet you both," I said. They both looked at me and then looked at each other before they continued to watch the road out ahead of them without a reply. My eyes narrowed on them. Something definitely wasn't right.

"Get some rest, Acalith," Azrel said. "We should be at the barracks soon."

Right. Like that was going to happen with these two hanging around. I gripped my sword tighter and repositioned myself so I was sitting up against the back wall of the cart and could keep my eyes on the two mysterious mercenaries. I wasn't taking any chances, not with this lot. I knew better.

SIX

AZREL

The ride was uncomfortably quiet for hours. Night had long fallen, but I wasn't stopping until we got to those barracks to get the healing aids. I was hot and I was absolutely, completely and utterly exhausted. I had been beyond any normal level of exhaustion since that earth-wide earthquake had hit. I wasn't sleeping, though I pretended to so no one would worry about me. Since then, though, I was barely holding it together. The word "terrified" didn't do justice to what I was feeling.

I'd had a few scary moments on this journey over the past three months, but this was different. This fear was deeper than any I remembered ever feeling. How could the entire earth shake like that, all at once? Worse, how was I able to see and hear it happen all over the globe? I could not get out of my mind what that sensation, the feeling, was like.

Now, on top of all that, my friends and family were in this condition, and I couldn't bloody heal them! The fear, the terror, the helpless feeling of not being able to do anything was eating me alive. I honestly wasn't completely sure how I was even vertical and lucid. I felt like I was sinking into an abyss of madness while being yanked and torn to shreds in fourteen different directions. So much fear surrounded me, and there was nothing I could do about it.

To add to the list of things making me lose my mind, Addredoc was not answering my communications. I hadn't heard from him for two days since Tabway Pass. My fear for him kept me constantly trembling. I might have killed him. I could have drained him of his power completely in order to kill those Stone Trolls. I tried to comfort myself by chanting, "Two Ancient Wizards. Two Ancient Wizards," as a reminder of how powerful Addredoc really was. He could kill a dozen Stone Trolls easily with the amount of power he had. But then the pessimistic thoughts would settle in—he was guarding the entire massive mountain range of Godel with his magic, retraining soldiers, and fighting a civil war on top of what I'd asked him to do from 2,000 miles away.

The silence surrounding me at the moment was hurting my ears and giving me a terrible headache. With little hope, and driven only by desperation, I tried to reach Addredoc again. Long agonizing moments passed like they always did, and he didn't answer. I bowed my head and let the loneliness and fears surrounding me tighten the noose around my neck. I was going to hang by it soon if something didn't give; of *that* I was certain.

I suddenly felt the air move in a strange way and, without realizing why immediately, I ducked and then heard a thump. Snapping my eyes to the side, I saw an arrow sticking out of a tree trunk next to me.

"Azrel," Acalith called weakly from the back of the cart, "what was that?"

I looked in the direction from which the arrow had come and saw a pack of half dozen Spar Ridgian mercenaries inside a thicket of brush. My lip twitched in rage. I was *so* not in the mood for this!

I stopped Ceco and jumped off her back. Drawing my Sword and my Salynn blade, I headed straight toward them. A few arrows flew at my head but, as with Yaljasa and Onofreo when they attacked, the air went very thick around me, and everything got very slow. The same kind of thing had happened months ago when the Dirty 30 tried to ambush me in Oaksher Village. I only hoped that the natural reflexes of the White Warrior, not my magic, were responsible for this. I had to keep that hidden!

I spun and dodged and ducked under every arrow they shot at me. Each time a carefully aimed arrow missed, and I got closer, the eyes of the mercenaries got wider and their shots became more desperate. I knocked a few arrows to the side and out of my way. A couple of others I cut right in half with my Salynn blade, which sliced through the wooden shafts like a blade through cream.

One arrow was aimed low as a mercenary attempted to take out one of my knees. Instead, I took up my Sword and knelt down, putting the arrow right in front of my blade. I watched as, slowly, the metal tip and the shaft of the arrow split right down the middle, each half sailing past my head on either side.

The world snapped back to normal and I stood. "Drop your weapons!" I yelled as I approached them without yielding.

Their response was one last shot from a bow. I guess they

thought I wouldn't have enough time to deflect it, as I was so close to them now. Stupid bastard. Immediately the air went thick again and I saw the arrow coming at my face. I crossed both of my blades in scissor formation under it and, pulling them apart, I snapped the arrow into two pieces.

Everything went normal again and I was standing right in front of them—and they were terrified. "I told you to drop your weapons," I said slowly. All of their bows clattered to the ground. I glanced at their belts before looking back into their softly glowing green eyes. "*All* of your weapons." As if suddenly remembering the blades in their belts, they quickly pulled them out and dropped them to the ground. They even pulled out weapons from places I didn't know they were hiding them. "Is this all of you, or can I expect more intruders?" I asked.

"Intruders? You're in *our* woods, lady!" a courageous man to the left said. From what I could see under the black ensemble, he was big. Tall and broad shouldered with narrow, suspicious glowing green eyes.

"Peace, Orrin," a man in the front said taking a step forward. He was tall and lean with a dark tan and a rather beautiful, if slightly weathered, thin face. I could see a neatly trimmed gray beard under his softly glowing eyes. He pulled off his hood, and I blinked in wonder when I saw a few brown Sallybreath flowers in his short, kempt gray hair. He was a Salynn of Spar Ridges.

I didn't know much about Spar Ridge Salynns, but I did know they were extremely rare; there were perhaps a half dozen in the entire kingdom of about three million people. They were usually held in great honor because of their rarity, and their magic was pretty powerful. So what in the name of all that was Good was this Brown Flowered Salynn doing in the woods, in a position just barely above a slave? Whatever the reason, I didn't have to time find out.

"Who are you?" the Salynn asked.

I started to back away towards Ceco. "Someone you don't need to concern yourself with. I'm just passing through."

He took another step forward. "No one passes through these woods, not without a good reason."

I shrugged a shoulder. "Then I guess I've got a good reason."

He looked at me skeptically. "Why you're holding two of our

own captive?"

I turned and mounted Ceco again. "They're free to go. They've just chosen to accompany me."

"Yeah! After she killed two Balyanas on her own, *with blades*, and didn't suffer a single burn!" Onofreo exclaimed.

"And after she unnaturally dodged all of our arrows like she just did yours!" Yaljasa added furiously.

I looked at them and shrugged. "Your reasons for accompanying me are your own. I'm not keeping you here. If you're afraid of me, you're smart, but that's your problem." The two of them fumed, still afraid to leave my side, for which I was glad because I still needed them to guide me.

"Where are you leading her?" the Salynn asked my two guards.

"To the barracks," Yaljasa said. "She needs medicine for these that were injured during the Balyanas encounter."

The Salynn looked at me again. "What *are* you?" he asked, narrowing his eyes at me in genuine concern and suspicion.

I sighed and gave him my best expression of boredom. "Nothing. Now if you'll excuse me, I have some medicine to acquire." I spurred Ceco forward.

The Salynn slowly but bravely moved into my path, forcing me to stop Ceco. "I don't know what you are," he said gently, "but you're definitely not nothing." There was kindness in his eyes all of the sudden, which made me suspicious. "My name is Aithyan. May we take a look at your injured friends?"

My eyes narrowed. "You expect me to trust you?"

"No, but I think someone of your abilities needn't worry about us. Betraying you is likely a death sentence." I couldn't help but grin at that one. He surprised me by smiling kindly in return. "Will you let us help you?"

I was about to refuse, when all six of the mercenaries in the trees, as well as Yaljasa and Onofreo, removed their black hoods to reveal brown Sallybreath flowers in their hair.

"What the...?" I gasped.

"Ah," Aithyan said, "I see you're aware of how far we have fallen."

I looked around at each of them with wide eyes. This was all of them. It had to be. All of the Brown Flowered Salynns. There was no way Spar Ridges had more than these eight in the entire kingdom. "What in the name of the Sky Sanctuary are all the Spar Ridgian Salynns doing in these woods?"

Aithyan sighed. "It's a long story, but the short of it is that two of our very own murdered our princess." My heart sank to my toes. "So the king banished all of my kind to the woods as punishment for the killers he was never able to catch."

I swallowed and was about to say something to him when Yaljasa spoke. "Well Aithyan, look who isn't dead." I rolled my eyes, suppressing a groan.

His brows drew together curiously and I kept an eye on him as he quickly approached the side of the cart. His eyes went wide. "Princess!"

"Hello, Aithyan," I heard Acalith say in a tired voice.

Aithyan jumped up into the cart, and I quickly scrambled off Ceco to watch him to make sure he didn't try anything.

"What? You....you're alive?" the Salynn gasped.

"Barely."

He gave a small shake of his head, as if trying to wake himself up from a dream, and then quickly moved to kneel next to her as his hands started to glow with brown shimmering magic. He held his hands over her injured arm and I watched as the black burned skin lightened to a normal shade and knitted together until her arm looked completely normal. If there was one thing the Brown Flowered Salynns could do well, it was heal.

For the first time in two days, I felt the tightness of fear loosen in my chest a little. I had healers now. At least my friends would be okay.

"Here," Aithyan said, offering Acalith his water skin. Acalith drank from it eagerly. "How are you alive? What are you doing with these people?"

Acalith sighed and leaned heavily against the back of the cart in massive relief, no doubt. "I staged my murder, Aithyan. I had to leave Spar Ridges. That's all you need to know. Now will you please heal my friends?"

He nodded. "Of course, your majesty." He moved to examine everyone else in the cart. I saw his face cringe in dread after a moment. "Elreol," he called to the group near the trees, "come help me."

The largest of the Salynns passed me. He had broad shoulders and thick arms on top of a straight, narrow torso. His shaggy blonde hair grazed his shoulders and his skin was tan. He looked at me with big eyes and an almost childlike wonder as he climbed up into the cart. His stare was making me squirm a little. The green glow didn't help either.

"Elreol. Focus," Aithyan scolded.

Elreol blinked and then looked down at Ortheldo. "Oh dear," he said in a deep voice that made my eyes widen. I hadn't expected such a deep voice to come out of someone so innocent looking. Elreol's hands started to shimmer with brown magic as Aithyan moved over to Moifulyar. I watched eagerly as Ortheldo's burns also began to heal. Finally, his eyes opened and Elreol jerked away from Ortheldo so fast that he landed on his rear end in the cart. "Oh my! You have strange colored eyes!"

Ortheldo blinked and looked around, dazed. Before he could sit up all the way, I was crawling up into the cart and lunging at him. I was practically airborne when my lips met his, and both of us went sprawling to the floor of the cart with his arms wrapped tightly around my back and my arms around his neck. It took me a long time to finally let him go, but even then I immediately rested my forehead on his shoulder and desperately continued to hold on to him. "It's okay, sweetheart," he whispered gently in my ear as he held me tightly in return. I pressed my face into his shoulder so his shirt would absorb my brimming tears. The last thing I needed was for these Salynns to know I was the White Warrior.

"Oh, I see who gets the brunt of your attention!" I suddenly heard next to me.

My head jerked up to see my brother fully healed and smiling at me. He had his arm around Acalith, who was smiling like a fool with her head resting on his shoulder. I laughed and crawled over to him, and threw my arms around his neck too. He eagerly and tightly embraced me in return. I couldn't help it. I had to press my face tightly into his shoulder so I could cry. It was too much to hold back. I started sobbing like an infant, allowing his shirt to absorb my white tears, keeping them hidden.

"Hey, hey," Rabryn said gently as he held me tighter and buried his face into my neck.

Eventually, I felt Ortheldo press his face into my back and

wrap his arms around my stomach. Both of my boys were holding on to me tightly.

"I was so scared," I whispered. I never liked to admit I was scared, but it was the truth.

"We know," Rabryn said softly.

My sobs eventually quieted down a bit. I pressed my face into my brother's shoulder one last time before I pulled away, wiping my face. Looking to the side, I saw Moifulyar smiling shyly at the scene before him. I grinned, then gestured him closer to me so I could embrace him as well without leaving the vicinity of Ortheldo and Rabryn.

When I pulled away, I looked at Aithyan and Elreol, who were still crouching in the back of the cart, gently smiling at the scene that had unfolded. "Thank you," I whispered.

"You're welcome," Aithyan replied kindly.

When I met his eyes, I realized suddenly that he knew who I was. How *could* he know? He must have seen my tears just now. Damn it. But oddly enough, he said nothing about it. Reading his eyes, I actually saw excitement and joy and relief. That he was happy about who I was, though, made me suspicious. Spar Ridgians had the least love for the White Warrior than those of any other realm in Casdanarus, and maybe the world.

"What is your name?" he asked softly.

"Azrel," I answered, wondering why he wasn't trying to drive an arrow through my back.

"I am pleased to meet you, Azrel." Tears suddenly sprung up in his eyes. He bowed his head and pressed his thumb and index finger into the corners to hide them.

"Aithyan, are you all right?" Elreol asked.

"Yes. I'm just tired," Aithyan replied. "Come"—he looked up and smiled knowingly at me—"we need to get back to the barracks."

"Since your friends are healed," the one called Orrin said to me, "can we have our two best swordsmen back?"

I met his eyes, which were incredibly unfriendly. All their eyes were, except Aithyan's and Elreol's. "I told you, I wasn't keeping them captive. They can go."

"Actually," Aithyan said, "I was hoping you would join us, Azrel. We can give you all a place to clean up, rest, and eat, and we can talk."

He probably had a million questions that he couldn't ask in front of the others. I glanced at my companions and got a unanimous nod from them.

"Sure," I responded. "But um…" I hopped out of the cart and gestured for Aithyan to follow me.

I went to Ceco, who looked awful. Her head was low, and her one good eye was heavy and sad and tired. She was still pretty badly injured from her fight with Acalith. She had a deep wound in her shoulder, a few bruised ribs and probably a fractured skull, not to mention her destroyed right eye. I'd had to stop once to cut a slit in the wound to drain it because it had swollen so badly. I'd also been driving her like a pack mule through unbearable heat.

I sighed and petted her neck. "My wolf is also pretty badly injured. Could you…"

"Of course," Aithyan said, and his hands immediately started to shimmer with brown magic. He gently touched her as her wounds healed, and I heard her sigh in relief.

I smiled at her. "Better?"

"Yes," she whispered. Aithyan only showed slight surprise at the sight of a giant, talking wolf. I suppose they'd seen stranger things here in these woods. Ceco still looked exhausted and even a little dehydrated. I wasn't sure when she had last eaten or drank anything. All I knew was she'd been following us for weeks, since we left Fayithjen, and I certainly hadn't been taking very good care of her. Not that we had many resources to take care of her with.

"Aithyan, is there any water or food close by for her?"

"We have food and water at the barracks. It's only a couple of hours away."

I nodded. "Are you okay to wait that long?" I asked her.

She nodded her head. I nodded back and petted her head once more. I went to the side of the cart and addressed my companions. "Are all of you well enough to carry your packs?"

"Why?" Acalith asked stubbornly.

"Because Ceco doesn't look very good and I want to lighten her load. The Salynns' barracks are still a couple of hours away."

Ortheldo scooted to the edge of the cart and hopped down. "I can carry mine."

"Me too," Moifulyar added.

"I think we're all okay to do so," Rabryn added as they all climbed out of the cart.

"All right," I said. "Ortheldo, will you help me unhitch this cart from her?"

Ortheldo nodded and came toward me, but Orrin stepped forward quickly. "Actually, if it's all right, could she bring this with her?" I looked at him, confused. He shrugged. "We could actually use something like this there."

I looked at Ortheldo, who shrugged. I walked over to Ceco. "Are you feeling up for it? If not, tell me." I would have no issue telling Orrin no.

"I'll be fine," she said softly.

I nodded at her and then looked back at Orrin. "Okay." I looked at my group again. "Everyone else get your stuff. Let's go."

We were on our way quickly, Ceco even having a little pep in her step now. I was feeling pretty great at the moment. All my friends were walking and talking and everything seemed okay for a while. I was still stressed about that earthquake and where Addredoc was, but at least the sky had waited to completely fall on my head.

About an hour passed when I started to hear some hushed whispers among the Brown Flowered Salynns as they walked behind us. I immediately looked over at Rabryn, who met my eyes at the same time, hearing what I heard. Moifulyar also glanced at me with concern. Some of them were insisting it was a bad idea to travel with us, but Aithyan kept saying that everything was going to be okay. Another few moments passed and the debate got a little louder behind us. I looked at my brother again, who shook his head, indicating things were not sounding good for us.

I spun around. "Is there a problem?"

All the Salynns looked at me, startled. I resisted the urge to roll my eyes. I did have two Gold Flowered Salynns with me who had impeccable hearing just like they did—like *all* Salynns did.

"No, not at all," Aithyan said with a forced smile.

"Really? So I *wasn't* just hearing you argue about whether you should be traveling with us?" The Salynns looked around uncomfortably at each other. "Yes? No?" All their eyes went down. "Let try this again. Is there a problem?"

Yaljasa's head came up and she daringly met my eyes. Her

teeth were clenched and she looked like she wanted to say something, but with a tiny glare from me, her upper lip twitched and she looked away again.

"No?" I said. "Shall we keep going then?"

Aithyan smiled at me a little nervously. "Of course."

I nodded once and put my back to them and we all kept walking.

Another tense half an hour passed, during which I was constantly glancing over my shoulder. The Salynns weren't talking much. Most of them seemed lost in their own worlds. Aithyan and Elreol, however, were enjoying a light conversation. As another half hour passed, I began to notice the Salynns' formation started to shift. The majority of them started to fall back a little past the cart and fan out behind us. My eyes narrowed when I suddenly saw brown swirling magic in the eyes of one of them, the kind of magic Rabryn used when he wanted to communicate in thought.

They were plotting!

I spun fully around, but before I could say anything, Yaljasa cried out, "Now!"

All of the Salynns except Aithyan and Elreol held out their hands, and a wall of brown sparkling light lit up the entire forest and came at all of us. The light swept through all of our bodies, in one side and out the other. I felt something strange inside of me. It was like a hurricane force wind that was trying to push my heart through my back. Before anything happened though, a door inside of me seemed to slam shut on the wind and I was fine. Nothing was happening to Acalith or Ortheldo, but everyone else was clutching their chests and doubled over in pain. Thinking quickly, I clutched my chest and pretended to have the same reaction.

Ceco dropped down to her forelegs in agony. "What...is...happening?" she whispered.

"Oh nothing," Orrin said, stepping forward, "we're just taking away any and all magic inside of you. Can't have our prisoners making a break before we bring them to the king."

SEVEN

I glared at the Salynns, and my teeth clenched. They wanted to play this game? All right. I was up for it, so I continued to feign being in pain so they wouldn't know I was way more powerful than they could even imagine. They couldn't take my magic, no matter what silliness they tried with their Brown Salynn magic. That privilege was reserved for the Light Gods.

I'd play along until we could quietly get away. I needed to not use my magic at the moment, but I certainly wasn't as powerless as they'd attempted to make me. I just needed to bide my time.

Aithyan looked at me, panicked and confused even as he was panting from the pain of his magic being taken away. I could see in his eyes that he was wondering if he was wrong to believe I was who he thought I was. I gave him a quick comforting wink and relief instantly flooded his expression.

"My father will recognize me, you morons!" Acalith screamed as she attended my brother, who was still doubled over in pain.

Orrin met her eyes coolly. "Princess Acalith is dead, remember?"

He held his hand toward her and a cloud of brown smoky magic wafted from it. It snaked around her body. I straightened up, my act forgotten, and I watched her appearance started to change. Her perfect beautiful blonde ringlets of hair went stark straight and turned from blonde to black. It also shortened to a length that didn't even touch her shoulders. Her gently glowing green eyes dimmed and changed from bright green to an ugly, unlit mud brown. Her light porcelain skin darkened to a rich tan color and small freckles appeared, dotting her face.

Acalith stood trembling for a moment, pulling at the ends of her now short, straight black hair and looking at the darker skin on her arms. Her eyes met mine, and I gave her my most determined look. She didn't have to gaze at me long before she swallowed heavily and nodded. She knew I wouldn't let them get away with this.

Acalith let out a slightly shaky breath and shifted her gaze to the Salynns. "Azrel is going to kill every single one of you bastards," she said. "You can kiss your entire race goodbye now."

I glared back at the Salynns. Orrin crossed his arms and smirked as he took a few steps toward me. His face was one of a human in his early forties, but angled and severe. He had prominent cheekbones, a wide square jaw, and smooth, rich tan skin. He would have been handsome if he wasn't so evil. His loosely styled brown hair fell over his forehead and nearly into his glowing eyes, giving the illusion of softness; however this guy was anything but.

"I'd like to see that happen," he said, stooping to bring his eyes level with mine. "What are you going to do with no magic?"

Clenching my teeth, I brought my arm back ready to punch him, but he shot a small blip of brown magic at me. Something hit my wrist that kept my arm from moving. I cried out in surprise, and a bit of pain, when my arm was suddenly wrenched behind my back; then my other was, too, though no one was touching me. A few of the other Salynns shot little blips of brown magic at my friends as well, binding their arms behind their backs.

I panted heavily through my nose. My temper clawed at the inside of me, ripping and tearing at the walls of my chest, begging to be released. I could not stand being controlled or bound by anyone. My entire body pulsated with the heat of my heartbeat. I was going to rip this guy to shreds. I looked over my shoulder at Ortheldo, who gave me a look of reserved determination as he stood there bound. Our eyes met and gave me a small nod that said, "I trust you. I'm following your lead until you're ready to do something." His faith and trust in me meant everything in this moment.

I looked back at Onofreo with a dark smirk. "Mark my words, you'll be dead before the sun comes up today." The arrogant smile melted right off his face. I kept my eyes locked with his. "Well," I asked tersely, "what are you waiting for? Let's go."

Orrin cleared his throat and looked at the other Salynns. "Each one of you takes a prisoner."

I smiled another dark smile. "One of you on each of us?" My lip twitched. "I'm insulted," I said, narrowing my eyes.

He came forward and punched me in the jaw, which actually hurt. "Shut your mouth, bitch."

The rage beast inside of me roared and pounded at my chest so hard I felt it in my temples. I looked back at him and took a menacing step forward, leaning in until he backed away. "Make me," I dared him.

"Orrin," Aithyan suddenly spoke, "listen to me. You don't know who Azrel is. She can help us! And if Princess Acalith is brought back to her father, he will forgive us and restore us our honor. Change her back so her father can see her! What you're doing makes no sense."

Orrin looked at Aithyan. "Makes no sense? What about the past three months we've been banished to these hellish woods? Who's going to pay for that?" He looked at Acalith. "I'll tell you who. She is. She's the one responsible for us being sent out here."

Oh man, this guy. "You're an idiot," I said in disgust. "You're really going to piss and moan about being out here for three measly months? You're going to exact revenge over *three* stupid months?" I narrowed my eyes. "How old are you? 1,000 years old? 2,000? And you're bitching about three damn months?" I shook my head as the rage beast settled. "You're pathetic." Suddenly this guy wasn't worth killing. He'd probably been pampered from the day he drew breath and was now simply throwing a temper tantrum for being forced to "rough it" in exile for three silly months.

An idea suddenly occurred to me out of nowhere, and my eyes went wide. Addredoc, the Stone Trolls, and the fire! Addredoc could not conjure fire; no Wizard could. He had to have used my magic to kill the Stone Trolls. But it was red! My jaw went slack. He'd changed the color of my magic, which could only be done by changing the properties of it. If the properties of my white fire magic were changed, Hathum wouldn't be able to detect it.

No wonder Addredoc wasn't answering me! Changing the properties of my magic, *my* magic, would have put him into a coma. Granted, the color and property change dumbed down the power of my magic, but it was still formidable, and it was still *my* magic! It was still my power, just undetectable by Hathum.

I bowed my head and closed my eyes and concentrated on the source of my magic, the depthless pool of energy that sat in my chest. Could I do it? I was more powerful than Addredoc even, so I *had* to be able to do it.

I'd only heard of a magic user changing the color of magic

once—when magic was first created. One being, whoever it was that created magic, was able to make it different colors, hence the color array we had today. Now Addredoc, one of my closest friends, had the ability. He was so unbelievably powerful. I had to get to him soon, though, so I could heal him.

I pictured the pool of energy in my chest as a fathomless glowing white mass of fire and light. I concentrated hard on it and began to picture the pool of energy in black. I watched it darken more and more, until I was seeing a glowing mass of depthless *black* fire and light.

Let's see Hathum trace *this* color!

I opened my eyes and knew they were glowing black.

Orrin gasped and backed away so fast that he tripped over himself and fell onto his butt in the mud. I put a stream of my magic into the cuffs on my wrists. They vanished immediately. I sent a stream of black fire to each of my companions, releasing them as well. They stared at me, terrified and confused. I could have sworn I heard all of their heartbeats pick up pace in unison. I would have to explain later. I held out my hand to Acalith and sent a stream of black fire to her, changing her back to her regular form.

I slowly turned to face the Salynns. They each were frozen in fear with terror-filled eyes. I shifted my gaze to the one on the ground. Orrin began to crawl backwards, but ended up trapped between me and the cart.

I slowly crouched down in front of him, my black glowing eyes meeting his green ones. "You're lucky you just proved to be an idiot and not evil. Otherwise I would end you. Now, if you would be so kind, give my friends back their magic."

Orrin looked at all the Salynns and nodded. They held out their hands, sending another wall of brown sparkling magic toward Rabryn, Moifulyar, and Ceco. I heard them sigh in slight relief.

"Everything in order, guys?" I asked without taking my eyes off Orrin.

From the corner of my vision I saw short bursts of gold magic from Rabryn and Moifulyar and a brief flash of pink from Ceco. "Good here," Ceco stated.

"Ortheldo, please unhitch Ceco." Ortheldo immediately moved to do as I asked, with Moifulyar at his side. "We're going to leave now. I have business elsewhere that you will not interfere with." Orrin looked completely terrified of me. I felt a little bad for him, seeing such a big being trembling in fear. He wasn't evil, just stupid. I sighed and put my magic away, turning my eyes back to normal blue. "Listen, if you want to come with us, I have no objections, but you will come peacefully. Either way, when we get to Spar Ridges Kingdom, I will see that your king restores your honor."

Orrin swallowed uncomfortably. "You don't have the authority to do that."

I smirked at him. "Oh yes I do." I stood to my full height and looked at Aithyan and Elreol. I doubted they'd want to stay among the people that had just attacked them. "The invitation extends to you as well."

Aithyan glanced at Elreol and then smiled at me nervously. "If you'll have us, my lady,"

I nodded. "Of course I will. Come. We have to go." I looked at the rest of the Brown Flowered Salynns. "I'll leave you all to ponder the choice before you. We'll be at the palace if you decide to join us."

I turned to leave and saw that Ceco had changed into her full human form, wearing brown leggings and a long pink tunic, and carrying her tall wooden staff. Without a glance back at the Salynns behind us, we walked on.

I was eager to put some distance between us and the Salynns so I could use my magic to safely heal Addredoc. After nearly three days, his condition couldn't be good. I was glad my companions were up for the walk, though it was the dead of night. They'd likely gotten enough rest being injured and unconscious in the back of the cart all day.

They were uneasily quiet for the next half hour. I knew they were waiting for an explanation from me as to why my magic was black, but they were cautious to not broach the subject with the Salynns' prying ears too close by.

We finally reached the edge of an incredibly vast bog. It looked a lot like Vefur Swamp, only miles and miles bigger. The sparse land available for us to walk on was nothing more than incredibly wet and decayed patches of soft moss, intermixed with puddles of water ranging from fifty yards wide to three feet wide.

I was in absolutely no hurry to start trudging this thing, so I paused and finally sighed. "All right, wait," I called to my party and faced them.

Rabryn was immediately in on me. "What the hell was that, Azrel?" he cried, throwing his arms out to his sides.

"Just wait. I—"

"Your magic was *black*!" Ortheldo added.

"I know. I—"

"What have you done?" Acalith gasped.

"Is something wrong with your magic?" Ceco asked, crowding around me with the others.

"What? No! I—"

"Black is Hathum's magic!" Moifulyar said.

I pressed my fingers into my temples. "Will all of you shut up for a damn second!" I cried. Aithyan and Elreol were the only ones to hang back, for which I was grateful. I sighed, lowering my hands. "I changed the color of my magic." Their eyes all went wide. "It's still my own magic, just a different color."

"You...you shouldn't be able to do that," Ortheldo said. "I don't think."

"Yes I can. Addredoc could."

"When did Addredoc change it?" Rabryn asked.

"In Tabway Pass when I killed the Stone Trolls. He was able to muster my own magic from inside me, no doubt with the White Warrior's help." I glanced at Aithyan and Elreol, who looked amazed and thrilled at having heard that out loud. "He changed the white color to his red so I could kill those Stone Trolls without Hathum being able to track me."

Ortheldo and Rabryn gave each other worried glances before looking back at me. "Azrel," Rabryn said, holding up his hands and taking a step toward me. "To change the color of magic, you have to change the properties of it, the essence of it. To change your magic to red, Addredoc would have had to give it Godel's essence." He looked panicked. "To change yours to black, you'd have to give it Shadow's essence. That is not a good thing, Azrel! It can't be! Shadow and Light are separate for a reason!"

"It's still my magic," I said stubbornly. "My magic itself has not changed. I would feel it if it did."

"But it has Shadow properties now!" he cried.

"What was I supposed to do?" I yelled. "I can't let Hathum

find me! You felt that earthquake, little brother!"

"I did," he said, more softly, taking another careful step toward me. "And I know it scared you, Azrel. It scared me too. But this is not the way to deal with it."

My brows drew together. "I'm dealing with it the best I can, Rabryn." I said slowly. Then a flash of anger erupted in my chest. "But the Light Gods have yet to lift a damn finger to come to my aid!" I shouted. "Even as the entire world heads for the abyss!" I pressed my lips together, forcing myself to calm down, and silently begging him to understand. "At least this way I can use the Shadow properties of my magic for something good; I can stay hidden from Hathum!" Ortheldo and Rabryn exchanged worried glances again. "I can always change it back to white, but this way I can get some crap done without the stress of Hathum finding me hanging over my head."

"Azrel," Rabryn said shaking his head slowly. "I don't think it's a good idea to keep your magic black."

I glared at him and felt an unfamiliar anger burn towards him. "Then you go pray to your precious Light Gods and tell Them to get Their asses down here and help me! Or give me my crown or something! Until then, I'm improvising."

I looked at all of them in turn, daring them to challenge me again. I was way too exhausted to deal with their lack of faith in me right now. Rabryn and Ortheldo exchanged weary looks, then Ortheldo and Acalith, then Acalith and Rabryn.

I rolled my eyes. "Are you all quite done questioning me now?"

Rabryn and Ortheldo gave resigned sighs. "Yes. All right," Rabryn said, though his eyes betrayed a lack of conviction and were even a little fearful still.

Despite that, I felt my shoulders loosen. They may not have liked it, but they were trusting me, and that felt good. "Listen, if Addredoc changed the properties of *my* magic, I know he can't be in great health right now. I need to heal him, but it will probably weaken me to a point that I'll pass out, or at the very least, be stumbling like a drunk from exhaustion."

Ortheldo nodded. "We'll help you."

I nodded. "Thanks. If I heal him now, it will probably weaken me for the usual span of about six to eight hours."

Ortheldo nodded again. "Perfect. Just in time for you to be fully powered up for when we reach the woods."

"Exactly."

"Okay," he said with a forced smile. "Get to healing him then, and give him our best."

I nodded, took my pack off, and got on my knees. I lit my eyes up and pushed my black magic toward Godel, 2,000 miles away to the south. It felt like riding Lightning, speeding across the landscape of Casdanarus until I finally saw the Godel mountain range before me. Yet I still felt the soaking wet ground of the bog's edge seeping through my pants.

I entered the mountain, flying right through the earth and rock, and began feeling for Addredoc's presence. I felt the energy of his powerful magic pressing against mine and followed it. When I finally arrived in Addredoc's chambers, I covered my mouth with my hands. He was unconscious, like I knew he would be, but he was bone thin and as white as the sheets upon which he laid. The Red Sallybreath flowers in his smooth, straight black hair were all brown and shriveled. A few of them were even on the pillow, surrounding his head in a death halo.

"Oh Addredoc," I whispered as tears sprung up. I pressed my fingers into my eyes to keep from crying. "All right, all right," I whispered, looking at him again, and moved to the side of his bed. "I'm here, sweetheart. I'm here."

I rested my hand on his forehead and made his eyes open first. His stare was as blank as death. With a sniff I leaned over him, looking into his beautiful dark brown eyes, and concentrated on the reflection of my own black eyes. I waited a moment, but my brows dropped when no color pooled into my vision like it usually did when I did a massive healing.

"Crap," I muttered to myself when I realized what was wrong.

Disease or illness, like I had healed in Cairikson, was a black color when I saw it inside of someone. I wouldn't see a black sickness reflect in my eyes if my eyes were already black. I would need my magic to be white in order to heal him.

I sighed and pinched my forehead with my thumb and index finger. Was healing Addredoc worth risking Hathum's finding out where I was? I felt incredibly ashamed for even hesitating. He was my friend, and he was dying. Of course it was worth the risk.

I sighed and concentrated on my magic in my chest and lightened it, removing the darkness until it was pure shining white again. I heard my companions breathe a very unsubtle sigh of relief when they saw my eyes go from black to white.

I looked down into Addredoc's eyes again and concentrated on the white reflections of my own. Soon enough, the black color of his weakness filled my vision. I pushed my white magic against the black until it slowly started to disappear. Addredoc sucked in a large gasp of air and sat up straight in bed.

I didn't even have time to say goodbye to him because I was suddenly back in the bog and falling over. With a light splash, I landed on my side in the soggy earth. Rabryn, Ortheldo and Acalith were quickly next to me. Oddly enough, I didn't pass out. I supposed it was a good thing because it meant I was getting stronger. But it was going to be a very long six-hour walk across this bog with me on the verge of passing out the whole time.

Ortheldo scooped me up in his arms. "Rabryn, grab her pack." Rabryn nodded and picked it up, slinging it over his shoulder. "Let's go," Ortheldo said. "We've got to get to those woods."

"And out of this swamp," Acalith said, irritated.

"Try to rest a bit, Azrel," Ortheldo said softly to me. "We need you powered up for the forest."

I rested my head against his shoulder and nearly fell asleep. I wasn't quite exhausted enough to do so—well, I actually was, but I didn't want to sleep if I didn't have to. I had to keep my guard up in this place, so sleep wasn't really an option. As Ortheldo began walking, I concentrated on my magic once again and changed it back to black. I didn't know if Hathum would track the healing I'd done for Addredoc. But even if he did track it, I hoped he would track it to Godel and not Spar Ridges.

I just had to wait, hope, and see.

EIGHT

The first three hours through this bog passed surprisingly peacefully. I gained enough strength over that time to walk on my own, but I still felt incredibly heavy. It was like a hand was reaching from the sky, pushing down on my shoulders and trying to squish me into the ground. Ortheldo had his arm around me. I half rested, half dropped my head on his shoulder when it became too heavy to hold up. He tightened his arm around me and kissed my forehead, and we kept walking in heavy silence.

All of us were soaked up to our hips, our boots filled to the brim with mud and water. Even our sleeves were wet from the occasional tumble to the ground when a puddle ended up being deeper than we'd thought. We were all too tired to speak. The only sound around us was the plunk, plunk, and splash of our walking.

Something inside of me suddenly shifted. Or fluttered. I wasn't quite sure which. I thought I felt a very faint pressure of Shadow there. I stopped walking, which made Ortheldo stop walking, and I looked around with wide eyes. I wasn't really looking at anything, just trying to figure out what was happening inside my chest.

"Azrel?" Ortheldo asked.

It could have been a warning, but I just wasn't sure. I was too tired to know. I didn't answer him, only turned my head to look at Acalith. We had more than one warning system here. I watched her eyes for a moment, and saw their green glow very slowly brighten.

"Azrel?" she asked.

"Crap," I said to myself, and glanced at Aithyan and Elreol, only to see the same steady brightening of their eyes.

"Azrel? What?" my brother asked.

"Our eyes!" Aithyan said suddenly, and everyone drew their blades.

I looked around at the wide open clearing of the bog and saw nothing. The tree lines in front of and behind us were three hours in both directions. We would be able to see if something was coming at us from here. Where could the danger be coming from?

A few moments passed before we saw some thick black dots come from behind the distant tree line and start to fly across the bog. Ortheldo and I watched carefully with narrowed eyes, trying to identify the creatures in case they came our way. Wings. What creatures in Spar Ridge's woods had wings? The quiet was heavy as we watched, not sure yet what they were or if they knew of our presence here.

"Maybe they'll miss us," Ceco said.

It was quiet for a few more moments, and I dreaded the fact that they seemed to be getting bigger—which meant closer.

"Deeks," Ortheldo finally said.

"Damn it," I said under my breath and bowed my head. I was too tired for this. Deeks were magically immune creatures, so Ceco's powerful pink magic was useless. So was all the Salynns' magic. I felt so completely done with everything that I nearly went to my knees, but Rabryn spoke before I could.

———

"Are Deeks killable?" he asked.

"Yes," Ortheldo replied. "But they are immune to magic like the Balyanas were."

"Finally," my brother said with, oddly enough, genuine excitement. My brows dropped and I looked back at him, confused. My eyes went a little wide when I realized he was smiling and taking his bow into his hands. "Something I can shoot at," he declared, adjusting the belt across his chest that held his quiver of arrows.

I couldn't help the broad smile that pulled at my mouth. Leave it to Rabryn, in a moment of utter despair, to make me grin. I was still so weak, though, that my legs suddenly gave way and my head fell forward. Ortheldo was the only thing holding me up right now.

"It's all right, Azrel. It's okay," he said, gently lowering me to my knees. "We've got this one." My arms slid limply to my sides as he set me down. I couldn't fight this battle. I was useless like this. He looked steadily in my eyes for a moment, reassuring me. "It's okay," he whispered, and then kissed my lips before standing and arming himself with his own bow.

I gave in. And for some reason that bothered me. I'd never given in before, to anything, especially when the people I loved were facing danger. I'd always fought until I was dead, or nearly there. Why was I letting weakness win now? I couldn't deny that my strength was gone, yet I'd felt like this many times in the past few months and had always managed to summon it back somehow, from somewhere. Right now, it was like reaching into a black hole and trying to pull air out. As I slid down, letting myself lay in the wet mud of the bog and closed my eyes, I wondered why.

———

When I awoke, the sun was up. By the look of it, it was about nine in the morning. I slowly sat up and found myself on the edge of the bog just inside the forest tree line. Seeing all of my friends surrounding me, sound asleep, I sighed with relief. We'd made it. They'd survived the Deeks. Granted, I saw scratches and claw marks and bruises on them all, but Ceco and the Salynns could heal those injuries easily enough when they woke.

I chuckled to myself. They didn't need me, and I was proud of them for that. My humor died, though, when I realized all of them were grouped together here sound asleep—*all* of them. No one was on watch!

I quickly tried to stand, but hit my head on something. "Ow! What the—"

Crouching, I looked up above me. At first I saw nothing. But moving my head slightly from side to side, I managed to see a faint shimmer of pink light. I looked over at Ceco, asleep in her human form. Next to her, the top of her rugged wooden staff glowed pink with her magic. Looking up again, I ran my fingertips over the shield of her magic around us, a shield she was able to sustain even in sleep. I was impressed.

I sat back down on the ground with my knees up and just watched my companions sleeping. I was incredibly glad at that moment for Ceco and her magic. My friends needed rest, and they were all sleeping deeply and peacefully right now. We had a very long two-day journey ahead of us through these woods, and they would need all the strength they could muster.

I looked into the woods, waiting for them all to wake, and found myself brooding. I was hating The Light Gods for sitting by idly, hating the White Warrior for not telling me who the damn necklace's owner was, hating myself for being so utterly powerless to do anything of use, hating Hathum and his Shadow Gods for being so greedy and power hungry so as to mess with the world again, and hating how afraid I was about that earthquake. For five days it had been amazingly quiet since then, though. I'd thought that with a force like that the Shadow Gods Themselves would be walking the earth! But there was nothing. Not one unusual occurrence in the world since that quake. I was certain if something were out of balance with Shadow and Light, I would know about it instantly. There weren't too many more places in Casdanarus that were so riddled with Shadow creatures as Spar Ridges, but so far, our encounters here had been relatively normal.

Unless *that* was the abnormality.

Copper for your thoughts, Azrel?

My heart leapt up into my throat and I could barely breathe. *Addredoc!*

I heard him chuckle. *Hey.*

You're okay! Are you okay? How are you feeling?

He chuckled again, and it was the most wonderful sound to hear in that moment. *Yes, I'm okay. I tried to contact you sooner, but you must have been asleep or passed out. Thanks for coming to heal me.*

Please. If it hadn't been for me, you wouldn't have nearly died in the first place.

You had a dozen Stone Trolls on your butt. It's okay. A three-day coma was worth the price of your life.

I found myself smiling, and missing him terribly. *So, you changed the color of my magic?*

He chuckled again. *Yeah, I guess I did.*

Addredoc, seriously. Do you have any idea the amount of power that takes? No one has been able to do that since magic was first created, and my magic isn't any regular old magic! It's the Light Gods' magic!

Sheesh! We haven't spoken in three days, and you already doubt my exceptional abilities? I feel insulted.

I had to press my face into my knees to keep from laughing too loudly. I didn't want to wake my companions. I hadn't realized until this very moment how much not hearing from him had weighed on me and drained me of strength. Hearing from him now, I felt unbelievably refreshed and genuinely happy—even as my heart sank at the subject that needed to be discussed.

So, about that earthquake…

I felt his light-hearted mood immediately shift. *Oh, Azrel,* he said in a low tone. *You would not believe what I saw.*

Oh, I have an idea. I told Addredoc everything that had happened to me when that earthquake hit. I gave more detail about how I seemed to be in every single place all over the earth at the same time, yet still on my knees, in pain, in Tabway Pass. I told him how Rabryn and Moifulyar had felt the same thing, but Acalith and Ortheldo had not.

My brain almost turned to soup again, Addredoc. I said. *Why would that have happened to me?*

He sighed. *I don't know, but I think it probably has something to do with you being the White Warrior. There was enough black fire that erupted from the Black Mountains to allow me to see it from 200 miles away in Godel. That's probably something the White Warrior should know about, so you were warned.*

Warned by whom?

Probably the Light Gods.

I flinched. *You…you think the Light Gods did that to me?*

They're pretty much the only ones that could.

I took a moment to contemplate that. I was terribly confused. I'd thought the Light Gods were sitting on their lofty perch ignoring what was happening down here. They sure hadn't taken any significant steps in this war yet. They *certainly* hadn't taken any significant steps to interact with me until that earthquake hit.

I swallowed heavily. If the Light Gods had seen the need to intervene and show me what was happening, then something was really wrong!

Azrel, I have a feeling things are about to get really, really bad.

Yeah. Me too.

Just then, I felt that strange feeling in my chest again, a weird fluttering pressure that built when something of Shadow was happening. What was wrong with my warning system? It felt so strange. Usually it was an undeniable, almost painful pressure, pushing its way out of my chest. Now it felt like a light, fluttering caress in my chest wall, nothing urgent or worrisome.

Crap, I said as I slowly stood up. I couldn't worry about it now. Something was on its way.

What is it? What's happening?

I sighed. *Addredoc, listen to me. I need you to squash that civil war in Godel immediately. I don't care what it takes. You give that land an ultimatum to join me or die, and you kill anyone and everyone who refuses.*

What?

I sighed. *I can't give Hathum more soldiers. If anyone in Godel is on the fence about whose side they're on, end them. I know you can.*

Well, sure I can, but I never thought you would want me to waste a massive amount of innocent people!

They're not innocent if they refuse me and join Hathum! I argued. Was he actually questioning me?

Azrel, some of them just want to live in peace away from you and Hathum.

Then end them! I cried. *War is coming whether they want it or not! If they won't fight for me, they cannot fight for Hathum.*

He was silent a moment. *Azrel, are you okay?*

I'm fine. I'm just frustrated and angry and sick and tired of everything.

Everything?

Everything! I'm sick of this hatred towards me. I'm sick of the struggle to fight this Shadow. I'm sick of the Light Gods idleness. I'm sick of this necklace. I'm sick and tired of everything! I sighed. *Do as I say, Addredoc. You've got two days.*

Two days?! he cried.

Two days! Then bring whomever you've got to Spar Ridges. We'll be there by then and we can figure the rest out there. If Hathum is at the Black Mountains, he'll be at Godel in no time, so get whomever is willing to fight for me out of there. Kill everyone else. Do you understand?

Yes, White Warrior, he said in resigned defeat, and left the communication without a goodbye.

I should have felt guilty about the lives I'd just ordered Addredoc to take, but I could not risk Hathum gaining another million or so soldiers. There was no room for emotion in this. It was war, and I was already at a massive disadvantage.

"Hey," I called out and went around waking everyone. "Get up. We've got to move."

Everyone woke up looking fairly refreshed, though still pretty banged up.

"Is something coming, Azrel?" my brother asked.

"Yeah."

"What is it?"

"I don't know, Rabryn!" I snapped.

He looked at me, confused and hurt.

I sighed. "I'm sorry. I don't know. I just know something is coming."

"Okay." He glanced at Ortheldo before getting to his knees and starting to pack everything up.

My face scrunched up in annoyance. I squatted down next to my brother and took hold of his arm, examining the numerous, long, deep scratches on his skin. "Why aren't any of you healed?" I met my brother's eyes. "What happened when I passed out?"

Ortheldo squatted down next to us, looking worried. "We ended up in a battle with a Queen Deek."

My heart jumped into my throat. "Oh crap." Wounds from Parent Deeks could not be magically healed. They had a rare magic in their claws that was as old as time, preceding every other kind except good and evil magic itself—my and Hathum's magic. I could heal my companions, but it would be better to save my strength for whatever was coming at us right now. My companions would live. They seemed to be doing all right as it was.

"So I'm guessing we can expect some repercussions from the King Deek at some point," I said flatly.

Ortheldo nodded. "Likely."

I sighed. Deeks were also rare in the fact they formed strong bonds among their species. Loyalty ran deep under their leathery skin. If my friends killed the Queen, and they must have in order to still be breathing, the King was going to find out sooner or later and hunt us down until he killed us or died.

"Well, all right then," I said. "Come on. Let's go." I was so done with this journey to Spar Ridges.

As we started to walk, I gradually felt the flutter of Shadow get faster. I could only assume it meant that whatever it was, was getting closer. I really missed my horse right now. I was sick of walking, I was sick of trudging, I was sick of my pack on my back. I shook my head. The nearly four days since the earthquake was taking its toll on me. I was just sick and tired and angry at everything.

The necklace's owner had better be in Spar Ridges. I began trembling at the thought that she very well might not be. If she wasn't, I was going to take the entire civilization of Spar Ridges down to its foundational studs just on principle! There was nothing in creation I was more sick of than that necklace. I had far more important things to do than indulge this wild goose chase.

That's when the sound came.

I stopped in my tracks and closed my eyes, more in annoyance then weariness. I needed my armor on, but not my white armor. I glowed too brightly when I was in my White Warrior form. Tapping into the black fire in my chest, I transformed into a Black Warrior form.

My hair went raven-feather black and lengthened to past my waist. My skin darkened to tan and I softly glowed with a menacing black glow. My outfit looked and felt exactly the same except for the color—a billowing black cloak, a light, smooth, silk black top and leggings so I could move with ease. I realized quickly, though, that something felt different. It only took me a moment before I looked down at my hands. It was my gloves.

Instead of the fingerless white wool gloves I usually wore, they were made of a strange black mesh material and covered my entire hand, including my fingers. My three claw-like knives didn't appear either. I stared at this oddity. Why would my gloves change?

The sound was closer. I supposed the gloves didn't matter. I sighed and pulled out my sword. From the corner of my eye, I saw my companions grouped together, gawking at me with wide eyes and seeming to be frozen in terror. Well, not exactly frozen—more like trembling.

I turned to them and resisted the urge to roll my eyes. I wasn't that scary, was I? "What?" I barked at them.

"Azrel…" Rabryn said with a distinct tremble in his voice.

I shook my head and looked away from them all. I didn't have time to alleviate their doubts or indulge their questions. "Better arm yourself, Rabryn," I said without looking back at him. "This battle is going to suck."

I shifted my gaze to the treetops just as a massive army of

giant black beetle creatures, the size and weight of baby cows, skittered over the branches above. Some leaped down to lower branches, while others jumped down to the ground and continued toward us.

I sighed and brought my sword up, slicing one of the bugs in half as it leapt toward my face. I was fighting off a few other ones when I happened to look down at the ground at the first bug I'd sliced in half. I watched with wide eyes as both halves began to quiver. Suddenly, the top half grew a bottom half, and the bottom half grew a top half, and two beetles came to life. I felt like I was being choked.

"They won't die!" Rabryn screamed before I could recover from my shock.

I didn't have the energy or wits to reply because I was too busy defending myself against the volley of endless attacks. All of our swords swung wildly, but it only did more damage to our survival. The beetles just healed or multiplied. I soon felt stinging wounds on my arms, neck and ankles from the prickly claws on their feet.

From the corners of my eyes, I saw flashes of gold and pink magic as Rabryn, Moifulyar, and Ceco tried magic on them. But like most of the other creatures in Spar Ridges' woods, the bugs were invincible to magic. My companions' blasts of gold and pink managed to blow some of the beetles back, but they just leapt to their skinny, scratchy feet, time and time again. All of us were spotted with blood from close calls with the giant insects.

I panted and sweated as dread boiled up in my chest. This was not going well. The beetles were piling up in front of us, jumping on the backs of other beetles, and those on the backs of others. I knocked a few pillars down occasionally, but three more would take their place. The entire mass of black bugs rose like a tidal wave in front of me. The beetles were stacked taller than me, and even more, relentlessly, were coming up from behind!

I clenched my teeth. Hell no. I would not go down like this!

I quickly sheathed my sword and turned my eyes black as I dug deep into my magic. I put a thick black shield around myself. The bugs bounced off it, sounding like raindrops on a glass window. With a smirk, I changed the magic from a solid shield to a flaming one. The beetles that jumped at me were incinerated instantly.

Watching them evaporate in the black flames, I allowed myself to throw my head back and laugh. I'd won.

"Azrel!"

Someone let out a strangled scream, and I turned around, confused. All I could see was a wave of black beetles as tall as my throat.

"Azrel!" It came again, more strained. I thought it might be Rabryn.

My eyebrows dropped. Why was I not more concerned? My heart wasn't racing. I wasn't worried or afraid, though I couldn't see him. Why was I... Something was wrong! What was I doing?

I turned around frantically, looking through my shield at the sea of beetles. I didn't see anyone! I was the only one protected! I'd thought...I'd thought I had covered them all in it.

I had to do something, *now!*

I pooled and concentrated all of my magic in my chest. I could only hope that my companions would be in magical shields of their own, as I wasn't going to have complete control over the blast I was about to unleash.

When I had gathered all my magic from every fiber of my body and soul, I lifted my arms up in front of my chest, and sucked in a breath. Everything went suddenly still for a moment. The wind stopped blowing. The bugs stopped attacking. Time seemed to stop in a painful moment of unnatural quiet.

I screamed at the top of my lungs and threw my arms out to my sides, sending ripples of black fire in every direction. The bugs were obliterated. The trees, some three feet thick, snapped in the wake of the blast. An explosive sound of simultaneous trunks breaking filled the entire world. Whatever didn't break was incinerated instantly from root to tip. Every fallen leave or blade of grass was burned to ash in three seconds flat.

Panting, I looked around at the gray, charred landscape that surrounded me now. My eyes went wide. I couldn't comprehend what I had done. I'd just burned an entire square mile to ash! My eyes slowly panned left to right in disbelief as I gaped at the damage. I was standing in a smoldering, gray wasteland now. There was *nothing* left.

I looked around frantically. I was alone! I placed a hand on my chest, trying to keep the panic from rising into my throat. Had I killed them? My eyes searched the ground. Were they among the ash I had created?

Suddenly, a soft thump and the sounds of breathing—and life—filled my ears. I spun around. There Acalith stood with Ortheldo, Rabryn, and Moifulyar. I slumped with relief. Ceco appeared next to them in a pink flash with Aithyan and Elreol at her side. My relief quickly turned to concern, though, when I saw how badly injured they were. All of their necks, faces, arms and legs were cut up anew with smaller claw marks of the bugs, adding to the damage the Deeks had done to them just yesterday. Their sleeves and pants were torn to shreds. Blood dripped off the torn pieces of their clothing.

Before I could ask if they were all right, Rabryn's fierce blue eyes were on me. "You almost killed us, Azrel!" he exploded. "You're lucky Acalith and Ceco were smart enough to get us out of here before you made that attack!"

He looked both very afraid and very angry. I tried to read his eyes but couldn't. All of them stared at me in the same horrified way. Wait, were they blaming me? I'd just saved their asses from those bugs!

"What?" I asked. "You're fine, aren't you?"

Rabryn shook his head. There was a heavy silence for a moment as he looked at me in disbelief. "You almost obliterated us."

I rolled my eyes. "Calm down. You're *not* obliterated, are you?"

Rabryn got quiet again. He looked odd to me for some reason. Almost like a stranger, like I hadn't practically raised him. Why did he look so strange?

He took a step toward me, slowly shaking his head. "You don't even see it, do you?"

"See what?"

"Azrel," he said slowly, "you have *got* to turn your magic back to white!"

I smirked. "You're joking, right?" I held my hands out to my sides and looked around the gray wasteland I had created. "Do you see what my black magic just *did*?" I chuckled gleefully. I was feeling so great. Everyone was okay, and damn my black magic was powerful. Why was he trying to ruin it?

The anger completely melted from his expression, leaving only horror. He looked at me like he didn't know me, and I couldn't even bring myself to care about it.

I sighed and shook my head. "No, Rabryn. I'll not be changing my magic back to white anytime soon. Having it black protects me from Hathum and lets me do things like this." I pointed around us again. "Hell, my magic actually has some juice to it now. I can actually *do* what needs to get done."

Rabryn visibly trembled. "Azrel, that's because black magic is fueled by hatred and malice. It is the power of destruction, which is why, when you destroy things, it's so efficient."

I knew I should care about that, but I really didn't. All I knew was I was safe from Hathum and I could still use my magic. That was all that mattered.

"Come here," Rabryn said, taking a step toward me. He held out his torn up arm. "Try to heal this."

I sneered at him and backed away. "Look, I may not be able to heal with my black magic, but I sure as hell can protect myself with it. Ceco and Moifulyar and the Brown Flowers have healing abilities. We don't need mine. We need my magic to keep us safe! And that's what my black magic does."

"Azrel!" Rabryn cried, gripping my shoulders firmly in his hands. "It's destroying who you are!"

I clenched my teeth and gave him a hard shove. He stumbled back a few feet and looked at me with horror and disbelief again. Oh, how I hated him right now. I'd never before hated my brother, but he had pushed it today.

"I'm fine," I growled at him.

Rabryn's eyes ignited with intensity. "No you're *not* fine!" he screamed as he took a threatening step toward me.

I was about to defend myself when Ortheldo stepped between us, shoving Rabryn's shoulders back and keeping him away from me. "Stop! Stop!" I couldn't see his face, but whatever Ortheldo's expression was, it was drawing Rabryn's full attention. "We have more important things to do then bicker here," Ortheldo said. "This isn't getting us anywhere. You and Ceco and Moifulyar and the Brown Flowers can heal us. We have to go."

I watched suspiciously as Rabryn looked back at me. He

pressed his lips together and reluctantly nodded. "Fine. Let's go."

NINE

AZREL

An uncomfortable heaviness fell over my party as we continued toward Spar Ridges. Even though I had changed out of my Black Warrior form, everyone except Ortheldo kept a fair distance from me. Even Ortheldo's proximity seemed forced, though. He barely looked at me. When he did, it was with a brief, false smile before he would look away again.

I shook my head. *Screw them.*

I picked up my pace and took a significant lead. I wasn't going to be questioned by them. They had no clue what I was dealing with! Who were they to judge me? I was the White Warrior, and I was going to handle this in the best way I could. Right now, that involved staying hidden from Hathum, finding this stupid necklace's owner, and then joining up with the army that Addredoc, Lisswilla, Reese, and Yarin were gathering for me. *That* was how this was going to unfold!

I shook my head again. Now, when I needed their faith in me the most, they were shaken. Figures.

We eventually got to the edge of the gray area that I had destroyed and headed back into the green of the forest. We were only a half a mile into it when out of nowhere something heavy landed on my shoulders and took me to the ground.

"Oof!" I spun onto my back to see what it was, but pain exploded in my forearm and I screamed.

"Azrel!" Ortheldo called, and all of my companions ran toward me. I hadn't realized how far ahead of them I'd gotten.

I shifted my gaze to my arm to see the source of the pain. The creature was unlike anything I'd ever seen or heard of. It was a tiny, gray skinned thing that was only a bit bigger than a large house cat. Its head looked too big for its body, and so did its very big, very human-looking green eyes. Its wide mouth extended across its entire face—a mouth that was now clamped down on my forearm with my blood bubbling up around its lips and dripping off its chin.

"Azrel!" My brother and Moifulyar had paused their running

and loaded their bows.

"No!" I cried and, before I even knew what I was doing, I threw my free arm up in front of the creature's face. I screamed again as both of their arrows impaled my forearm. I went completely limp, my arms injured and bleeding, and stared blankly up at the sky.

Slowly, I turned my head to get a decent look at the creature. Gazing into its eyes, I instantly knew I had been correct in taking those arrows for it. It looked like a mix of a four-year-old human child and a shriveled old man. It was hairless and had pointy ears that stretched out behind its head. Its enormous eyes were filled with fear and terror and pain. It wore only torn and shredded pants that barely stayed on its bone-thin frame. Its sickly looking body was covered with old scars. The creature was so filthy and so afraid that I wanted nothing more than to bathe it and cradle it in my arms to protect it.

Even as I thought that, it clamped down on my arm so hard I heard the bone snap. I screamed again as my blood splashed onto its forehead, yet the creature just looked even more afraid. Though my vision was blurring, I'd swear I could see tears in its eyes and undeniable regret.

"It's okay, little one," I said, breathing heavily. "I won't hurt you."

The creature seemed to understand my words, and its eyes widened a bit. It made a soft purring sound and released my arm before it slowly backed away from me in a strange frog-like manner. Its large eyes were already filled with tears, but then I saw its wide bottom lip start to tremble too.

Suddenly a rapid fluttering of Shadow inside my chest made me snap my eyes to my companions. Rabryn was coming toward me with his hand already glowing gold. Was he the threat?

No.

I look past my brother and clenched my teeth when I saw Aithyan and Elreol raising their bows and aiming at him. I barely had time to suck in air. "Rabryn!" I screamed as they fired.

I was frozen as my little brother's upper body jerked forward from the impact and landed hard face down on the ground. I started panting as I looked at the two brown-feathered arrows sticking out of his back. He wasn't moving. His eyes were closed, and he *wasn't* moving!

My entire body started shaking, and slowly I moved my eyes to the trees. That's when all of the Brown Flowered Salynns appeared in the shadows. All of them were here, and all of them had their bows loaded and aimed at us.

"Well done, Forgius," Aithyan said, looking past me.

I turned and realized he was addressing the little trembling creature that was now cowering under some low brush. I looked back at Aithyan with as much hatred as I could muster. I fed that hatred, pouring it into my gaze so he would feel it burn even from five yards away.

He only blanched a little before he nodded his head toward my fallen baby brother. "Afraid I can't let any healing happen, my dear," he said. "We need you injured to take you in."

"Ah ah!" one of the brown flowers said, aiming his arrow at Ceco. "Don't even think about it. I'm a quicker shot than you are, princess."

Aithyan shook his head at me. "Foolish child. We are tasked to capture intruders and protect our woods. Granted, this was forced upon us, but we're honorable people. We do our job and don't let our prisoners escape. But then you turned out to be more powerful than we'd anticipated."

Orrin stepped forward from the trees with his arrow aimed at my head. "We clearly needed a better surprise tactic for someone as powerful as you. That's where Forgius came in. He's got a hell of a bite, huh?" Orrin smirked.

"We couldn't let you just walk away. Bringing you to our King might just earn us favor back into the city," Aithyan concluded.

I slowly sat up. With this, with everything, I was done. I lit my eyes up black and slowly got to my feet.

"Ah ah ah!" Aithyan warned, bringing his bow up higher. "I wouldn't."

I started toward them.

Aithyan's eyes widened and he fired his arrow into my left shoulder. I jerked with the impact, but I didn't even feel it. I relished the fear in his eyes as he loaded his bow again and fired into the same shoulder. My body jerked again, but I was still coming at him.

All eight of them, in a panic, forgot their other targets and fired at me. Every single arrow hit my body somewhere, but I didn't even stumble. The rage beast pounded my skull and clawed at my chest to get out. I didn't fight it this time. I released it.

"Foolish child?" I hissed in a voice I didn't recognize.

They all fired another round of arrows, and still I moved toward them. I imagined them all at my feet and not breathing. It would happen slowly, though. I would make it happen slowly.

My eyes found Ceco as I passed my brother's fallen form. I pointed down at him without pause. "Fix him," I said, my voice sounding like I had gargled with gravel. Ceco flinched from the sound, but she didn't dare hesitate. She went to my brother quickly as another volley of arrows hit me in the stomach.

Focusing back on the Salynns, I lit my palm up with black fire and, without thought, healed the bite on my arm right down to the broken bone. My black magic *could* heal! Maybe I couldn't heal others, but I could heal myself, and that was all that mattered! I summoned more of my black fire, healing the arrow wounds, at the same time, burning all the shafts in my torso to ash.

The Salynns started backing away from me. When I transformed into my Black Warrior form, all their eyes went wide with terror.

"I not only warned you," I began, my voice now sounding like a menacing low gurgle, "but I *showed* you on several occasions that I was formidable, and not to be trifled with." I tilted my head to the side. "But you went ahead and trifled anyway, didn't you?" I put a wall of black fire up behind them, leaving them nowhere to go. "*I'm* foolish?" I cried, my voice clear and loud now. "*You* are the ones that have challenged *me!*"

My hands flew out in front of me and a wall of black flames rushed out like a title wave towards the Salynns. They screamed and writhed in agony as their skin steamed, bubbled, and boiled. I watched for a few moments with satisfaction. This was what happened when you crossed me! They clawed at their own faces in pain. I clenched my teeth and grinned, baring all of my teeth, when long bloody scratch marks blossomed on their cheeks and arms.

"Azrel!"

I thought I heard someone calling my name, but it sounded too far away. I just kept watching as the Brown Flowered Salynns ripped at their own skin, intentionally causing themselves one pain to try and relieve themselves of another. It was actually pretty amusing.

"Azrel!"

It was my brother screaming, I thought. But he sounded miles away.

Suddenly, my arm was yanked. I was spun around and Rabryn stood in front of me, healed and alert, and took my face in both his hands. "Azrel, stop! Stop!"

I gazed at him, confused. "Why?" I asked.

He swallowed and leaned down so his eyes were level with mine. "Because my sister doesn't torture people."

He was concerned for these Salynns? Seriously? I jerked my face out of his hands, "Well, maybe it's about time I did." I started to turn toward the screaming Salynns again, but Rabryn took hold of my shoulders keeping me still. My eyes narrowed as I slowly looked back at him. The most pathetic pleading look came over his features.

"Azrel, please stop." His voice was trembling. "Please? For me?"

I glared at him. When did my brother become such a wussy wet blanket?

"Please?" His voice cracked at the word, and his eyes glossed over with tears. "I'm begging you. I'll get on my knees if you want. Just stop."

He was begging and pleading with those ridiculous blue eyes of his, and I wanted to retch. I huffed and rolled my eyes before I looked back at the Salynns. With a flick of my hand, I stopped the black fire from eating their skin alive.

Rabryn looked over at Moifulyar and Ceco. "Help me," he said, and all of them rushed over to begin healing the Salynns.

I threw my arms out to my sides. "Great! That's just fantastic, Rabryn. Good idea. Take the bad guys' side. That's smart."

Rabryn looked at me over his shoulder as he healed a red-headed girl. "This isn't about *sides*, Azrel!" He stood up and walked over to me, keeping his eyes locked on mine. "Hathum tortures people. Shadow creatures torture people. Shadow Gods torture people." He stopped in front of me and shook his head.

"You do not. The White Warrior does not. The Light Gods *do not!*"

My lip twitched and I crossed my arms. "You're right. The Light Gods don't torture people. In fact, They don't do much of anything these days, do They?" Rabryn's eyes widened. I wasn't sure if it was horror or shock. Maybe both. "As for me? Maybe I ought to start torturing people. I might actually make a little headway in this war if I did."

Rabryn stooped to put his eyes level with mine. He gently took my face in his hands again, and I wondered why I nearly flinched at the tender touch. "Azrel," he said softly, "listen to yourself. Something is wrong."

He wasn't getting it, and I hated him for that right now. "The only thing wrong with me," I said, glaring, "is my aggravation with the overwhelming odds I'm facing and with absolutely no help from the Light Gods!" I knocked Rabryn's hands off of my face and grabbed fistful of his shirt yanking him towards me. I clutched the material so hard my arm trembled. "You felt that earthquake, didn't you? I *told you* what Addredoc saw in the Black Mountains." I was panting. "I am in serious trouble here, Rabryn. I need to do something different and drastic, or everyone I care about is going to die!"

"Azrel," he said gently, encircling my wrist with one hand and lowering it so he could lean down to meet my eyes again. "Answer me something. How is torturing eight Salynns going to help you defeat Hathum and save us all? Hmm?"

I felt something strangely familiar, yet at the same time alien, flutter alive in my chest. I quickly dismissed it and hardened myself against it. There was no room for emotion! "It won't help me save the world," I said through clenched teeth, "but it sure makes me feel better." I shoved Rabryn to the side and took a step toward the Salynns still cowering on the ground.

Before I could even light up my hands to finish what I started, Rabryn jumped in front of me. "Will you listen to yourself?" he cried desperately. "You just said torturing people makes you feel good! That's something Shadow beings enjoy. Not you! Something is *wrong*, Azrel!"

"Nothing is wrong!" I screamed at him. All I wanted to do was watch those traitorous Salynns clawing at themselves for a little while. They deserved it! They'd shot him! They'd attacked me!

They'd tried to imprison us!

Rabryn's entire body was trembling. "You added Shadow properties to your magic, and now those Shadow properties are showing up in your actions. How can you not see that?"

The rage beast was pounding at the door in my head and chest again. This again? "My magic is fine," I growled, barely getting the words past my clenched teeth.

Rabryn shook his head and held his hands up. "No, it's not," he said more gently.

"It's —"

"I know you," he interrupted softly, taking a step towards me. He rested his hands on my cheeks again and stooped to meet my eyes. "I know you better than you know yourself. And I know that if you took the Shadow properties out of your magic right now, you would see what is happening and be just as horrified as I am."

I glared at him, my heart racing with the pounding rage. "I'm *so* sorry," I sneered. "I forgot that you were perfect."

Rabryn flinched. "What?"

"You're the self-righteous golden boy, aren't you?" I practically spat the words at him. "The Light Gods beloved, huh?" Rabryn's hands slowly slipped off my face as he stared at me. I felt like I was going to throw up from how pathetic he was. "I am not going to apologize for slowly and painfully killing a half dozen enemy dicks."

Everything was so quiet for a moment. I could just barely hear the soft breeze blowing through the woods. It lifted a strand of my brother's long hair off his shoulder and made it dance for that quiet moment, until it fell behind him out of sight. Rabryn turned his face away and squeezed his eyes closed, allowing a large tear to drip down his cheek.

I felt a flash of satisfaction seeing that. Maybe he would shut up now. He opened his eyes and pressed his lips together. Wiping the tear, he slowly nodded as he stared at the ground. I waited quietly for the useless, spineless thing he was going to say next.

A strained, "I won't let you do this to yourself," finally came out, and suddenly he punched me so hard in the mouth that I landed on the ground on my back. Pain flashed through my jaw and up into my skull.

I lay there staring blankly up at the sky for a moment, trying to comprehend if that had really just happened.

I was on the ground.

My jaw was throbbing.

I tasted blood in the corner of my mouth and felt it drip down my chin.

He just hit me!

Slowly sitting up, I fixed my eyes on him. His nostrils were flaring and he was trembling and breathing heavily with fear, but his eyes and jaw were stubbornly set. "I won't let you torture innocent people. You want those Salynns," he said, pointing back at them without taking his eyes off me, "you're going to have to kill me. Is that's something you're willing to do?"

I slowly wiped the corner of my hand across my lip and saw the blood smear my skin. He was actually going to try to fight me? Something was wrong. My brother was acting like my enemy. Suddenly it dawned on me, and my eyes went wide. Hathum must have gotten to him! He'd turned on me!

I slowly got to my feet. Well, if there was one thing I was good at, it was destroying my enemies.

I lit myself up with black magic, lifted my hands, and shot a continuous blast of black fire at him. A golden shield of light developed in front of him and he ducked behind it, crouching before me and cowering. The fool! I was going to obliterate his magic in an instant, and then him!

Ortheldo, Acalith, and Moifulyar ran at me with their weapons drawn. I glanced at them and only took a brief moment to be shocked; Ortheldo was leading the pack! He drew his weapon against me! Hathum had gotten to him too! He must have gotten to all of them! No wonder it had been so quiet lately. Hathum had been plotting this the whole time!

Clenching my teeth, and with zero effort, I lifted all of them off their feet and pinned them up against some trees. Growling, I added pressure to the force holding them up, crushing it against them and making them all cry out in pain. I looked at Ceco, who just stood there, staring at me in terror for a moment before vanishing in a flash of pink magic.

My lip twitched briefly before I looked back at Rabryn. He was on one knee, desperately holding his shield in place as my black fire assaulted him. I took a step closer, my face trembling from how hard my teeth were clenched, and I released the rage beast. I poured all of my hatred into my magic. My hatred for Hathum, this mission, the Light Gods, the people of The Pitt, everything! The blast of fire assaulting Rabryn intensified. He screamed. I knew I should care about that, but I didn't. My chest was empty, black. I felt nothing but the hatred and the rage.

I watched the edges of his golden shield started to give way. I was going to kill Hathum for taking away the people who were closest to me. Screw this necklace, and screw this mission! I was heading straight for the Black Mountains once this was over, and I was going to stab Hathum in the throat!

I took another step towards Rabryn. Then another. His eyes were squeezed shut, and I saw a tear slide down his cheek. There was no sympathy left in me for any more betrayal. I was done. I screamed, intensifying my assault and concentrating my magic harder on him.

I would not lose this war!

Behind that thinning golden light, he was curled up into a ball in front of me, shaking. In that moment, everything went quiet somehow. I didn't hear my screams or the roar of my magic, but as plain as day, I heard the soft whisper of my little brother. "I love you, Azrel."

Then I overcame his shield. Throwing his head back, he screamed in agony as my black magic overwhelmed him, and I watched him burn to ash.

TEN

I ceased my attack and put my hands down. It was quiet again. I blinked a couple of times. The ash still held the shape of his face and his body, like a naked, bald, porous stone statue of him down on one knee, arms crossed in front of him trying to shield himself from an attack he had no chance of escaping. His eyes were closed. His mouth was open. He was the perfect likeness of utter terror and sadness.

I blinked again. Something stirred in me. It felt strange. I didn't know what it was. Deep in my chest, something was bubbling to awareness. Curious, I let it surface.

It was memories. Memories in The Pitt. My eyes went wide. They flashed by in sequence faster than I could really watch them all, but at the same time I didn't miss a single thing. It was my memories with Rabryn.

My entire body went still. No, that wasn't true. I stumbled backwards a few steps, barely able to keep my balance. He was so full of life and beauty, the embodiment of kindness and love. I remembered the innocence that had been in his bright blue eyes. I remembered all the times he draped an arm around my neck and kissed my temple when I was down or depressed. He'd always managed to find a smile for me, no matter how bad things got, no matter what he was dealing with by watching me go through that torture.

Quickly the memories faded…and Rabryn was a pile of ash before me.

My breathing became rapid. I blinked and stumbled backwards. My back hit a tree trunk and I began to shake so badly my legs collapsed under me. I wasn't seeing this. I was not seeing this!

"Rabryn," I choked out, my voice sounding like someone had sanded my vocal cords. "Rabryn…"

This wasn't real. It wasn't real! My…my baby brother.

Dead. Killed.

Killed by me!

I heard the grunts of Ortheldo, Acalith and Moifulyar as they fell from the tree to which I had pinned them. I wanted to look at them, but the pile of ash in front of me…the ash that looked like my brother… I couldn't look away.

The rage beast roared to life again, only this time when it clawed at my brain, I wished it really would. I wished it would tear my brain matter, my eyesight, my life, my feelings to shreds!

Kill me, I begged it silently.

No, death was too easy. I deserved this. I deserved to be suffering by looking at the ashen remains of my little brother. If there was an eternal torture chamber in the Abyss, it would be a vacation for me if I killed myself right now. So, no. I wouldn't die. I would endure this. I would suffer this because I deserved to.

My brother. My baby brother. Burned alive. Burned to death. Dead. By me.

My vision went black, but I didn't pass out. I realized tears had filled my eyes. I touched them quickly because they blocked the view of the ash that was left of my brother.

My brows dropped, and somehow, amidst this torture, I had a rational thought: How did my tears *darken* my vision?

I looked at the hand that had just wiped my tears, and my eyes went wide; my tears were black!

Trembling, I yanked my gloves off in a panic, hastily rubbing my hands over my wet eyes and cheeks, and looked at them. They were covered with black water!

No. That wasn't right! My temporarily changed magic color shouldn't change my tears!

"Azrel?" Ortheldo said, carefully approaching me with his weapon drawn. Acalith was on her knees next to the ash, her head bowed and crying. Moifulyar was with her, but his eyes were on me.

What had I done? *What had I done!?*

I desperately reached for the communication link in my mind. Something was wrong! Something was wrong! I had to dig to find it. I screamed into it as I accessed it.

Addredoc!

Azrel? Azrel! What is it? What's wrong?

I couldn't breathe. I couldn't think. *My…my tears…they're black.*

What? He shrieked. *Azrel, what did you do?*

I...I changed my white magic to black.

Addredoc made a strange noise between a gasp and choke. *Azrel! You don't add Shadow properties to Light magic! That taints it!*

I looked at the black water on my hands and felt my lungs constrict, like an invisible fist had just plunged into my chest and squeezed them together. I was only capable of quick, shallow breaths, but my vision was already pulsing from the lack of air. I desperately rubbed my face. Maybe if I looked at the black tears on my hands enough times they would magically change back to white.

No.

No.

No! They were black! *Black!* And now my hands were shaking.

Suddenly, with a bright flash of red magic, Addredoc appeared before my eyes. I wailed his name and, as the floodgate of tears opened, reached for him like an infant needing to be picked up by a parent.

He ran and dropped to his knees in front of me and held my face in his hands. I looked at him and his big, soft, wise brown eyes and his pale white skin. My heart raced as I clutched his red robes in my fists in a panic. I hadn't seen him in so long, and he looked so beautiful. His hair had gotten longer. It was still pin-straight black, but now choppy at the ends, and came down to nearly brush his shoulders. He looked at me with such compassion, such sympathy, that I nearly went completely limp.

"I knew something was wrong with you during our last communication," he said as he searched my eyes, like he was looking for signs of life in a wounded soldier. "*Any* color Azrel! *Any* other color would have been fine!" He gripped my face more firmly in his hands, and I found myself just staring into his as I cried. His brows went up sympathetically. "Why do you think a Shadow being can never touch your Sword? Because Shadow and Light cannot coexist."

I took in a few rapid sobs. "I thought it would hide me better from Hathum."

Rabryn. I couldn't even defend myself. I'd killed him. I'd killed my brother.

More black tears spilled over from the panic, but this time I didn't wipe them away fast enough and Ortheldo saw them. Behind Addredoc, his eyes flew open wide. Throwing caution to the wind, he ran up to me, falling on his knees beside Addredoc. Ortheldo grabbed my face from him and looked at my black tears closely with horror—not sympathy or compassion, but fear and horror.

"Where's Rabryn?" Addredoc asked.

I wailed, and in that instant any strength I had left drained away. I collapsed in a ball with my forehead on the ground, feeling the weight of the entire world pressing into my back. I couldn't live with this. I couldn't live with what I'd done. He was dead, *dead* by my hand! And I couldn't do this without him.

"Oh no," Addredoc breathed, likely seeing the remains behind him.

The agony seemed to take on a life of its own, and before I realized what I was doing, my hand was pulling out the Salynn blade from the holster on my thigh. Sitting up, I plunged it deep into my chest. I felt the sharp pain as it pierced my skin and bone and heard the faint pop when it hit my heart.

"NO!" both Addredoc and Ortheldo suddenly screamed as they faced me again.

Life immediately began to seep out of me as my hand became soaked in blood. With it came relief. No more pain. No more burdens. No more world without Rabryn. No more knowledge that I had killed him. Gone. All of it gone.

I started to fall backwards, but Addredoc caught me. He was looking down at my face saying something, but I didn't care enough to try to hear him. My vision was already fading as my hand holding the knife went limp and dropped to the ground. Addredoc suddenly seemed to want to help me along as he yanked the blade out of my chest. Life slipped away faster, but I could still see his face. He was holding me up and looking down at me, and though I could barely see him, he seemed to be fearful. Why was he so worried about me? Death was what I deserved. I'd killed my innocent, sweet baby brother. This was what I had coming.

Before I could pass into oblivion, I felt strong healing magic enter my skin and mend my stab wound from the inside out. As life filled me once again, I gasped deeply and my eyes flew wide open. Addredoc's eyes were the first thing I saw.

"Not yet, Azrel," he said softly. "Not yet."

I wanted to die! Who was he to stop me? I would *not* live with the fact I had killed my brother!

"Azrel? Azrel listen to me," Addredoc said gently, still holding me with his arm around my back. I had no strength to even sit up. "Azrel"—he rested his free hand on my cheek and gently caressed my skin with his thumb—"how long have you had your magic black?"

Leave me alone! I wanted to scream. *Just let me die! Please just let me die.* But I had no strength.

Addredoc kept holding me tightly, pinning me against his chest so I couldn't reach for another weapon. "How long have you had your magic black?" he asked again, searching my face.

"A day," I finally moaned and weakly looked around for my Salynn blade to thrust into my chest again.

"Good! Good. That's good. Now listen"—with his hand still on my cheek, he slightly moved my face, drawing my attention back to his brown eyes—"you've got to pull that Shadow taint out of your magic." I tried to look away, but he moved my face again, keeping his eyes locked on mine. "Listen. Listen. Turn it white again. Turn your magic white again, Azrel."

Why? What did it matter? Rabryn was dead. Dead because of me.

"Come on, sweetheart," he said urgently. "Try. At least try."

I closed my eyes and begrudgingly began to do what he was asking.

"Can she do it?" Ortheldo asked.

"I think so," I heard Addredoc respond. "I just hope it's not too late."

"Too late? What do you mean too late?" Ortheldo asked.

Addredoc waited a moment before he answered. "Hathum can feel Shadow magic just as much as he can feel Azrel's white magic. It's *his* magic." He paused. "If he knows it's her using Shadow magic, he can manipulate and control her via that Shadow magic. He can increase its power until it consumes her in some way, either mentally, physically, or magically." Addredoc blew out a breath. "She might be okay, magically anyway. It's been very quiet since that earthquake. He may not have detected her use of it."

Slowly, I saw the magic pool in my chest begin to brighten and turn white. I waited. Something else came out of me suddenly that made my eyes fly wide open and I gasped. Darkness. A filthy taint that I hadn't realized was there came out of my soul. I actually felt it lift out of me as my magic brightened to white again.

After a few fearful moments, I felt the purity of my magic fill me, and my entire body went limp in Addredoc's arms from unbelievable and overwhelming relief. I felt so light and cleansed, just clean all over. Panting, and in a strange stupor of regret and cleanliness, I lit my eyes up and saw white light reflecting off Addredoc's skin. A single tear dripped down my cheek and I touched it. I felt a flash of fear that it would still be black when I pulled my hand away, but all I saw was white water on my fingertips.

Ortheldo and Addredoc both sighed and sagged in relief. "Thank the Light Gods," Addredoc said.

I slowly sat up with Addredoc's help, wiping my tears of relief and regret. I kept checking my hands to make sure they were still white. Once I was sitting up, I knew something was different. It wasn't just my magic either, but me. Something, a presence it felt like, was near me, or in me, or with me somehow. I felt an unbelievable peace and calmness, even as my eyes rested on the pile of ash that had been my brother. It wasn't The White Warrior though. I knew what she felt like, and it wasn't anything like this. She tended to stress me out. This was bigger and more peaceful and more calm and beautiful then anything I'd ever felt before.

It was almost like the strange state of nothingness I had reached outside White Veilvin during the battle on their border. Only I wasn't dying this time. I wasn't fading. The exact opposite seemed to be happening. I felt *everything*. I was aware of *everything*.

My eyes scanned the ground slowly. I was aware of every single insect under the forest vegetation. There were countless numbers. I couldn't see them; it was more like I felt their energy. Each tiny life force of every insect seemed to reach out towards me and physically touch me. I could even feel a snake slithering near a log a mile away to the north.

I felt and saw everything in a very strange way. I could feel their life force with my very own, from the insect to the snake and everything in between and beyond. Plants, trees, fish in a stream along the bank of some island far to the south. The oceans. I felt every single life force of each sea creature across the planet, even in places seven miles deep. I felt the sea and plant life at those depths. In some obscure ocean far in the east, a pod of Bur whales was gathered for the birth of a newcomer. I felt the instant that calf was born because its life force was added to everything else I was feeling. I could feel all of it. I could feel the world.

I looked down at myself and realized I was in my White Warrior form. Without fully realizing it, I was slowly reaching into my pocket, pulling out the necklace with the Anarran Gem. The orange glow was so dim that I couldn't even see it inside the layers of the clear stone anymore. It didn't pulsate with warmth any longer, but it wasn't dead yet.

I knew that because I felt its life force, too.

I held up the gem and smiled. I became suddenly aware that the Anarran Gen actually belonged to me. I knew it, because its life force matched my own. It was a part my *own* life force.

In this strange state of awareness, I felt three major pieces missing from my own life force. One was my crown, one was the untouchable energy in my Sword, and the other was this tiny gem.

The gem was mine. It had always been mine. I was the necklace's owner. I knew everything about it—where it had been found first, where it had been found when protecting the gems of healing had been mandated. I knew every hand that it had passed through in history and every person that had protected it before The White Warrior had been created.

I pinched the gem in my thumb and index finger and ripped the chain off, tossing it away. Most importantly, I knew how to keep it alive. My own life force kept it alive when it was a part of me. As long as I lived, so did the gem.

I looked down at my White Warrior ensemble and focused on the small fire-shaped diamond broach fastened to my chest. With a soft smile, I brought the gem forward and touched it to the diamond broach. Like a small piece of a puzzle, it fit into my life force perfectly, filling the tiny gap that had been missing. There was a small flash of orange, and the gem vanished in my fingers. My diamond broach began to softly glow orange deep in its core.

I looked around, realizing fully for the first time that energy was the core of everything, everywhere. It was in plants, in animals, in magic, even in emotions like love and friendship and hatred. All life, healing, creation, everything was energy...Light energy. But there was also energy in destruction and hatred, and that's what Shadow energy was. The two energy forces, Light and Shadow, destruction and creation, were at odds with each other, always, for eternity. There was no gray area between them...until now.

My brows dropped when that thought came out of nowhere. No gray area between Light and Shadow until now?

Before I could contemplate longer, the energy of the strange state I was in seemed to rise out of me. From my toes, up out of my shoulders, it disappeared from me and floated away. I blinked once as the world's beating heart faded from my awareness. Then my eyes rested again on the pile of ash that had been my brother.

My entire body trembled as I carefully stood and stumbled toward him. The wind had started to blow away some of the ash of his resemblance. I wasn't sure what I was feeling. It wasn't much. If I felt anything it was shame and exhaustion. Without shifting my eyes, I pulled out my Sword. Moifulyar saw me coming and took Acalith's shoulders, gently pulling her away from the ash heap.

I stopped in front of it. I stared down at it. Then my heart got hard, righteously hard, and I shifted my eyes up to the sky. Taking my Sword up in one hand, I gripped the blade with my other and squeezed! My lips barely twitched as the blade cut into my palm and blood immediately started dripping to the ground.

"You *will* give me back my brother," I said, glaring up into the blue sky that I could see through the canopy of the forest. "Fully intact. Or I swear to you, I'm done."

I waited. They knew I was talking to Them. I knew They could hear me. The Light Gods, the ones with the power of creation and life.

Nothing happened.

"Look at my face," I said in a hiss, "and tell me if I'm bluffing." I gripped the blade harder, letting the edge cut down to the bones of my fingers, and then bent it upwards. I heard the soft crack, like a tiny bit of breaking glass, as the metal slightly gave way under my White Warrior strength. "Test me in this. I dare you."

I waited, blood and tears steadily dripping to the ground.

Nothing happened.

I bent the blade up again and heard another soft crack. I waited again, keeping my eyes on the sky.

Nothing happened.

I gripped the blade tight and prepared to snap it in half when finally I heard a long gasp at my feet.

I looked down just in time to see the gray ash of my brother fade. It gave way to the peach color of his skin right before my eyes. I dropped to my knees in front of him as the ash solidified and took form—first his face, and then all the way down his body. His hair came into view; his clothes appeared on him. Eventually his arms dropped to his sides and he slumped over, whole again.

My White Warrior form faded as I threw myself at him, holding him up before he hit the ground, and I wailed so loud it sounded more like a scream. I sobbed. Everything I had inside of me spilled out in those tears as I held my baby brother in my arms.

"I'm sorry," I said, though it sounded so hollow compared to what I had done. "I'm sorry."

He hated me. I knew that much. I could feel his guard was up and the only reason he weakly returned my embrace at all was out of sheer politeness. With every fiber of my being I knew that and I didn't blame him; I hated myself more than he could hope to hate me. But as long as he was alive, he could hate me until the end of time. I would understand if he walked away right now and never spoke to me again. As long as he was alive.

I pulled away and looked at his face. He refused to meet my eyes, as I knew he would. He looked at the ground and then off to the side. "I'm sorry," I said weakly.

Without a word, he pushed himself away from me and up to his feet. I couldn't take my eyes off him as he walked past me. He and Ortheldo embraced tightly for a long time. Then he hugged Acalith. When he pulled away, he kissed her lips quickly before embracing Moifulyar, and finally Addredoc. A few words were murmured during the whole exchange, but I couldn't make them out.

Rabryn walked over to his packs and slung them over his shoulder. He held out his hand to Acalith, who accepted it eagerly and instantly melted into his side, and started walking into the woods toward Spar Ridges again. Acalith didn't look at me once. I met Ortheldo's eyes. He gave me a forced, sympathetic smile before he turned and followed Rabryn into the trees. Moifulyar gave me a wary glance over his shoulders before he, too, followed suit and brought up the rear of the group as they disappeared into the woods.

I shook my head and looked down at my lap. I'd never felt so cold and alone before. I deserved it though. I knew I did.

Someone kneeled next to me. I looked up and saw Addredoc's kind eyes, which held absolutely no trace of scorn. "Give them time," he said softly. "That was probably the most terrifying thing they could have ever seen in this life—the White Warrior, you, succumbing to Shadow. Not even killing your brother could compare to witnessing what just happened with your black fire."

I looked over in the direction of the twelve Salynns I had tortured, but they were gone. No doubt they'd escaped the first chance they gotten, and I didn't blame them. I didn't have the strength to speak. I just kept staring down at my lap.

"Well, now that begs the question," Addredoc suddenly said, a little lighter, "of why the hell Hathum didn't know about you using Shadow magic. He should have pounced on that immediately."

"Who cares?" I said miserably, hardly interested in Hathum at the moment. "As long as he wasn't aware, that's all that matters."

"The 'why' may be more cause for concern than you think, Azrel." Addredoc sighed and I forced my eyes up to his face. "It also begs the question: What have we learned from this experience?"

I nearly smiled…nearly. "Don't turn my magic black."

Addredoc shook his head. "More than that." He shifted his position so he was kneeling in front of me and stooped so his eyes were level with mine. I nearly glanced away, but his eyes held mine firmly. "Nothing good comes from fear." My heart softened at the truth of that. "You are so fearful, and so desperate to stay hidden from Hathum, that you endangered yourself, your friends, and really the world."

I swallowed heavily as the weight of his words settled like a rock in my chest and then plunked down into my stomach. He was right. And I knew it. The rock quickly became wrapped with a layer of guilt, and that guilt burned, seeming to spread like a fire in my veins.

Addredoc sighed softly and glanced around. "I know you don't do very well with pressure, Azrel, but there is *nothing*, no hope, without you." He met my eyes intensely again but touched my cheek with his fingertips in a small gesture of comfort. "The Shadow Gods will win and we will all die or be enslaved. The world *will* end."

He reached up and gently tucked a loose strand of my hair behind my ear, his fingers caressing my cheek again as he dropped his hand back into his lap. "I don't want to sound like a mean dad, but you have got to do something about this fear of yours. There is no room for it as the White Warrior. It causes panic and makes people do foolish things. You've done well up until that earthquake hit which"—his brows went up and he tilted his head—"I honestly can't blame you for panicking about that, but you're supposed to be braver than me."

I managed a small smile. "You don't sound like a mean dad. You actually sound like *my* dad." Addredoc blushed and gave me a sweet half smile. I swallowed as the shame melted the smile off my face. "It would just be easier to be brave if I wasn't so damn limited in my magic."

Addredoc's tone stayed sympathetic as he reached out and petted my hair. "I know." He sighed and his thumb gently touched my jaw. "But at least you know the Light Gods are actively with you now." I glanced up at the sky self-consciously. "They brought Rabryn back. And They didn't just warn you about the effects of that earthquake, They *showed* you."

I looked down at my hands in my lap and something dawned on me. "They did more than that."

"What do you mean?"

I sniffed and met his eyes. "When I changed into black armor, my gloves changed." I recalled the times I'd found a strange mesh material wrapped around the hilt of my Sword. It was enchanted cloth so my Sword was protected from any Shadow that might try to touch it if it was ever out of my hands. "My black gloves were made of the same strange mesh material that protects my Sword from Shadow, and they covered my hands completely."

Addredoc brightened a little and nodded. "To protect the Sword from the Shadow in you while you used it." I smiled a little. Addredoc sighed as peace and hope filled his eyes such as I'd never seen since meeting him. "That's more than The Light Gods have done in the midst of humanity for over 3,000 years." He smiled at me and looked me in the eyes. "I really think you need to sit down and try to have a nice long talk with Them. I know your faith is small and limited after what They did to your dad, but you have got to at least try. You've got to pray, Azrel. If They'll listen to anyone, They'll listen to you."

I felt a small amount of dread seep into my heart. "What if They do nothing even after I talk to Them?"

Addredoc shrugged. "Then at least you tried."

I looked away. "I don't know."

"Try," Addredoc said. I looked at him helplessly and he petted my hair again in comfort. "Listen, I have to go." I felt like I'd been stabbed in the chest again. "I left in the middle of a civil war meeting. Are you going to be okay?"

"I think so," I replied, knowing it was a lie. I was not okay. I was nowhere near okay.

"Are you sure?"

I looked into his compassionate eyes and shook my head as new tears filled my eyes, blinding me until they fell down my cheeks. "No," I sobbed and leaned into him, resting my forehead against his chest.

He quickly wrapped me tightly in his arms. "It's okay, sweetheart. It's okay," he whispered.

I cried for a while. Addredoc just held me and whispered softly, comforting me until I managed to settle down a little. Rabryn hated me with good reason. None of the others could trust me now. They'd all walked away without a word to me and had given me wary looks as they'd left. I had given in to Shadow, and they had seen it. The White Warrior didn't give in to Shadow. What use was I now? I'd betrayed my father and my life's mission, and I had killed my little brother.

Addredoc was here, though. He was holding me and comforting me at the worst possible moment of my life. He didn't see any of that—the shame, the guilt, the betrayal, the mistakes. He was just here, staying with me and holding me together as the questions ran through my head.

"I love you, Addredoc," I said in a stuffy voice.

I felt him freeze for a moment before he relaxed and his arms wrapped more securely around me. "I love you, too."

I knew I needed to pull it together, but the strength wasn't there at the moment. So I waited in Addredoc's arms. I waited until the tears had totally stopped. I didn't feel better—I still felt empty and ashamed—but I had to keep going because I didn't know what else to do.

I was done with the hunt for the necklace's owner. Now, it was time for Hathum and me to face off. I needed my army and I needed to kill him. And if I was successful, I would likely end up like my father, wandering the earth aimlessly trying not to be recognized by the world for thousands of years, or until I died. I didn't know what my natural life span was, but I was certain I would find out soon enough.

I slowly sat up. My heart raced when Addredoc pulled away, looking into my eyes with the most loving, adoring look I'd ever seen on his face. He caressed my cheek again. "Are you all right now?"

I nodded and then, as if it was the most natural thing in the world, I leaned in and pressed my lips briefly to his. His hands came up to my face and touched my cheeks just as I pulled away. "Yeah, I think I'll be all right now."

Addredoc stayed quiet a moment, and I was afraid it was about to get awkward, but he unexpectedly leaned in and kissed me quickly one more time before he stood up and held his hand out to me. I smiled and took it, and let him pull me to my feet. When I reached his eye level he was smiling a little playfully at me.

"So is it okay to assume I don't have to follow your last order to kill half of Godel in a day and a half?"

I actually grinned. "No. We'll figure out what to do about Godel later. But I really do need you to squash that civil war as soon as possible. I may need you to get a little more aggressive on that front." I smirked. "I found the necklace's owner. Now I need my army."

He nodded once. "I understand. I'll do my best."

"I know."

"Are you still going to Spar Ridges?"

I nodded. "Yeah. I need their army and we need supplies. We have to."

Addredoc nodded again. "Their army is said to be the best in Casdanarus, better than even Dwellingpath's."

"Oh I know," I conceded with small enthusiasm. "They're also the ones with the most hatred for the White Warrior."

Addredoc nodded sadly. "That's true, too."

I met his eyes. "Thanks for coming, Addredoc." I swallowed hard. "I really, really needed you, and I missed you."

He smiled and tucked another loose strand of hair behind my ear. "I missed you, too."

He met my eyes, and I could tell he wanted to kiss me goodbye but wasn't sure if he should. Instead, he kissed my forehead and pulled me into another warm embrace. We stayed like that for another moment before he pulled away. "Bye."

"Bye," I replied.

He quickly leaned in and kissed my lips firmly one more time. I giggled as he pulled away and looked at me with some playful mischief before vanishing in a flash of red light.

As soon as he was gone, I got incredibly cold, and it had nothing to do with the temperature. I shivered and crossed my arms tightly over my chest and rubbed my upper arms vigorously. It was really lonely out here, when I was alone in every way possible.

ELEVEN

I slowly started in the direction of Spar Ridges again. I took my time, kicking a few rocks here and there with the toe of my boot, seeing if I could hit a not-so-far-off log. My mind and emotions were all over the place. I shook my head. I couldn't believe what had happened in the last day.

I sighed and kicked a loose rock, hitting the log dead in the center. Why hadn't Hathum pounced on me the second I'd changed my magic to black? Rubbing my forehead with the side of my hand, I found myself thinking about what Addredoc had said about the silence being more of a concern. If Addredoc found a reason for concern, that only made me more nervous.

I couldn't help but be grateful, though, that nothing had come out of that. Well, besides the fact that I'd murdered my brother.

At that thought, my legs suddenly went numb, and I had to get down on one knee and one hand or I was going to fall flat on my face. I stared at the ground with wide eyes for a few seconds, trying to stop my trembling. *Rabryn is okay. Rabryn is okay. Rabryn is okay*, I kept telling myself. *He's alive. He's okay.*

I blew out a breath when my trembling finally subsided and I got back to my feet. I hadn't gotten twenty paces when I heard a strange sound. I stopped and looked around for the source. It wasn't threatening. It was a soft, gentle purring sound.

I shrugged my pack off my back and put it on the ground. A slight rustling of some brush caught my attention. Slowly crouching down I looked under it, and I couldn't help the surprise at seeing the little gray-skinned creature that had nearly bitten my arm off. Forgius, the Salynns had called him.

He was crouching in his strange frog-like manner and cowered against the tree where he was trying to hide. He looked completely terrified, ready to dart away any moment, but he just kept staring at my face.

I smiled at him and sat myself comfortably on the ground. "Hello little one," I said. "Did you stay here with me this whole time?"

The creature relaxed slightly and looked down at the ground. He nervously poked at it with his fingers before nodding his head and lifting his eyes back up to me.

My brows dropped. "Can you understand me?"

Forgius lifted his head a little and nodded again.

My eyes went a little wide. "Really?" When I'd spoken to him earlier, I hadn't known for sure that he could actually understand me.

I smiled and held my arms out to him, gesturing him closer. He looked at me confused, his face twisting in such a strange way that it actually made me chuckle a little. "Come closer," I explained. Keeping his eyes on me, he lowered his head so his chin was level with the ground. I smiled. "I won't hurt you, little one. I want to hold you."

He made that purring sound again and carefully brought one foot forward. He hobbled toward me in that strange way, hands down first and then moving his feet forward. When he was in front of me, he paused and looked up at my face.

"May I pick you up?" I asked.

Shifting his weight to his heels, he brought his hands up in front of his chest and interlaced his fingers in a gesture that looked like nervousness before he met my eyes and nodded slowly.

I placed my hands under his arms, ignoring his pungent odor, and brought him slowly toward my chest. I kept my eyes on his face to make sure I didn't scare him too badly. I cradled him in the crook of one arm and held him close to me. It barely took a second before his head relaxed against my shoulder and he closed his eyes.

He was so little and so cute—in a really repulsive way.

"Are you hungry?" I asked. He opened his eyes and moved them up to me, keeping his head on my chest. "Do you eat?"

The creature lifted his head and nodded, looking almost hopeful, as he interlaced his fingers together in front of his chest again.

I slowly and carefully reached into my nearby pack with my free arm. "I don't have much left, but luckily I don't eat anymore." I felt a specific item and looked down at the large-eyed creature. "Do you eat human food?"

He nodded again.

I smiled and pulled out the last of my dry meat, bread and

cheese and handed it to him. He shifted his position so he was crouching right on my thigh, surprisingly keeping his balance well. He took the food in both hands and began eating it like a chipmunk, small quick nibbles and full cheeks. I laughed a little.

I watched him eat for a few moments, since it was a pretty comical sight. With my heart getting heavy again, though, I looked in the direction of Spar Ridges, where my companions had headed off. I didn't see a single one of them.

I sighed and looked back at the filthy little creature crouching on my thigh. He gave me a wide grin with bread crumbs all over his mouth and chin, which made me smile again as he finished the last bite. I carefully reached up and petted his shriveled, nearly bald, head.

"Thanks for sticking with me, Forgius."

Seeming to read my mood, the creature deflated and little and rested his hands on my chest as he looked up at me with sad eyes.

"Addredoc would have stayed, but he's busy getting me an army. So are Lisswilla, Yarin, and Reese." My heart sank again. "All of them are very far away from me, but"—I sighed and looked into the forest towards Spar Ridges—"one of them still managed to be here for me."

I couldn't be upset with Rabryn, Ortheldo, and Acalith. I really couldn't. I deserved whatever treatment they gave me and worse. I had killed my brother. But even if I deserved it, it hurt so much to have them walk away from me.

I looked in Forgius' eyes again. "Shadow is tricky, little one." I shook my head. "I didn't even realize what was happening." I petted his head, making him purr. "It's so easy, under Shadow's spell, to blame everyone else for what is really wrong with you. I thought they were all turning on me, but"—I shrugged weakly— "turns out I was turning on them." I looked out towards Spar Ridges again. "It sounded so rational, blaming them, and telling myself *they* were changing, not me." I shook my head again and looked back at Forgius. "Shadow is tricky."

I sat on the forest floor for a while with this sweet, strange little creature standing in a frog-like crouch on my thigh. I felt no rush to even catch up with my party. I felt no rush to do anything. For the first time in four months, I wasn't in a hurry. I didn't need to save a dying gem because I already saved it. My life force, my own life energy, kept it alive.

I took a moment to ponder the fact that I was the damn necklace's owner. I was finally able to absorb that for a second. For the past four months, I'd been on a goose chase to find the elusive owner of this gem, yet it had been me the whole time. And now that I didn't have a hunt, a chase to pursue, I didn't know what to do. I pondered something else. The White Warrior knew we were the owner of the Anarran Gem, the gem of all healing, so why had she sent me on the goose chase in the first place? She'd released the gem from its holding place, which I knew how to do now that I was thinking about it, and had sent it to Ortheldo. In turn, Ortheldo had come to find me. Why?

I sighed and reached into my mind, deep into my subconscious where I knew The White Warrior liked to hide. I found the barrier she could always be found behind and poked at it, but she didn't stir or speak. She had been unusually quiet lately. The earthquake must have taken more out of her than it had from me. I didn't want to disturb her, though, because I wanted to put off hearing her reaction to my turning my magic black. I hoped doing that didn't have long-term effects on her. I cringed at the thought. She would be okay, I reassured myself. The Light Gods would have done something about it. I hoped.

I paused my movements before I shifted my eyes to the sky, thinking about Them. My eyes narrowed a little, not in anger this time like I usually looked at Them, but in curiosity. Addredoc had told me to pray, to talk to Them. I wasn't completely sure I was ready for that, but then again, I wondered if I really ever would be.

"You are there, aren't You?" I blurted out before I could hold it back.

I didn't hear a response, but I definitely felt the growing warmth of a presence looking at me, or possibly even coming near me. Forgius looked around, terrified, as he got off my leg and slowly started to back away with his eyes searching the sky. As the presence increased, my breath quickened and I shifted my eyes back down again. But it seemed to be too late; the presence didn't leave.

My mouth went dry as I felt eyes watching me. They were kind, unthreatening eyes, but huge and powerful—intimidating. They felt as big as entire world and, for some strange reason, they felt familiar, too, even loving.

I suddenly felt... I wasn't completely sure what. Whole? Complete? Not lonely? I couldn't describe it. I felt almost alive on the inside in places I didn't even know were dead, or places that I didn't even know were there. This warmth and love penetrated places I'd sooner forget, and some places I *had* forgotten. I felt exposed, like these eyes were seeing and feeling every dark place inside of me, but because the presence was nothing but loving, I didn't feel ashamed. I didn't feel like I needed to hide those places from these eyes. The presence was so accepting that even my darkness and my flaws were okay, and maybe even beautiful.

I started trembling as tears rolled down my cheeks. "Is that You?" I said in a shaky whisper without taking my eyes off the ground. I was terrified of what I might see if I looked up. "Are you one of the Light Gods?"

Yes, an ethereal voice responded. The sound made me jump, though it was as soft as a whisper carried by the wind. It was a male voice that seemed to slowly sweep through me like a warm liquid, filling every empty and dark place I had inside.

I swallowed heavily, trying to moisten my throat and still fearful of lifting my eyes from the ground. "You're real," I breathed.

Yes, Azrel. It's nice to finally hear from you.

I shook my head vigorously, desperately trying to shake away the voice. I even backed up on my hands and knees away from the current spot I sat. As if I could crawl away from a God! This was too much. I couldn't communicate with these beings!

I immediately felt the presence being to fade. *Be strong, Azrel,* the voice said as it faded away. *Things are about to get worse. But we are always with you. Watching over you. Never forget...*

The eyes and the presence faded, and I was left sitting with my back against a tree, breathless. I remained in thought for a moment. I felt so...clean. I didn't know how else to describe it. It was as if that presence had reached the darkest, ugliest parts of me and somehow purged me of them. I felt lighter, not so weighed down by every mistake I'd ever made in my life. Everything that had ever gone wrong, or I had done wrong in my past, was somehow healed. It wasn't gone, but it was okay. It was like I still faintly felt that presence inside my soul, or a piece of it anyway, and it was somehow helping me carry these burdens now. And this being, a God, was a lot stronger and far more capable of carrying my burdens than I was.

I sighed and wiped my cheeks free of tears. For a moment, I just breathed. I leaned back against the tree, pulled one of my knees up, and just breathed. It was silent, my little Forgius nowhere to be found, and I sat there for a long time doing nothing but breathing. At least an hour passed, and I allowed myself to rest in the peace that Light God had just given me. Peace deep inside of me that was beyond comprehension.

I thought about the Light Gods, *really* thought about Them for the first time in my life. I didn't know anything about Them. My father hadn't put high priority on religious teachings while I was growing up. All I really knew, mostly from Rabryn who had grown up knowing about Them because of my mother, was that there were three. Just like there were three Shadow Gods. They were opposites in every way. The Light Gods had two females and one male. The Shadow Gods had two males and one female.

That was it. That was the extent of my knowledge about Them. My heart fluttered a little when I realized it was the only male of the Light Gods that had spoken to me a moment ago. For some reason that felt good. Had it been one of the females, I'm not sure it would have had the same impact. I almost felt special, singled out, to have the only male talk to me.

I sighed and got to my feet eventually, brushing the leaves off my clothing, and then went over to my pack. It was still a two-day walk to the kingdom of Spar Ridges. The peaceful feeling inside of me dimmed slightly, but I was happy it was still there. It gave me strength to carry on. I reached down and picked up my pack, threw it over my shoulder, and then turned to begin in the direction of Spar Ridges.

"Azrel?" I suddenly heard behind me.

I spun around to the astonished faces of my entire party, including Ceco. All of them had stopped walking and were looking at me with wide eyes. My brother quickly looked away, keeping his eyes on the ground and his jaw tight.

"What are you all doing behind me? I saw you leave east over an hour ago."

"We did leave east," Ortheldo said. "We haven't stopped

going east. What are you doing in front of us?"

My face scrunched up in confusion. "What? Ortheldo, I've barely gone ten yards from the spot you left me. I haven't moved."

His eyes got wide. "That's not possible," he said approaching me. "We've been walking for over an hour."

I smirked up at him. "Did you get lost?"

"No." He shook his head.

Awkwardness loomed, but I was enjoying this peace so much I didn't want to let it go by allowing myself to get upset about it. Peace was a powerful thing.

I glanced at my brother who met my eyes briefly before looking away. "Listen, I deserve every bit of distance you all want to put between us. I do." I shook my head. "All I can say is that I'm sorry and that I tried to fix what I did." My brother swallowed without looking at me. Him being unable to meet my eyes stung, so I shifted my gaze to Ortheldo. "I'm sorry. I didn't know what was happening." I shrugged helplessly. "That's all I can do. It's up to you if you want to forgive me, or if you want to brood over something I did everything I could to fix."

One glance of all their faces and I sighed as the reality settled in that they were not going to forgive me. Something was broken.

"Come on," I said with resign. "I know your supplies are low. Let's get you out of these woods. I've had it with this place."

TWELVE

"Way to get us out of the woods, Azrel," Rabryn said flatly, only without the playfulness which he usually addressed me with. It was pure annoyance and anger still. I rolled my eyes and shook my head. This was getting ridiculous. I supposed I should be glad he was talking to me at all, though.

More than two days had passed. The sun was now going down on the third and we should have been out of Spar Ridge's woods and at the kingdom at least twelve hours ago. My companions had been out of food for a full day already. The woods were still hot, and all of us were filthy. You could see the sweat streaks through the dirt on our faces and necks. We were out of clothes, too. What we wore now had been on us for the entire two days through the final trek of these woods.

It had been surprisingly quiet. Not a single battle to be had, aside from our supplies being low, the heat, and the fact we could not get out of these woods for some reason. With every hour that passed we'd told ourselves, "Maybe the kingdom is just a little farther." And an hour later, "Maybe it's just a little farther. Let's give it another hour." Another hour would pass until a half a day had gone by.

Right now all of us stood in the middle of the woods, completely helpless. The trees all looked the same; some of them even seemed familiar. Ortheldo and I glanced at each other particularly often because we knew our distance perception was not off this much, not by twelve hours. There was no way both of us could be this wrong about it.

Ortheldo and I glanced at each other again and he shrugged a shoulder. "Maybe another hour?"

I looked around, shaking my head. "No way. Something's wrong." I turned my eyes to Acalith. "This is your Kingdom. Do you have a clue as to what's going on?"

She sneered. She still hadn't met my eyes in two days. "We're just not there yet. That's all."

My eyes narrowed. "Excuse me?" I said, walking toward her.

"Hey. Look at me!" Acalith crossed her arms and set her jaw before turning her glowing green eyes towards me. "First of all, grow up. All of you," I said, glancing around at all of them. "Second of all, if you want to continue to hate me, fine. But don't talk to me like I'm an idiot with this, 'We just haven't arrived yet,' crap. I k*now* we should have been there by now!"

"Then why aren't we?" Acalith asked, throwing her arms out to her sides.

Oh, I wished I could have slapped her. I just glared instead. "If I knew the answer to that, I wouldn't have asked you if you knew what was going on."

"Well, I don't!" she said snottily.

I smiled in disbelief. "You know what," I said, shaking my head, "when we get to Spar Ridges, all of you can consider yourselves dismissed from my services." It felt like the air had been sucked out of the forest. I particularly eyed my brother, who was looking at me with wide eyes, "All of you." I glanced at Ortheldo, who had the same expression.

"But you need us, Azrel," Ortheldo said.

"Do I? Really?" I asked, narrowing my eyes at him. "I need this cold shoulder you all are giving me? The attitude? The talking to me like I'm an idiot whenever you *do* decide to talk to me?" I glanced at all of them and shook my head again. "No thanks."

"Azrel," Ortheldo began, "you need—"

"You know what I need?" I interrupted, holding my finger up at him. "I need people like Addredoc, who stayed by my side during the worst moment of my entire life. What were you all doing while I was dealing with that? You went walking on without me for over an hour." I felt a tear drop down my cheek and quickly wiped it away. I shook my head at all of them. "No. I don't need that. We're done once we get into the city." I eyed my brother again. "Done."

I turned in the direction towards Spar Ridges and started walking. That peace from the Light God was still strong inside of me. It was strange how having to dismiss them all hurt me, but I was still at peace. It was like this iron strength was inside my soul now, holding me together, even while the world around me seemed to be flailing around and falling apart. I couldn't believe the kind of strength that came with peace and knowing the Light Gods were with me and always would be. Rejection from other people, even my brother, didn't affect me as badly as it would have two days ago without that Light God paying me a visit.

I stopped in my tracks just a few paces away from the group when I noticed something odd. A particular tree trunk caught my attention. It had an unusual and irregular pattern in the coloring of the bark that looked like the face of an owl. My brows dropped as I turned to look over my shoulder behind me. Sure enough, I had noticed the same exact markings on a tree behind me while I had been talking to the others.

"What the..." I said aloud, walking toward the markings behind me.

"Azrel?" Ortheldo asked.

I stepped in front of the tree and pointed to it. "Look at this."

Ortheldo came up beside me. "So?" I turned around and pointed to the tree markings behind me. He turned and looked and his expression dropped. "What the...?"

I nodded. "Yeah."

"What is it?" Moifulyar said. stepping forward. I indicated the two exact markings on two different trees. Moifulyar looked back and forth between the two, and then he began to look back and forth in other directions as well. As he did that, his face dropped, too. "Oh no."

"What? What is it?" I asked.

He met my eyes briefly before glancing down. "It's a Circle Mirror spell."

"A what?" Ortheldo and I both asked.

"It's a spell," Moifulyar replied. "It likely encircles the entire kingdom of Spar Ridges and is their very last defense." He pointed to the two owl markings. "The markings are mirror images of each other. You see here." He indicated another tree nearby with a unique butterfly-like pattern in the coloring of the bark. Moifulyar then pointed across the way to another tree with the exact same butterfly-like discoloration.

"Wonderful," Ortheldo said flatly.

Moifulyar shrugged deeply. "It keeps intruders out by keeping them lost in the woods forever or until they turn back."

"Great," I said flatly.

"How do you know this?" Rabryn asked.

Moifulyar looked back at him. "All Wizards know how to do it." His eyes got wide when a hurt look passed over my brother's face. Rabryn didn't know how to do it, and he was a Wizard. "I mean, experienced Wizards, my king." Moifulyar said quickly.

"How do you break it?" Ortheldo asked.

Moifulyar shrugged helplessly. "You generally can't. Only the Wizard who created it can break it, especially one this size. A very powerful Wizard must have conjured it." He tilted his head to the side. "I'm thinking it might have even been an Ancient Wizard. Modern day Wizards don't have this kind of power anymore."

"Well," Ortheldo said stubbornly, "Spar Ridges hasn't been in complete isolation for the past 3,000 years. They would need supplies and trade from somewhere. There has to be a way in."

Moifulyar shrugged. "I'm guessing only the Wizard who created this spell and the King of Spar Ridges will have that knowledge."

Ortheldo sighed in frustration. Rabryn and Acalith deflated slightly, Rabryn putting his arm around Acalith's shoulders.

I pressed my lips together and huffed an annoyed breath from my nose. "I've got a way in." I turned around and started walking towards the owl discoloration in the tree, snatching up a rock from the ground along the way. I was sick of these woods! I lit up the rock with white fire and hurled it into the owl's face, nailing it square between the eyes.

A sound exploded all around us like ten thousand windows breaking at the same time, and a blinding white light flashed in the woods in front of us. We all quickly ducked down like the sky was falling on our heads. When we looked out ahead of us again, we saw the vast opening of the woods not ten yards in front of us. I slowly crept closer to the edge of the trees and couldn't believe what I was seeing.

We were out! We made it through Spar Ridges' woods and were finally looking upon the expansive kingdom. I'd never seen Spar Ridges before. Beldorn had never taken me here for the obvious reason that it was far too secluded to warrant a visit. I doubted even Beldorn would have been welcome amongst these people. No one was.

The land before me rested in the middle of four majestic mountains to the north, south, east and west. The kingdom was so large that the mountain farthest east across from where we were was blue and indistinct in the distance. Massive irregular rock structures that resembled stalagmites jutted up tall throughout the land, looking like a thousand fingers reaching from underground to touch the sky. They ranged from two hundred to seven hundred feet high. They weren't just pretty decorations either, as I saw staircases carved into of some of them. I could even make out a few houses placed in large crevasses along the rock faces.

Most of the rock structures went up to a point, and each of them had a war beacon built into it. From what I could barely make out from the ground, small hutches for the watchmen had also been built at the top of the stone peaks. These rock formations allowed Spar Ridges to see everything for miles. No matter what came at them from their woods, from any direction, they would have more than enough time—days even—to rally their army and prepare a defense.

A few of the massive stalagmite-like structures had large holes carved into their bases, where wide dirt streets ran underneath for easy commuting. The rock structures and the holes also allowed strategic advantages for the ground troops of Spar Ridges' army. Looking around, I knew I would hate to get into a battle with these people on their home turf because this landscape would be a strategic nightmare if I were their enemy. Well, chances were I *was* their enemy.

No sooner had the thought flown through my brain than over ten thousand bowmen appeared along the faces of the nearest rock structures. At the same time, streams of spearmen marched forward from every direction toward where we stood at the edge of the woods. They were ready for us.

I sighed, crossed my arms over my chest, and waited for them. I cast a cool glance at Acalith over my shoulder to see her reaction to returning home. She looked petrified. Her soldiers would recognize the Princess, no doubt. She'd barely been gone four months.

"Acalith," I called, drawing her attention. "You want to come up here next to me? Or are you going to stay back there and cower, *Deralilya?*" I stressed the word so she would remember who the hell she was—the right hand of The White Warrior. Narrowing of her eyes at me, she took a few steps forward to stand closer to me and waited for the army to approach.

I heard a single command in their own language over the stomping of boots. The infantry troops instantly halted in front of us and lowered their spears in such perfect unison that I flinched. Oh man. I could use soldiers like this in my army—pristine, precise, and perfect in form on every level. A sea of fierce, glowing green eyes waited before me, and my heart raced with excitement over the possibility of recruiting them. Spar Ridges had over two and a half million soldiers like this. I wanted them badly, all of them.

A lone rider came forward through the ranks. He was a barrel-chested man with steel gray hair and a neatly trimmed matching beard. His face was weathered. He stopped his horse at the very edge of the soldiers, his glowing eyes scanning us carefully. The silence stretched on until it got uncomfortable.

I sighed and rolled my eyes. "What's wrong, commander? Are the six of us too much for your 30,000 scouts to deal with?"

Every soldier in rank narrowed their green eyes at me. Great. This was about to erupt into a battle. I really didn't want to waste such magnificent soldiers. I needed them desperately!

The commander glared hard at me. "Do not speak unless spoken to, woman. Which man is in charge here?"

I immediately held my hand up to stop Ortheldo's advance. "I will speak, commander," I said slowly, "when I have a mind to." I wanted to give this guy a nasty piece of my mind, but my desperation to try to make at least a decent impression helped me keep my temper in check. "I am in charge of this host, so you may speak to me if you wish."

Rage blazed in his eyes. So much for a good impression. "I will not barter with a woman!"

I sighed, shook my head, and looked at the ground.

"Run them through," the commander ordered.

My eyes were already glowing white by the time I flicked them back up to the army. With a single intention, and barely any effort, all their spears started glowing white, and I lifted them up out of the hands of every soldier. The 10,000 bowmen on the rock formations fired their arrows, but they didn't get three feet from the strings before those, too, were glowing white and were halted. Ripples of terror went through the entire army as I slowly lifted the spears and arrows above their heads and turned them upside down so the points were aiming down toward their skulls.

I met the commander's eyes. "How about you barter with me now?" I said slowly, eyeing him with my glowing white eyes.

"Wh...White Warrior," he said in a breath.

"The one and only," I replied coolly.

He wanted to attack me, but his men were at the mercy of my magic.

I held the spears and arrows in place with ease because I felt the energy coming from them. It was the same sensation as when I felt the energy of everything's life force in the world. Everything had energy; everything was made of energy, even inanimate objects like these spears and arrows. I felt the energy of the trees that the shafts were cut from, and the rock that the tips were hued out of. Most strange of all, I also felt the energy of each person who had labored over making each part, of each spear and arrow, as well as the soldiers who had used each weapon in the past. I felt their life force as keenly as if they were embedded inside. It was a ton of information and energy to feel since there were 30,000 soldiers and several life forces attached to each weapon.

"Azrel, don't," I suddenly heard my brother mumble. I looked over my shoulder at him and saw his pleading eyes. "Please. I'm begging you. Don't."

My brows dropped. He actually thought I was going to slaughter 30,000 people. It was like he didn't know me! I shook my head sadly at him. Something was lost between us. With a soft sigh, I turned to the commander again. My brother was something I'd have to deal with later.

"What do you want here?" the commander asked, trying to harden his voice as he glanced between me and the spears that I held over his soldiers' heads.

I scoffed softly to myself and glanced to the side; that was a loaded question. "How about your army?"

"What?" he asked, his brows drawing together in confusion and anger.

"I believe..." a female voice said from the back of the crowd. The soldiers before me slowly started to part down the middle, making a pathway for someone else. I quickly linked the energy of the weapons and the soldiers so that if the soldiers moved, the weapons moved with them. "The White Warrior declared she wants our army."

I searched down the narrow path and soon saw a small figure approaching. From the way the soldiers bowed slightly at the waist, she was someone of importance. My eyes narrowed slightly as she emerged in front of them. She was very youthful, with long silky looking honey blonde hair fanning out against her shoulders. She had a narrow jaw, a pointed chin, and big, soft brown eyes. Her eyes were a nice relief from the sea of glowing green in front of me, which meant she wasn't from Spar Ridges. She was slender and small—about five feet, two inches—and she wore a long sky blue robe that swished around her feet, with a white rope cinching it closed at her waist.

My left brow went up. "And you are?"

She surprised me by smiling. "I'm the Wizard whose circle mirror spell you just broke." My eyes went a little wide at that. Female Wizards were incredibly rare. She peered at me, keeping a soft smile tugging at her lips. "Not an easy feat, since it has been in place for nearly 3,000 years." Female Ancient Wizards were rarer still! Her eyes then moved to my left, and she took the edges of her robe and gave a small curtsey. "Princess Acalith."

The entire army gasped, and noise rippled through the ranks as all of them finally noticed her standing near me. I wasn't sure if it was strange or flattering that I had drawn so much of their attention that they didn't even see their dead Princess standing there. Admittedly my party stood mostly behind me, but they were in plain sight.

The Wizard straightened again, even as noises continued to go through the ranks. "It is wonderful to see you alive and well, Princess, though I fear you have a lot of explaining to do to the King and Queen."

Acalith tried to keep a passive expression as she nodded, but I could see her entire body trembling. "I imagine I do, Soheela."

"May we escort you to the palace, or will the White Warrior just impale us all?" Soheela asked. She kept that small, playful smile on her face, which made me sneer at her for some reason. Wizards weren't inclined to be playful.

I looked at Acalith. She glanced at me before pulling her shoulders back, held her head high, and looked back at the Wizard.

"The White Warrior won't harm these soldiers."

My eyes went wide. "Oh won't I?"

"No," Acalith said calmly, shifting her gaze back at me, "because she needs them in her army."

I narrowed my eyes, and before I knew what I was doing, I moved quickly to stand in front of her. Acalith cowered slightly, and I tried to ignore the fact that I saw Rabryn step forward, readying himself to protect Acalith from me.

"First of all," I said, "you don't tell me what I will and will not do. You've been by my side long enough to know that the fact that you're the Princess here means *nothing* to me. Secondly, no one said that they were even going to join my army, so you'd better believe they are going to stand with spears and arrows above their heads for a good long while until we are guaranteed safe passage out of here."

"We?" Acalith said, her eyelids dropping halfway. "I thought you told us we were dismissed from your services once we arrived here."

I smirked at her. "You want to stay here, be my guest." We stared at each other quietly for a long moment. Her glowing green eyes locked on my white ones.

"So how would the White Warrior like to conduct this meeting?" Soheela said from behind me.

I narrowed my eyes at Acalith and then panned a glance over to my brother, Moifulyar, Ceco, and lastly Ortheldo. Seeing the distant, indifferent looks on their faces, I shook my head before walking toward the soldiers.

"I'm not with them," I said as I melted into my White Warrior form and passed the Wizard.

"White Warrior?" the Wizard asked. "Where are you going?"

I ignored her as I created a shell of white fire around myself, forcing the soldiers to back away more as I went down the line of them that had parted. Everyone seemed confused and stayed quiet. I wasn't completely sure what I was doing myself. All I knew was that I needed to meet my horse, my sweet Lightning, who I hadn't seen in nearly a week, on the eastern side of the mountains. He and I needed to discuss what my next move was. The hunt for the necklace's owner was over, so now what?

"Follow her," I heard the Wizard say faintly behind me. "Send a messenger to the east. Tell them the scouts have been compromised and to ready the entire army." The scouts followed me but kept their distance.

I needed to have a long, uninterrupted talk with the Light Gods. It was exciting and terrifying to admit, but I needed to pray. I also knew that I had to get away from my brother, Ortheldo and Acalith. The way they were treating me was useless. I couldn't lead them, or anyone, if they didn't trust me. No one trusted me now. Not my friends, not my brother, not Spar Ridges. There was no point to me lingering here. Addredoc, Lisswilla, Yarin and Reese were my last hope. They trusted me still, and they were getting me an army to fight this oncoming Shadow.

It had been so quiet the past week, though. Barely a Shadow creature stirred. Sure we had been attacked a few times in Spar Ridge's woods, but that was more a result of our presence disturbing them, not a command from Hathum. We would have had a more difficult time if Hathum had orchestrated attacks on us. Addredoc's warning rung clear in the back of my mind though. The lack of response from Hathum was not to be dismissed lightly. He was up to something. He had to be.

No sooner had the thought crossed my mind than I stopped in my tracks, my shoulders sagging as a Shadow formed in my chest with intensity I hadn't felt since that earthquake. It nearly took my breath away. Then an increasing breeze started to come up from the west from the direction of the woods we had just left. The soldiers felt it, too, and soft murmurs rose up behind me.

"Full alert!" one of the bowmen from atop one of the nearby rock structure called out. "Incoming attack from the west! Light the warning beacons! We need the full army!"

Craning my neck, I could just make out a figure pointing to the west. Holding a small torch, a second black silhouette started running toward the fire tower. The breeze intensified until my white hair blew wildly around my face, and I inhaled deeply. The beacon above me blazed to life, and an instant later I saw a faint flash of orange far to the east. Magically enhancing my sight, I zoomed in until I saw the eastern side of Spar Ridges, a four-day walk, also lighting the warning beacons. It was across the entire realm of Spar Ridges, so I knew the east had an incoming attack of their own.

"Oy!" one of the watchmen atop the rock formation cried. "The north! The north! To the north!"

My eyes went wide at that! There was nothing north of Spar Ridges besides Miick, an extinct and abandoned Shadow Humount realm that my father had destroyed long ago. There hadn't been activity there for three millenniums!

With my heart pounding and my eyes wide, I bolted up the stairs carved into the side of the rock formation, passed all the bowmen lining the steps, and headed toward the watchmen and the warning beacon at the top. I ran two steps at a time, enhancing my speed, and scaled the 200-foot rock face in moments. Reaching the narrow top, I saw the two watchmen, still held hostage by the arrows above their heads, staring at me with wide glowing green eyes—eyes that were steadily growing brighter because of the danger Spar Ridges was in. I jogged past them without any resistance. They just silently gawked as I hurried up the stone ramp to the upper section where the blazing beacon stood.

It was cold and windy up here, and my hair was blowing all over the place as I went to the edge of the low rock wall. I focused on the mountain to the north and saw the whole canopy of trees swaying violently. I stepped up onto the rigged rock wall and waited, the Shadow in my chest growing heavier and heavier.

All of the beacons atop the rock formations across Spar Ridges were lighting up, most of them looking like candles in the distance. The east was harder to see since it was so far away, but I magically zoomed in to watch the army there as it started to muster. The western army below also started to muster, as did the north. I even saw the south armies mustering, though I wasn't sure if they had their own attack to deal with or if they were coming to aid the north, east, and west.

"Azrel!" I heard Ortheldo call behind me.

He was coming up the rock face. I really wasn't in the mood to deal with him right now. I kept my eyes on the trees to the north, ignoring him completely as he reached the top of the ramp. He was quickly detained there by the bowmen.

"Azrel," he panted.

"Go away, Ortheldo," I said, concentrating on the woods.

"Sorry girl," he said in a breath, making me look over my shoulder at him. He was dripping sweat and his gorgeous light eyes were on fire as he looked at me. "But you're stuck with me. Forever."

I couldn't help the tears that erupted in my eyes. Momentarily forgetting the dire peril we were in, I hopped off the rock wall and went toward him. The bowmen stepped aside as I approached and I threw my arms around his neck and pressed my lips to his. He quickly gathered me tightly in his strong, brawny arms. I needed this. I hadn't realized until this moment how desperately I needed this.

Pulling away, he quickly kissed my cheek and my jaw before he buried his face into my neck. "It's all right," he said gently into my hair. "Everything is going to be all right."

I simply nodded against his shoulder, unable to speak or even breathe past the lump in my throat. He hadn't given up on me. I'd thought he had, but he hadn't. He was here. I pulled away, and a single tear fell down my cheek that I couldn't hold back. With a soft smile, Ortheldo tenderly wiped it away with his thumb and then touched his forehead to mine.

"Now do what you've got to do," he said.

I smiled, and the crinkling of my eyes caused the rest of my brimming tears to fall. Both of his hands were on my cheeks, wiping those away too. The fire in his periwinkle eyes burned into my soul before he leaned down to kiss me one more time. He pulled away a moment later, and I was able to turn around and head back to the low rock wall to overlook Spar Ridges.

Spar Ridges had two and a half million soldiers, and all of them expanded like spilled ink on the ground in the emerging twilight. As the sky got darker, so did the growing Shadow in my chest. I wasn't sure how I was able to bear the magnitude of it. It was so heavy it felt like it could yank me to the ground and drag me straight to the core of the earth if it wanted to. But my shoulders didn't sag and my head was held high. I listened to the commanding officers of all four gathered armies below hollering orders. I watched as those orders were obeyed with incredible swiftness and precision.

The moment all two and a half million soldiers were gathered in the four corners of the realm, the whipping wind suddenly stopped. It was so sudden that my hair dropped limply and the world went quiet. Even the hollering went silent. Ortheldo silently stepped up to my side and looked over toward the north with me. I saw the ink stain of the soldiers below shift slightly as they all looked around at each other, wondering what was causing such sudden and unnatural stillness.

Suddenly, an explosion of black erupted from the trees in all four directions! It was so unexpected that everyone, including me, ducked and shielded our heads. When I looked out again, it wasn't black fire like I had assumed, though it might as well have been. It was a tidal wave of Deeks, the ugly flying beasts of Spar Ridges' woods, rising in unison above the treetops, blacking out the sky. My eyes went wide because there was no way this many Deeks had been hiding in these woods. There was no way this many Deeks even *existed* until ten seconds ago! It was Hathum, multiplying his poisonous flying beasts right before my eyes to attack Spar Ridges. I hadn't known he could do that. I didn't even know that was possible for anyone besides the Gods.

I hopped up onto the rock wall again and looked out. I knew what I needed to do, but I was just afraid to do it here in Spar Ridges because passing out in this place was probably not the wisest idea. I would be executed instantly or wake up in a cell. Most likely—executed.

I looked back at Ortheldo, who just nodded once. "I know," he said and slowly pulled out his sword. "I told you: Do what you've got to do."

I looked at him with deep gratitude. He would do everything in his power to protect me from these people when I passed out. We both knew he would be overwhelmed quickly, but he also knew I couldn't let two million soldiers, and countless civilians, die if I could stop it. I hopped off the rock wall so I wouldn't plummet to my death when I fainted, and looked over at the soldiers below.

Let's go!

The unexpected voice of the White Warrior made me jump. I'd only heard from her once in nearly three weeks since we left Fayithjen Forest.

What the hell? I screamed internally at her. *Where have you been?*

Busy. Do it.

Busy? I shrieked. *What the crap could you possibly have to do? You're stuck in my head!*

Azrel! she cried. *Deeks? Soldiers? Death? Let's handle it!*

I suddenly felt my magic come to the edge of my skin so hard and fast I gasped. I gripped my Sword and pulled it out of the diamond-studded scabbard at my hip and it exploded in white fire. Once again I was made aware of the immense power source hiding in the blade that I couldn't tap into, one of the pieces I was still missing of myself.

I clenched my teeth in frustration, pushing that agony away, because I could really use that magic right about now! I slowly turned in a circle, looking at the ring of Shadow filling the sky on every front that surrounded me, and then I looked down at the soldiers below. Licking my lips, I held out my hand and felt for the energy of the weapons below. The ink spill of human beings on the ground, as well as the bowmen on the side of the rock formations scattered over the land, slowly began to light up as my white magic surrounded every single weapon—from spears and arrows, to swords and axes and anything and everything I felt in between.

The army cried out in panic, with no idea what was going on, most of them without a clue I was even here, as I raised each weapon out of their hands and belts and scabbards. I even raised the scout's weapons, which I had used to hold them hostage with, and pointed the tips toward the black oncoming mass. Sweat immediately began to drip down my temple from holding at least four million weapons in the air with my magic.

I waited a moment and even sent up a little prayer to the Light Gods. "Let my aim be true. Please!" I begged quietly.

A prayer? The White Warrior suddenly said, sounding offended. *Since when do you pray to Them?*

Since one of Them was there for me when I needed Them the most, I responded.

What? she cried.

You've missed a lot in your busyness, I sneered slightly.

Clearly.

The Deeks came closer, the breeze from their wings causing my hair to fly out behind me. The army below was in a panic, wondering what was happening with their weapons floating above them. I felt sweat start to drip down my neck and back.

When I could just see the shine of the Deeks' beady black

eyes, I took a deep breath and lit with white fire every single weapon that faced every direction. I screamed at the top of my lungs and thrust my Sword arm forward, making the first wave of weapons fly forward toward the black mass in the air. I controlled their fast flight, making sure that every weapon hit a target or maybe two. The black mass rolled over on itself like a wave in the ocean, as most of the beasts in front fell dead to the ground.

The expense of my magic had already made me collapse to my knees, but I was not ready to pass out yet! I thrust my Sword arm out again, sending the second wave of weapons toward the beasts. With a sickening splatting sound, another wave of Deeks rolled over itself to fall dead on the ground. I started trembling as tears fell from my eyes. I wiped them quickly to make sure it wasn't blood, and only saw white water. My eyes were not bleeding, which meant I still had strength to do this.

I clenched my teeth and with effort beyond what I knew I had, or The White Warrior had, I stood to my unsteady feet and sent the next wave of weapons, pushing them deep into the flying shadowy mass. Another wave rolled over itself, dead. I sent another volley of weapons, and another black wave crashed to the earth.

My legs went numb, and I collapsed to my knees again. I could see my Sword arm trembling in front of me as the edges of my vision started getting foggy. Another drop of liquid ran down my cheek, thicker, and I knew my eyes were bleeding. I had to stop. Lightning wasn't here to resurrect me.

I dropped my hand, my Sword clattering to the ground before vanishing in white flames, and then I fell to my side. I fully expected to hit my head, but felt Ortheldo's arm encircle my shoulders before I fully hit the stone. My blurry vision found the form of his face above me as he cradled me in his arms. He looked down at me, his pretty eyes standing out among the blur, before I went limp and everything went dark.

THIRTEEN

AZREL

My eyes slowly opened and I sighed in annoyance immediately. Well, I was alive, but I was in a dungeon. I rested my hand on my forehead and slowly sat up, feeling groggy. I looked around at the dark gray stone and grid pattern bars and bowed my head, shaking it slowly.

In the quiet, I realized the cell hummed with magical energy. I looked up skeptically. It was laced with Ancient Wizard magic. Did they really think ancient magic could hold me? My magic was as old as the Gods because it was Their magic!

I shook my head again and looked down at my lap. "Fools," I said to myself.

I was about to sit back and pray to the Light Gods when my brows dropped. I lifted my head, slowly looking out at the hall. Something felt wrong, *really* wrong! I stood up from the mattress and went to the bars quickly. Gasping, I clutched my chest and doubled over. The heaviness of Shadow in my chest could have pulled me flat to the ground. It was so massive! I glanced up and down the hallway of the dungeon but saw no one.

Sticking my fingers through the grid pattern bars, I clutched the thick metal, and yanked! With a loud clang and falling rock dust, I ripped the cell door off its hinges. Tossing it behind me, I stepped out into the hallway, looking left and right again. I'd never been here and didn't know my way out. Where was this wrong feeling coming from?

"Come on, Light Gods," I muttered to myself. "I need You right now."

What am I? Chopped liver? I heard The White Warrior, my second personality, say to me.

I actually sneered. It was irritating dealing with her lately. *You have limits, White Warrior,* I said. *The Light Gods don't!*

That's rude!

Will you just shut up and tell me how to get out of here? I cried.

Well which is it? Do you want me to shut up, or tell you how to get out of here?

I did not have time for this pettiness. "Light Gods, help me!" I cried up to the sky, ignoring her.

That warm and calming presence came to my side again and instantly calmed my heart. As I blew out a calming and cleansing breath, I swore I heard the White Warrior gasp. That confused me. When I focused on her and tried to reach her, I found that she had shut herself away again in that hidden part of my mind I could never reach. It was a place where I couldn't communicate with her, but I could still use my magic since she wasn't completely sealed off from me. The "window" in my mind separating the two off us had been thrown open months ago. It was curious, though. Why did she feel the need to hide in the presence of one of the Light Gods? We were all on the same side.

Hello, Azrel. It was the male Light God again.

"What's happening?" I asked out loud, looking up at the ceiling.

I told you things were about to get worse, and they have.

My heart was racing because his voice sounded tense and worried. I didn't know much about the Light Gods, but I knew that if one of them was worried about *anything*, it could not be a good sign!

"What do I do?" I asked in a choking whisper.

Do what you do best. Go fight.

I swallowed heavily. "What if I fail?"

Doesn't matter. You're a warrior. Warriors go to war regardless of the odds.

"I take it the odds are not in my favor at the moment."

No. Not at all.

I nodded and looked at the stone floor. "Great."

Don't forget though, Azrel. We're with you.

I looked up at the ceiling again, feeling softened by his kindness. He was not like the female Light God who had spoken to me when I'd first received the magic of the White Warrior long ago at the cave. "What is your name?"

Kadoma. My elder sisters are Unha and Aithrella.

I nodded and looked down at the floor again. I found myself swallowing heavily as I continued to absorb his strength and kindness and peace. I felt stronger with him near me. His presence took me to a place of confidence I could never have reached on my own, and it felt wonderful.

I looked back up at the ceiling and humbled myself to him. His kindness made it easy. "Stay with me?"

I felt his presence warm and intensify around me in what I imagined was a smile…if a God could smile. Maybe They could. *Always, Azrel. Always.*

With the confidence of the Light Gods with me, I darted up the hallway to the right as fast as I could towards where I felt the heavy Shadow. A spiral staircase was suddenly before me. Bounding up it, I melted my appearance into that of the White Warrior. The glow of my skin reflected off the stone walls, lighting my way.

I came to a platform in the stairs with a lonely wooden door in the wall to my right and paused. It was evident I needed to continue up the stairs, but something pulled me toward the wooden door. Before continuing, I turned and gripped the metal ring, pulling it open and stepping inside. A long stone hallway was before me with a ceiling at least forty feet. Cells lined both sides of the wall and stretched back farther than my white glow could even reach at the moment. I realized it was another level of the dungeon, but there had to be two hundred cages in here.

I suddenly heard a chorus of soft gasps from every cell down the entire dark hallway. I vaguely could make out shadows moving and, without even seeing details, I realized these cages were very overcrowded. There had to be fifty people in each cell that was only big enough to hold fifteen or so. The smell was rank, and I had to use a little magic to settle my stomach and keep myself from retching. There was no relief from the smell of human waste and body odor. It filled the entire corridor from floor to ceiling, and I could already feel it saturating my clothes.

The prisoners started gasping my name softly and with some reverence. "White Warrior."

I looked around, confused, as I slowly made my way down the hallway. Some arms reached out for me. Calling them skeletal would be generous. They were filthy, covered with oozing sores. Some sores had turned a gangrene color and a few had festered so long they'd turned black.

Halfway down the hall, I looked up, and my heart jumped into my throat. At the very end, under a brilliant spotlight of silver moonlight, a person was illuminated. He wasn't in a cell, but in a stockade. His head was bowed low, his hands hanging limp in the device. His black hair was so soaked with blood that it shined wet in the light above him. Recognizing his body and build, I knew, without seeing his face, that it was Ortheldo. I ran.

My heart raced as I collapsed to my knees in front of him and took his face in my hands. "Ortheldo?" I said softly. *Please be alive. Please be alive*, was all I could think.

His face was swollen so badly that both of his eyes were purple and pinched closed. He had lumps and long cuts all over his face and neck and shoulders and arms. I glanced above him and saw a tunnel of stone at least two hundred feet high where the moonlight was allowed in, but not fresh air, as there was glass above.

"Ortheldo?" I said again, putting my focus back on him and gently rubbing his face. I was desperate to revive him. He couldn't be dead. He couldn't be! I pressed my ear to his bare chest but heard nothing. "No," I breathed. Looking at his face as my tears fell, I instantly lit my hands up with healing white fire.

Save your strength, Azrel.

I jumped and snapped my head to look up at the moonlit tunnel above me. It was the female Light God! I knew her voice. It was the same cold, mean, hateful voice I'd first heard in the cave almost a decade ago when my father had handed me the Sword. It was the same voice that had insulted him as he lay dying on his bed. It was the same voice I had rebuked.

There is a much bigger battle, she went on. *Ortheldo will soon be home safe with us.*

I glared at the moon, glared at her like I had done the first time she'd spoken to me. "Listen to me," I said firmly as furious rage brought feeling back into my limbs. "There are two people in this world I cannot live without, whom I cannot do anything without— my brother and Ortheldo." I began panting in fear and rage. "I need them for reasons an emotionless bitch like you would never understand."

That being had zero respect from me. A single tear fell down my cheek as I continued looking up the tunnel.

"Kadoma," I choked out, softening my tone to a more

desperate and respectful one. "I am asking you for your help. I am *begging* you for your help. Will you please give me the strength I need to heal him and fight whatever is outside?"

He was quiet a moment before he said softly, *I will do what I can.*

I nearly went limp from relief as my head dropped down and rested against Ortheldo's. "Thank you," I breathed.

I wasn't sure what a God *couldn't* do in this situation. Something really awful must be outside. The pressure of the Shadow in my chest was tremendous. It felt like the entire palace could be brought down on my head by the heaviness of it.

I stood up and went behind Ortheldo, encircling his torso with one of my arms and holding him up. I ripped the padlock off the stockade and raised the top section to release him with my other hand. He slid out of the device and was completely dead weight in my arms, his body limp and lifeless. I gently laid him down on the stone floor and lit my hands up with white fire. Touching his cheek with my fingertips, I healed his face. When the lumps and cuts were healed and the swelling gone, I willed his eyes to open. They opened slowly and stared up at me in a creepy, blank, lifeless manner. Clenching my teeth, I stared at the reflection of my own eyes in his and saw a darkness expand.

Poison!

I gasped when I felt the evil energy of it. They had forced Ortheldo to drink fatal poison not ten minutes ago, probably just as I was waking up in my cell.

"Ortheldo," I whispered. "Hey." My tears ran in streams down my face. "You can't leave yet," I said forcing a smile, which leaked out more white tears. "We're not done." I poured my white fire into him to heal him of the poison in his system.

I waited a moment for the edges of the darkness to glow white and then fade as he healed, but suddenly the darkness of the poison thickened!

My eyes went wide. The edges should be glowing white right now! It should be disappearing! Instead it got thicker and darker. Layers and layers of darkness overlapped each other faster than I could heal!

I was shaking and near hysterical with the thought of losing him. No! My face shot up towards the tunnel. "What's happening?" I screamed at the sky.

I'm so sorry, Azrel, the male Light God said sadly. *I told you things were bad.*

"Tell me!" I screamed so desperately that my entire body shook with the force of my voice.

Go outside. You'll see.

All I saw was the white water of my tears. All I heard was myself nearly choking on my own air as I started to sob. I kept my magic inside of Ortheldo, healing him, even though the evil poison was overwhelming it quickly. I tucked one arm under Ortheldo's back and the other under his legs and lifted him up off the floor. I wouldn't leave him in this filthy, wretched place. With a passing glance from me at the cells down the long hallway, all two hundred doors started to glow white briefly before exploding open and releasing the prisoners.

In a burst of white flame, I vanished and reappeared outside the palace of Spar Ridges. I stood at the top of the castle's massively wide light blue metal steps, and I couldn't even comprehend what I was seeing fully. My legs began to tremble and, still holding Ortheldo, I sunk down to one knee, setting him down on his tailbone as I looked out over the massacre that was occurring. It was a sea of death happening in front of me. A massive, massive battle had erupted in Spar Ridges that filled the entire bowl of the four mountains. An expanse of land equal to a four-day walk was now a bowl of carnage.

People were screaming. Women were running wherever they could go, some dragging or carrying small, screaming children. Fires burned up homes. Even as I looked, one of the magnificent rock structures two miles away crumbled before my eyes, making the ground shake. Another smaller one collapsed off to my left as well.

Amidst the slaughter, I picked out the Shadow creatures easily enough, but I also saw enemy soldiers from Dwellingpath. This was the first time I'd ever encountered them, and my eyes went down to Ortheldo briefly; they were his people. Looking back out over the bowl, I couldn't even move or respond from the horror I was seeing. Hathum's entire army was in Spar Ridges.

Though as I looked around, I realized, so was *mine!*

My eyes went wide and my back straightened slightly.

Addredoc had brought my army!

I saw Sallybreath flowers of red, gold, white, light green and blue violet dotting the mass of movement in front of me. I also noticed the pointed ears of some of the elves from Alkgwathien! They were all here. Millions of beings had come to fight for me, forgetting their hatred of my father and the White Warrior. They had come…and they were all being slaughtered before my eyes.

"Azrel!" someone screamed.

I turned to the sound of the voice as another tear dropped down my cheek. A man dressed all in white whom I'd never seen before appeared at the top of the stairs and came toward me. He was handsome for sure, but unusual because, despite looking incredibly youthful, he had white hair that brushed his shoulders. Even more disturbing, his outfit looked a lot like mine, only tailored for the male physique and without a cloak. He had big brown eyes that somehow comforted me as he ran toward me.

He fell to his knees next to me and it only took an instant to realize who he was. The look in his eyes was way too familiar. "Lightning?" I said in awe. It was my horse! He was in human form!

He pressed his lips together and nodded. "What happened?" He glanced down at Ortheldo.

In panic and relief I gripped his shirt in a fist with my free hand. "He was poisoned! He's dying! I can't do anything! I tried! I couldn't…"

"Azrel," Lightning interrupted, firmly resting his hand on the side of my neck. "I've got him."

Smiling with tears still dripping down my face, I pulled him into an embrace. "Thank you," I said in a shaky voice. Backing away, I carefully handed Ortheldo to him.

Lightning took him tenderly in his arms and looked back up at my face, pressing his lips together in sympathy. "Go to your men," he said heavily. "Do what you can."

My brows dropped, "Do what I can?"

He sighed softly before tilting his head in the direction of the battle. "Go."

With my brows still drawn, I stood to my feet and headed down the stairs to the battle. Halfway down, I paused, my eyes darting around. I managed to spot Addredoc from the blasts of his powerful red magic among smaller blasts of red Godel Salynn magic. A few blasts of yellow magic pinpointed where Lisswilla was. A loud roar from Reese in his cat form gave me his general direction. I could also make out the half-human, half-animal forms of Fayithjen Forest. I saw blasts of pink and brown magic as well, which had to be Ceco and the Spar Ridgian Salynns that I had tortured. Among all this, I saw flashes of gold, white, and light green from the Salynns of White Veilvin, Galad Kas, and Triple Peaks.

Even as I watched, though, of the millions of soldiers before me right now, thousands were dying by the second. Bodies fell down in waves before my eyes, some burning alive in black flames or cut down by swords. Some were torn apart; some were mangled beyond recognition. Wave after wave of arrows from Dwellingpath archers impaled hundreds, thousands, with each volley. The blood was so thick in the bowl of Spar Ridges that it splashed up under the foot of the battle up to the soldiers' knees.

"Do what you can," Lightning had said. Right. There was nothing I could do to stop this. I was not this powerful. Not yet. I could barely deal with 60,000 Shadow creatures outside of White Veilvin, and that had even killed me. There were millions in front of me now. As far as my eyes could see, the bowl was a black sea of movement amidst explosions of different color magic as my troops tried to survive.

I sighed and looked up at the sky. "Any chance you want to give me my crown now, Kadoma?"

I can't yet, Azrel. I'm sorry.

"Why?" I cried out.

I'm sorry, he said softly. *It's out of my hands.*

I pressed my lips together and shook my head as I bowed it down. "I don't know what more I need to do to convince you to give it to me."

Please, I thought I heard him plead. But it was so soft that it was like listening to a distant whisper. *Don't give up.*

I nearly let myself give in to defeat. I wanted to badly, but I didn't have time for that. I raised my head again and looked out over the bowl as another wave of about five hundred of my troops fell to the Dwellingpath archers. I drew my sword and took a breath, preparing to do what I could, when a menacing, booming voice filled the entire sky.

"Is that my little flea?"

It was so big—not even loud just big—that I crushed my hands to my ears and ducked down. Watching in awe, the voice seemed to have a physical presence as the entire battlefield, Shadow and my army alike, looked like they were slowly pushed down onto the ground and forced onto their faces. It looked almost like a giant invisible foot the size of the entire bowl of Spar Ridges came down on top of all of them at once, forcing them down. The fighting stopped, and the sounds of metal clashing and magic exploding were replaced with the shocked groans and moans from everyone now lying prone in the blood.

An unnatural wind kicked up. It whipped my hair around my face so violently that I could only see a curtain of white before my eyes for a few seconds. When it slowed enough to allow me to see, a plethora of black smoky clouds appeared, filling the entire night sky. The heavy Shadow in my chest seemed to stretch outside of me, meeting up with the dark clouds in the sky and filling the entire bowl. I felt like a tiny, flickering white candle in the sea of black Shadow around me.

My heart was racing. I suddenly knew what I was facing. And I knew what that earthquake was that had terrified me so badly.

My first instinct was to run for it. I wanted to get as far away as I could, to bide more time and find out what needed to be done to convince the Light Gods to give me my crown back before I faced this. I refused to allow myself to do so, though. I didn't know what else I could to do to earn it, and a few more days wouldn't make a difference. Abandoning my men right now anyway, would be the dumbest thing I could do, even if doing so would save my life.

The smoky clouds rapidly folded in on themselves a few times before the shape of a giant face formed inside of them—a face with stark black puffs for eyes that looked down at me. It was a painfully beautiful face shape, and one I'd seen before.

"Hathum," I breathed.

The massive face floated down from the sky, shrinking the entire way, until a thin column of clouds touched down right in front of me. With a gentle swirl, the clouds vanished, leaving Hathum standing in their wake. He had changed.

His fingers had gotten longer and bonier, with long talon-like black fingernails filed into sharp points. His frame was gaunt and even more skeletal than those of the prisoners I had seen in the dungeon. His black robes were so massive on him that they nearly came off his shoulders, exposing his skeleton-like collarbone. His face was still generally the same, but thinner and more hollowed out. His blue eyes were more wide and crazy, reminding me of a rabid animal as they gazed upon me with a primitive evil and hunger that I'd never seen before, not even in a Gorkor's eyes.

"Hathum?" He said in a surprisingly smooth voice, "No no no no, dear." He smiled wickedly, exposing two rows of perfect white teeth. "My name is Elral. Hathum here is just my vessel. Do you know who I am?"

I wanted to be brave. I wanted to be tough. But I couldn't bring myself to speak. Maybe if I didn't, I could pretend this wasn't real.

His smile faded slowly, and I was left with his dangerous, wild eyes on me. "I'm the eldest of the Shadow Gods, dear." A burning sensation filled my left shoulder. I screamed and doubled over from the pain, and suddenly his face was right above mine and his long black talons were digging into my shoulder! "And *you* have been an epic pain in my ass since the day you were created." I hadn't even seen him move. He dug his talons deeper into my shoulder, sending the burning pain through my blood. It felt like boiling syrup was pumping through my veins.

Somewhere in the midst of my scream of pain, the tone shifted to a deeper tone of unbelievable rage and, risking him tearing my arm out of the socket, I head-butted him square in the nose. The force of the blow sent him backwards enough to get his hands off me. Before he could make another move to get closer, my fist flew out and I decked him right in the jaw, sending him stumbling down several stairs until he was on a knee.

"Son of a bitch!" I yelled. As he tried to stand, I jumped and spun my body in a windmill-like motion and slammed my fist down into his face so hard that his cheek slammed into the metal stairs.

Out of nowhere, I was lifted off my feet and thrown backward up the steps. I landed on the edge of the top step so hard that I heard and felt my spine crack inward toward my chest and my legs went numb. I gasped. I couldn't even cry out in pain, because there was no pain. I couldn't feel anything! I watched as the monster stalked toward me with such malice in his eyes that my breath got caught in my throat.

"Enough!" another booming voice cried out, filling the entire bowl. Then a blast of white fire from somewhere next to me slammed into Elral's frail frame, causing him to roll and bounce down a few of the stairs.

The terrifying Shadow God looked up and, next to me, I watched Lightning slowly come forward. His physical human appearance now had a captivating ethereal quality to it that I couldn't look away from. When he walked, it looked like he was moving in slow motion and floating just above the ground. Layers of white light that were somehow thick, but yet somehow transparent, surrounded him. Or came out of him. I couldn't tell which. His hair and ends of his clothes gently floated around him as if he were underwater. He was stunning and beautiful and unreal at the same time.

"Kadoma?" Elral asked, and my eyes went wide. "Is that you, little brother?" he said with sickly exaggerated sweetness, which sounded more menacing than anything.

A calming quiet seemed to come over the world as Lightning looked at the creature on the stairs. "You need to leave now," Lightning said. "You're weak. In this condition you're barely on par with me, big brother. And Xraun and Natsea aren't even awake yet." Lightning's eyes started to glow with a golden white light. "Unah and I, however, are at full power."

My heart swelled with pride, only to be quickly deflated. "Ah," Elral hissed mischievously as he got up to his knees. "But is Aithrella at full power?" Lightning pressed his lips together and sighed, which made Elral smile in a drippy evil manner that made me want to weep just from the sight of it. "I thought not. Very well. I shall gain some strength, and we will meet again. But before I go…" The creature spun around and flung a ball of black fire from his hand and deep into the crowd at the bottom of the stairs. Someone screamed.

Addredoc!

I gasped and desperately tried to sit up, struggling as pathetically as a stranded beetle, but my legs wouldn't work! "Addredoc!" I screamed.

Elral looked back at me and Lightning with his teeth clenched and bared. "Now I can go." The creature vanished in a plume of black fire, taking his entire Shadow army with him.

FOURTEEN

Slowly everyone in the bowl started to pick themselves up off the ground and noise began to rise up from them. It took a moment for some energy to ripple through the crowd, and even that wasn't much.

"Addredoc," I breathed and desperately tried to get up again, but it was like my entire body was severed from my chest down. It was completely useless!

"He's alive, Azrel," Lightning said, crouching beside me. I cowered away from him slightly, knowing who he was, and he looked at me almost like he was ashamed. I didn't know what to do. He was a God. He was a Light God and he was my friend…my horse.

"Come on, Azrel," he said and then touched my back. Feeling immediately flowed back down to my toes. "Let's talk."

I was too afraid to move. "I…I can't. Not right…" I looked behind me and saw Ortheldo as he sat up at the top of the stairs. He spotted me lying nearby and crawled over on his hands and knees. He dropped on his stomach before practically lying on top of me as he wrapped his arms around my back in a tight embrace.

"You're okay," I whispered with tears in my eyes.

"I'm okay," he whispered softly.

I met Lightning's eyes over Ortheldo's shoulder. "Thank you."

He nodded once in reply.

As I heard energy start to go up in the bowl, I pulled away from Ortheldo and sat up, looking over the crowd. So many bodies were on the ground and blood soaked the front of every single person who was just getting to his or her feet. All of them were looking at Lightning in wide-eyed awe. I stood, pulling Ortheldo up next to me.

Lightning, or Kadoma, looked at me. "I'm going to wipe everyone's memory of who I am. Things get awkward when I'm revealed."

I nodded, still barely able to comprehend what I was looking at.

"Please," he said in a soft pleading tone, "try to just treat me like your friend. People will get suspicious otherwise."

I couldn't move for a moment before I nodded again with little conviction. "I'll try."

He forced an empty smile before his eyes briefly flashed with a golden white light. Suddenly he looked normal again and everyone in the bowl took their eyes off him and was instantly moving with urgency to try and tend to the wounded.

I rested my hand on Ortheldo's chest and met his eyes. "How do you feel?"

"I'm all right, Azrel." He kissed my forehead firmly. "I'm going to find Addredoc."

I nodded because that's exactly what I was going to ask him to do. "Thank you."

Ortheldo rested the back of his finger on my cheek briefly before he left my side and quickly headed down the stairs into the bowl of bloody bodies.

"Azrel!" someone yelled.

I spun around. My brother and Acalith were coming up the steps toward me. Their clothing was soaked in blood and splashes of it were on their faces and necks. I sighed heavily in relief that he was okay. I wanted to run and embrace him and be thankful that he was all right, but I hesitated. The cold detachment was still in his eyes, but he seemed to be struggling with it now, like he wanted to forgive me but couldn't bring himself to.

I swallowed heavily and put my guard up so his indifference wouldn't hurt me. I didn't have time for it right now. "You all right?" I asked as he came to stand in front of me.

He pressed his lips together and nodded. "You?"

I nodded. "How long was I out?"

"Two days."

I shook my head and looked away. "What have I missed?"

Acalith stepped forward, and I noticed her reservations towards me were still heavily in place. In fact, she didn't look at me with any kindness or any struggle. "I reunited with my parents, and we've been discussing our next move." She narrowed her eyes slightly at me, "As well as discussing other political matters that are beneath you."

It was an intentional jab at me for my comment about her being a Princess not mattering to me. She'd gotten arrogant in the past two days of being royalty again, and I knew she and I were going to have issues again. I didn't bow to her, or anyone, and I had a feeling she might have a problem with that now.

My lip twitched. "Get the women in your land together and tend to the wounded."

Acalith crossed her arms, her eyes locked on mine in what seemed like a challenge. "And if I don't?"

My lip unintentionally pulled away from my top teeth, and I slowly shook my head at her. "You don't want to find out."

She took a daring step toward me and pointed her finger in my face. "You killed Rabryn," she hissed. The sting of that was sharp, but I firmly held my ground. I would not yield to her! "You don't get to tell me what to do anymore. I will not…"

"Enough!" My brother suddenly yelled. Acalith jumped and looked up at him with surprise. My brother was fuming! His face was red, and his nostrils were flaring. "Get the women together *now* and tend to the army. They are all we have, and we need every single one of them." Acalith hesitated, still staring at him in disbelief. "Go!" He cried, throwing his arm out toward the palace. With a glare, Acalith left quickly in that direction.

This was an odd quarrel. I looked at Rabryn curiously. He just closed his eyes and shook his head. "Don't ask." I wanted to argue, but my relationship with him was in severe tatters right now, so I bit my tongue. Eventually his eyes passed over my face before skirting away toward the bowl. "I left orders for Tinarandel to gather all the magic users and heal your troops."

I nodded. Glancing around, I realized someone was missing. Looking at Rabryn, I asked, "Moifulyar?" Rabryn just squeezed his eyes closed and bowed his head. "Oh no," I squeaked. I desperately wanted to gather my little brother in my arms and hug him, but I seriously doubted the gesture would be a welcome one, so I just reached out and gently touched his shoulder. "Rabryn, I'm so sorry."

"We lost a lot of people," he said, pressing his fingers into his eyes.

I just stayed quiet and nodded, offering him what comfort I could without getting too close. Rabryn collected himself, sniffing away tears, and then stepped out of my arm's reach. My hand slid off his shoulder and he gave me an awkward sidelong glance. My heart sank. I couldn't even comfort him from a distance.

"I'm going to see what I can do for healing," he declared without another glance.

Before he could start down the stairs, I heard "Azrel!" coming from within the crowd. It was Ortheldo. Both Rabryn and I took off running down the stairs toward the sound of his voice.

When I reached the ground, my boots sunk into blood that was nearly ankle deep. It made a disgusting, thick splashing sound as I ran through it. The hem of my cloak was instantly soaked as it dragged through the thick red liquid. The pile of carnage was up to the middle of my shins. I was leaping and stepping over bodies, and body parts, and insides, traversing a gruesome obstacle course.

Making my way to Ortheldo, I felt the weight of every eyeball on me. People were watching me while they pretended to be doing something else, healing wounded soldiers or carrying them, or administering aid by any means available.

Eventually, I heard Ortheldo yelling, "Move! Make way for her!" and the crowd began to part before me opening a path to where Addredoc was lying. Ortheldo had him cradled in his arms tightly and protectively. "He won't wake up. He's not responding."

I dropped to my knees by his side and took his handsome, beautiful face in my hands. "Addredoc?" His eyelids weren't even moving like when he slept. "Addredoc!" I said more forcefully.

I looked up helplessly at everyone that surrounded him— everyone close to me whom I hadn't seen in about a month. Reese was in his magnificent cat form, looking down at Addredoc with the most desperate expression of grief I'd ever seen. His sky blue eyeballs looked up at me helplessly as he whined with fear and loss. Lisswilla who, for as long as I'd known him, had had a problem with Addredoc—they bickered like an old married couple more often than they actually talked—was standing by looking concerned. Yarin kneeled behind Ortheldo, resting his hand on his shoulder.

I looked back down at his face. "Addredoc!" I cried again and rested my cheek against his chest. At first I felt nothing, but after a few stressful moments I finally felt it rise with breath. "Addredoc!" I cried in relief, gripping his face in my hands. My gorgeous Addredoc.

"Can you heal him?" Reese growled out sadly. He'd finally learned to talk in this form, though it was clearly a new skill since he sounded more animal than Salynn.

"I don't kn..." My voice trailed off as I looked back up the palace steps searching for Lightning, or Kadoma, but I couldn't spot him over the crowd. I clenched my teeth and bared them in annoyance for a split second before looking back down at Addredoc. His red Sallybreath flowers were gray and shriveled. My breath caught in my throat because that meant death was at hand, but none of his flowers fell out. They stayed in his hair even though they looked mostly dead.

Before I could analyze that too long, his eyes opened into slits. I gasped. "Addredoc!"

My heart jumped for joy when he actually smiled weakly up at me. "Hey."

I laughed loudly as tears of joy filled my eyes. "Hey."

I wanted to ask how he felt, but he was clearly not feeling well. He otherwise seemed okay, but my heart sank because I knew Elral wouldn't have singled him out for no reason. Addredoc had been hit with a Shadow God's black fire; I just didn't know what that meant yet.

He tried to sit up, but immediately fell back down against Ortheldo.

"Easy, easy," I said gently.

He blinked a few times and then an unsettling confusion came over his face. His eyes darted around to each of us in what looked like panic before they flew wide open. "My magic," he gasped. He looked down at his hands in and began to weakly struggle against Ortheldo to try and sit up. "My magic is gone!" He looked up at me with wide desperate eyes. "It's gone, Azrel! It's..."

"Shh shh shh," I said, quickly gathering him up from Ortheldo and holding him against me. "It's okay. It's okay," I said trying to soothe him. "As long as you're okay, I don't care."

He continued to breathe heavily, but slowly he went still. I held on to him tighter than I probably should have, but I loved him. I did love him. He'd stayed by my side when I'd needed someone the most. Through my darkest time, no matter how brief it may have been, he'd been with me.

"It's going to be okay," I whispered in his ear, petting his hair behind his head. I clung to him for far too long. I needed him to know I was here for him like he had been there for me. "You're going to be okay."

"Azrel," my brother ended up saying somberly. It was the gentlest voice he'd used toward me since the incident in the woods. I looked up and only realized I was crying when I felt a tear drop down my cheek. "Your troops need you."

I nodded and looked down into Addredoc's eyes. He was terrified. He was completely powerless for the first time in a 600-year existence. Worse, losing his magic meant he would die eventually if I didn't figure out a way to save him. The one upside was that I had time. The more powerful a Wizard was when he or she lost his or her magic, the longer the Wizard could live once it was taken away. Addredoc was incredibly powerful, with two gifts of Ancient Wizard magic, so he wouldn't actually die for years.

"You're going to be okay," I promised.

Just then, a racket of footsteps came out of the palace and down the vast stairs. It was the women of Spar Ridges. They had healing aids and bandages, water basins and herbs in their arms as they made their way toward my injured troops. To my dismay, there were only about 200 of them.

Acalith emerged behind the pack. Pausing at the stairs, she scanned over the crowd. Spotting Rabryn, she made her way toward him. She didn't even look at me as she approached his side. "That's all the women here in the northern side. I've send word to the west, east, and south to begin administering care."

Rabryn nodded once but had a hard time meeting Acalith's eyes. He shifted uncomfortably near her and made an effort to pretend he was not paying attention to her without being to rude about it. My eyes narrowed when Acalith just stood there by his side, looking up at him like she was waiting for further orders.

"How many total?" I asked, still holding on to Addredoc.

Acalith gave me a sneering glance before her eyes went right back to my brother. "There will be about 2,000 women attending the wounded troops across the land."

"That's not enough!" I cried. "It will take weeks to tend them all and most don't have that kind of time!"

Acalith finally looked down at me with a nasty glare. "And

what would you like me to do about that?"

That was it! I gently rested Addredoc on the ground and then jumped to my feet and stalked toward her. I would not take verbal abuse from her! Not her! I grabbed the front of her shirt in both of my fists and yanked her towards me. "I've had enough of you!" I growled with my nose a half an inch from hers.

"How dare yo—"

I didn't even let her finish her sentence before I slapped her across the face so hard that her shirt jerked in my fist.

She looked at me stunned then, "Don't you—"

I slapped her again, and then again, and again until her nose was bleeding.

"How dare I what?" I yelled, gathering her shirt in both fists. "Hmm?" I panted with barely concealed rage. "How. Dare. I. What?" I growled slowly.

"I'm a princ—"

I slapped her again. "You're a what?"

"I'm a princess!" she finally screamed and suddenly began to cry.

Now I knew something was wrong!

I gathered her shirt tightly in both fists. "There was a time, not long ago," I breathed, "when you didn't care about that." I jerked her once. "I *never* cared about that." My tone became lighter, but no less severe. "And I never will." I shoved her away from me hard enough to make her fall and splash in the blood on the ground.

As she landed, I saw it. A very brief and very thin flash of black light, like a crack of lightning that stretched from the left side of her chest to the right side of her head.

My eyes went wide. "Kadoma," I gasped. "What was that?"

Her shield is cracked, he replied urgently. *Get away from her!*

Suddenly Acalith's entire body went stiff and rigid. Her shoulders were up under her ears and her arms bent to her sides, and her fingers clawed into the blood-soaked ground. When her face came up to meet mine, her eyes were glowing black.

I felt like I was being choked. The air was stuck on an unfinished exhale and I started to shake.

Seeing my horror, she threw her head back and laughed like a maniac. "Oh, Azrel. I'm sad you figured out my little game so quickly! I was having so much fun with your friends and little brother."

"Elral?" I asked.

"Oh, indeed." Acalith's body suddenly rose from the ground without her having to use her limbs, like she had an invisible pulley attached to her chest that lifted her to her feet.

The creepiness of her movements made me stagger a few steps back while my heart pounded in my chest. "I thought...you were gone."

Acalith threw her head back and laughed again. "Gone? Gone? I'm never gone." She took a breath, "I'm a God!" she suddenly screamed, and the force of her voice became like a hurricane knocking me and everyone in a half mile radius onto our backs.

I splashed in the blood and suddenly Acalith was crouching next to the top of my head, though I hadn't seen her move. I was looking at her upside down, which somehow made her more terrifying.

"Don't worry, Azrel. You can have your little bitch back. I was just having some fun and, alas, I'm still too weak to sustain a good time, especially now that I've been discovered." Her eyes widened, and she looked down at me hungrily. "But not for long. We'll meet again very soon, my dear. By the way," she whispered, leaning down toward me like she was about to tell me an incredible secret. "In case you were wondering, this crack occurred because you killed your little brother." She looked down at me with false sympathy and tsked me. "Acalith really loves him. You kill him, and poof!" She grinned evilly. "Her loyalty and love for you cracked her shield nearly in half, letting me slip in with ease." She raised her eyebrows and looked like a mother about to chastise a child. "You really ought to pick better people in your crew, Azrel. I mean"—she chuckled and held her hands out to her sides—"if the Deralilya can't even withstand me, come on!"

I was frozen in terror on the ground. An invisible weight held me down that I could not lift, though I was trying. Why wasn't Kadoma getting rid of him again?

Acalith clicked her tongue in false sympathy again before she suddenly shifted her position so she was looking down at me from the front. She lifted her leg and put it on the other side of my body so she was straddling my hips. "Don't worry," her eyes got wide and hungry again as she began to caress my collarbone with one hand and eventually went down to my breast. "I've got tons more fun planned for you once I'm strong enough. Things you couldn't dream of!" She leaned down and kissed my chest just above my bodice before her black eyes shifted up to meet mine again. "Things you're not even aware of yet."

I was struggling to lift this damn weight off of me, but I couldn't! My arms wouldn't even move.

She hummed seductively, leaned down toward my face, and kissed my lips softly and briefly before meeting my eyes again. "You and me, dream lover," she said, caressing my cheek. "We're gonna have some fun."

Acalith threw her head back and laughed again before I saw a black fog seep out of the area where I had glimpsed the crack. It evaporated into nothing above her head. Acalith fell off of me and onto her side on the bloody ground.

The weight was suddenly lifted off me. I quickly crawled away from her until I had backed up into Reese's soft and strong cat form. His large head and a paw that was twice the size of my face came around partially in front of me, getting ready to pounce should anything go array. Everyone slowly got back to their feet, Rabryn looking horrified and stunned as he stared in Acalith's direction. I could tell he wanted to rush to her side but didn't dare. All of us stared at her in uncomfortable silence.

Acalith's body jerked once and I saw her head slowly start to move back and forth. Her face twitched and eventually her eyes flew opened. Everyone—Rabryn, Ortheldo, Reese, Lisswilla, Yarin, Addredoc and I—all backed away farther from her, clearing an easy fifteen-foot circumference. Looking confused, she sat up. Then her eyes went wide as the memories of what had occurred must have come to her. She frantically searched the ground, like an explanation would be in the mixed dirt and blood somewhere.

It was silent. She didn't know what to say or do, or what I would say or do. She glanced at me but couldn't even look long. She resorted to staring at the ground with her mouth moving up and down trying to form words, though none came. She finally was able to look up at Rabryn, but he turned his face away. Her eyes came to me again and she was petrified.

I wanted to look away, but I didn't. How could I?

"And you gave *me* crap for giving in to Shadow."

Acalith was stunned. I could tell she wanted to smile gratefully but knew there was no place for a smile at this moment. I crawled over to her on my hands and knees, sloshing through the blood, and wrapped her tightly in my arms.

"I'm glad you're back," I mumbled into her hair.

"I'm sorry," she said. "I'm so sorry."

"It's okay," I said. "It's not like you did serious damage." I sighed and pulled away, looking into her softly glowing green eyes. "And it's not like you're The White Warrior."

"But I'm the Deralilya; the one that's supposed to protect The White Warrior."

I shrugged a shoulder. "I guess we both suck then."

Acalith finally grinned, though nervously. "Yeah, I guess so." The smile quickly dropped. "What do we do now?" I looked at her, confused, and her eyes got worried and fearful. "A Shadow God has returned."

I sighed. "It's all right," I reassured her and gently patted her cheek. I scanned around quickly for Kadoma with no success. I managed to smile, though it was a little forced. "So has a Light God."

Her eyes got wide. "Seriously? How do you know?"

I titled my head uneasily from side to side because I didn't know what Kadoma's deal was, or if my horse was still my horse or, something else, or had always *been* something else. "It's a White Warrior thing," was the best answer I could give her.

"Azrel," Ortheldo suddenly said softly as he crouched down at my side. I looked over at him and saw his bright, unique eyes pleading. "You really need to do something about your wounded troops."

Yarin stepped forward looking worried. "*Can* you do anything?"

I gazed out over the bowl as a few of the women and able-bodied troops mulled around trying to do what they could for the injured, some severely injured themselves. All I could hear were moans and wails of pain, and distant muttering. It was suffering—unabashed, uncensored suffering.

I met Yarin's eyes and nodded. "Yeah. I can do something." I slowly stood up and turned to face the massive, milling crowd as I lit my eyes up with white fire.

"Azrel," I heard Ortheldo say in a tone of warning. "Just heal as many as you're able."

"Yeah," I said more to myself than him. "Sure."

An explosion of white fire erupted from the ground at my feet and rose up to consume me entirely. A few close bystanders jumped, and every eye was on me. I clenched my teeth as I pulled on my magic, the White Warrior, with every intention of draining her completely if I had to, to save my troops. I didn't care if she ceased to exist after this or if I did. Acalith or Rabryn or Ortheldo could easily take command of my army and fight, and Kadoma could take up the mantle for the Light Gods against Elral. I wasn't needed anymore, and that was okay.

As I let my magic build inside my chest, I realized that what I was mustering would not be enough to heal the over one million wounded. And I wasn't sure I would be able to cast my magic out across the four-day expanse of the bowl either. I needed more power. I resisted glancing at the Sword at my hip with a sneer. I could really use whatever powers were harbored in that blade. Alas, it wasn't to be for some reason.

Suddenly, an idea dawned on me from nowhere, and I felt my eyes go a little wide at the realization. Dropping my chin to my chest, I looked at the soft orange glow of the small flame-shaped diamond broach attached to the middle of my chest. I had the gem of all damn healing with me! I allowed myself a little smirk as, again, some knowledge from nowhere of how to use it came to my mind. *All* of my troops were about to be healed!

As my white fire blazed around me, I slowly reached up and pinched the diamond broach between two fingers and plucked it off my garment. Raising my chin, I looked defiantly out toward the middle of the bowl.

"This battle is mine, you bastard," I said softly through clenched teeth, knowing Elral was a God and he would hear me wherever he was.

I threw the diamond broach out toward the middle of the bowl letting it fly. I waited a moment, still feeling my connection to it since it was a part of my life force, my own energy. When I finished gathering all of my white fire, concentrating it in my hands, I screamed at the top of my lungs and fired a blast of my magic towards the broach. Enhancing my vision, I watched as the white fireball slammed into the diamond, causing it to explode into countless tiny drops of orange light that floated above the ground at eye level throughout the entire expanse of the four mountains. Slowly and gently, the sparks of light floated down to the ground, settling on all of the injured. There were a few dark gaps in the expanse of orange light where I assumed wounded enemy soldiers were left behind dying.

I was immediately weak and dropped to my knees. I forced my eyes to stay open so I could watch in awe as each of my soldiers began to glow with glittering orange magic. It looked like orange lightning bugs sizzling gently along the ground, and it was beautiful. My troops all gasped in awe or different levels of relief as their wounds were healed, and quickly I heard the noise level rising as life and energy returned to them. I smiled. I couldn't help it. Those sounds of life, those gorgeous sounds of energy and life, were music to my ears.

As everyone was healed and people began picking themselves up off the ground, the orange sparkles slowly floated into the air again above my soldiers. Then, with speed I could barely keep track of, they all formed currents and raced toward the center of the bowl again. With a final bright orange flash, my tiny broach was whole once more and flew back toward me. It slowed down as it got closer until it gently settled itself into my waiting palm. Closing my fingers tightly around it, I fell onto my side. My head splashing in the blood on the ground was the last thing I heard before I passed out again.

FIFTEEN

When my eyes snapped open I expected to be in a cell again. Oddly enough, I awoke to a strange green light surrounding me. My eyes went wide as I sat up and slowly looked around. There seemed to be no beginning or end. It was weird. I looked down at the "floor," though I didn't see any solid surface. Curious, I slapped my palm against it. Not only did I hit a solid surface, but I heard it echo off walls that didn't seem to be there.

"Like it?" an eerily familiar voice said.

I snapped my head in the direction of the sound and saw myself—or myself as The White Warrior standing there. I stared at her, dumbfounded, for a few moments. She was leaning up against a "wall" of green light, her arms crossed and one foot propped up.

I blinked a couple more times as I stared at her, trying to settle into the notion that I was seeing myself not in a looking glass, but completely apart and separate from me. I hadn't quite adjusted to the concept yet, but I couldn't help the odd grin that came to my face. As strange as this was, it was sort of nice to see her.

I picked myself up off the floor and stood. Still trying to adjust, I looked around the endless green light and shrugged. "It's not ideal, but a little interesting." When I looked at her— me—she smirked. It was slightly disconcerting, but I continued to smile at her. "It's good to see you," I said and started walking. "I think this talk is long overdue."

"Talk?" She kept her eyes on me as she pushed herself away from the wall and started toward me menacingly. I stood still. "Oh no, Azrel, we're not going to talk." Suddenly, I was thrown onto my back so forcefully that I hit my head on the floor. I tried to get up, but an unbelievable weight was on me, pinning me down. She came toward me and stepped one foot over my body, then sat herself down on my stomach. She leaned over, her face—my face—right above me. "You're just going to listen," she hissed.

She held a hand up and I watched in terror as long sharp black fingernails grew from the tips of her fingers. She slammed her hand down onto my face, and those fingernails went into my mouth, stabbing me in the tongue! Pain exploded in my face as those nails dug into my flesh, which should *never* have been injured like this. I screamed as best I could with my mouth full, and the pain radiated through my cheeks up to my temples. My eyes watered until tears were seeping out the corners. She ripped her nails down the length of my tongue as she took her hand out of my mouth, taking pieces of my flesh with her. I screamed, a wet-sounding gurgling, as blood bubbled up and dripped out both corners of my mouth to the floor.

"Ah," she sighed with exaggerated relief, looking at her long black talons as my blood and small chunks of flesh snaked down her fingers to decorate her pale, white palms. When she lowered her hand to her side again, her eyes were glowing *black!*

Panic clutched at my chest, and I started gasping as her form faded and melted into someone completely different—someone horrifying and incredibly familiar. I couldn't believe it. I'd failed. I'd failed just like my father had failed. Hathum, with his crystal clear blue eyes and his long blonde hair framing his painfully perfect face, was staring down at me with a grin that made my blood freeze.

"Well, hello again, Azrel."

I was shaking so hard I felt myself vibrating against the floor. I knew what had happened. In one terrifying, horrible rush, I knew what had happened, and I started sobbing.

"Oh shh shh shh," he said, leaning down and putting his face within an inch of mine. He stared at me with false sympathy.

Hathum had been The White Warrior in my mind since I'd first heard her voice in Rocksheloc.

"Oh sweet, stupid Azrel," he chastised softly. He lightly scratched his now normal fingernails down both of my cheeks repeatedly, almost like a caress. "You underestimated my power of mind corruption, didn't you, silly girl?" I couldn't respond, not only because my tongue was so damaged, but because I had no words to say. "Darling, there's a *reason* I perfected it over ten millennia."

"Nooooo!" I managed to get out in a wet sounding moan that sent flames of pain up through my face again.

That made him smile. It wasn't an overtly evil smile. In fact, it was pretty sweet and gentle. But the meaning behind it was what made me cold. I started shivering, though there was no real temperature here. He'd gotten the better of me. Before I'd even known what being The White Warrior really meant to me, or even the world, Hathum had beaten me.

How? I wanted to ask, but my tongue was so tattered it was useless.

"This is the real fun part," he said, shifting his position so his knees were up, his elbows resting on them. He looked at me with a sickly smile. His blue eyes glowed with an intense, hungry light. "This, Azrel, this moment, is what I've been looking forward to for over 3,000 years. The moment where you find out just how defeated you are."

I couldn't help it. My bottom lip trembled as tears poured from my eyes. His confidence was terrifying. I'd known I was out of my league when my father had first handed me that Sword, but my very existence had led me to believe I had a small chance. Hathum's confidence, his menacing glee, stole every ounce of hope I'd developed in myself.

Humming gently, he shifted his position again so he was on his knees, straddling my body, and leaned down toward my face again with that same false look of sympathy. He tenderly started playing with my hair, using his fingertips to brush it away from my forehead. "It's been a real pleasure, Azrel, being in your head. Gaining your trust. Making you think you were crazy." He chuckled gently before his eyes looked dangerous for a moment. "But I have been fucking with your life since the day you left the cave." His eyes lit up with a hateful gleam. "On the Ambuel River."

My breath caught in my throat as I remembered that day. It was the day that had defined me for as long as I could remember.

Hathum looked at my lips as he gently began to run his fingertips over them. "That bad feeling? That Shadow that grew in your mind just before the branch fell?" He smiled sickly. "That was me." My heart was racing. "That was the first time you ever felt my power being used, something you'd only feel as The White Warrior." He grinned evilly. "Also, your tremendous torture at the hands of the otherwise peaceful people of The Pitt? Me also." He scrunched up his nose almost playfully. "Their minds were easy to get into to make them do the things they did to you. And that, well, that was just fun."

He was enjoying this. I truly hadn't understood evil until this very moment. I scanned every memory I had in a split second, and then rescanned them as I tried to recall everything that had ever happened in my existence and analyze it with this new knowledge that Hathum was directly responsible for all of it. I had tried so hard to hide from him since the beginning. My father told me to hide. Beldorn told me to hide. And all of that effort had been wasted because Hathum had known all along.

How did you get in? I asked, realizing we were in my mind right now and, because Hathum was the master of mind corruption, he was hearing my thoughts. *I thought it was impossible.*

A corner of his lip went up in a smirk. "For your father, the *real* White Warrior, it was impossible because he wasn't human. Not until Unha turned him into one as punishment for his cowardice." Unha. I knew that name. She was one of the Light Gods, like Kadoma was. "You however, *are* a human, with natural born Shadow in you that I can access. Every human is vulnerable to me at some point in their existence. Yours was at Rocksheloc, at your lowest, when you actually gave up and decided to stop fighting. I was able to slip in easily."

I thought you were too weak to be that powerful, I choked out.

"Oh, I am," he said, and then grinned at my slight surprise. "But my God is not." I swallowed heavily, only to swallow some blood and little chunks of flesh that coated my throat as they slid down. "See, I've been trying to kill you your whole life, before you could reach any kind of potential as The White Warrior; hence, the river and the torture at The Pitt. But, unfortunately, you proved more resilient than any human I'd ever encountered." He shrugged a shoulder. "Naturally, I knew then that at least one of the Lighter siblings was helping you along. So in turn, I began contact with my Shadow God Elral. He's the one that came up with this brilliant plan."

You haven't won yet, I thought, but it was shaky, with no conviction whatsoever.

He smiled down at me and nodded. "Oh yes I have. See, no one even knows I'm in here. They think it's The White Warrior." He pinched my nose like he was playing with a child. "Just like you did." He leaned down toward my face again and dropped his voice low. "So here's what's about to happen. I left a piece of myself in you as soon as I was able to get into your mind in Rocksheloc, claiming to be your alter ego The White Warrior. That allowed me to give my body over as a vessel for Elral, and still survive...in you." My heart stopped and my eyes went wide. He smiled evilly. "I hope you like green because this place is the last thing you're ever going to see."

My breath started coming in ragged pants, and panic squeezed my chest as I began to realize that this was it. This was real. I jerked my shoulders, trying to sit up, but the invisible force was still on me, pinning me all the way down to my wrists. I floundered about with what little bit of room I could, but it wasn't much at all. I tried to access my magic, but I was empty of it. There was nothing there.

"Your efforts are useless," he said. "I created this hiding place, this prison in your mind before you even left The Pitt, with what little access I had because of your natural born human Shadow. You have no power here, I do."

I was panting, my heart was racing, my temples were throbbing. I threw my head back and I screamed helplessly in frustration. I was stuck. I was stuck! *I was stuck!*

"Oh shh shh shh shh," Hathum cooed softly and began to caress my cheek with the back of his knuckles. "Don't worry, darling. You didn't stand a chance. It's a plan that has been set in motion, starting with me and ending with Elral, since the day your father was turned into a human."

I breathed through clenched teeth as I lowered my eyes to meet his as defiantly as I could manage, which only made him smile.

"I've known about you your entire life and have been planning accordingly since that day." His brows dropped curiously as he looked upward in thought. "I think your father knew it, too."

My weak struggling ceased immediately at the mention of my father. Hathum met my eyes again and smiled.

"Which is probably why he didn't let you leave the cave until you could hit a bullseye with an arrow."

Tears filled my eyes once again as I remembered all the moments with my father when I had given him hell for being so overprotective. The times I had begged him to let me go outside and play at the stream but he never did. I remembered the first and only real big fight we'd ever gotten into about it. I was fourteen and I hurled insults at him, and the cave, and how it was a dungeon and a prison for me. I snuck out that night, planning to run away, but Ortheldo had followed me. Even at eleven years old, he'd been wise beyond his years, and he'd talked me into coming back. Thinking back, I realized now that my father had known. He'd known Hathum was after me—not *going* to be after me someday, but *was* after me.

Why didn't you kill me at the cave then? I asked.

Hathum looked down at me like I was daft. "How would that have helped me get my hands on your father's Sword?" He shook his head and held up a finger at me, looking at me condescendingly. "See, the main thing you learn from being an immortal is patience, the long game." He gestured with his hands. "You slowly set up your pieces; you take a few hits, sacrifice a little here and there, until you get your opponent right where you want her." He smiled down at me. "And that Azrel, is right here."

My chest was rising and falling rapidly. Hathum's eyes flicked down. He suddenly moaned and rested his hands over my breasts, pushing them together and groping them before he leaned down pressing his mouth against them. I felt his hot breath through my shirt and his nose against my chest.

When he sat up, he was breathing heavily. He moaned again as he leaned down to press his mouth against mine. It was firm, but surprisingly gentle—until he slipped his tongue past my lips. As soon as it touched the tip of mine, a burning flash of pain erupted in my entire head. I cried out and tried to jerk away from him, but he slapped his hands on each side of my head, holding me in place. I screamed around his mouth as best I could as his nails dug into my scalp, but it was a pitiful muffled sound. His tongue flicked lightly against mine, each time sending the burning pain through my skull. Squeezing my eyes shut, I had no choice but to endure it. He burned me for a long time—or it seemed, but time didn't seem to exist here.

He threw his head back and sucked in a big gasp of air when he finally pulled his mouth away from mine. He looked down at my face and licked his lips elaborately with a twisted expression hatred and adoration on his face. "I'm certainly going to have a good time with you here."

I needed to buy myself some time to figure a way out of here. *Was it you in my mind the whole time?* I asked. *Were you my other personality?*

Hathum grinned broadly. "You bet I was. I was slipping in and out of your mind before you and Ortheldo even reunited." He smiled. "Who do you think sent him the necklace in the first place?" My eyes went wide again. "Who do you think held those meetings with your protectors here? All me. It was all me playing my little games with you, getting you right here, where you would be done for. Little pushes and nudges and prods to get you right here with me, defeated." His grin got even broader. "Want to hear the kicker?" He asked. "Well, one of my favorite ones anyway."

I swallowed heavily, not really wanting to, but needing to. He slowly leaned down toward me again like he was going to kiss me a second time, but he shifted over to my ear and whispered softly. "Your brother is your true Deralilya." My eyes went wide. "*I* chose Acalith." He sat up, throwing his head back and laughing. "And you killed him with Shadow magic!" he howled. He was hysterical, barely able to contain himself. "Oh! If only I had been awake for that. This war would be *over!*"

Rabryn was my lead protector. He was the one who had so desperately tried to reach me when I turned my magic black. He'd known. Even if he wasn't aware of what he was, he knew. He'd still tried to protect me then. He'd always tried to protect me, even back in The Pitt. He was the best at protecting me.

My brother never left my side, I said, trying to muster some strength through anger, though I was completely helpless. *Why did you even waste your time choosing Acalith?*

"Waste my time? Oh no. It's all part of the game. Rabryn couldn't know he actually had some power under his belt. He's already powerful enough," Hathum said with a sneer, which was the first sign of something besides arrogance and glee I'd seen in him since I got here. "If you had named Rabryn the Deralilya, he would have taken full advantage of the responsibly and power and would have detected me inside of you in an instant!" He smiled again. "I handpicked Acalith because in all of Casdanarus, she was the one that was the most like you; that meant you two wouldn't get along, and she wouldn't look so closely. Plus, she was all stirred up about who she was loyal to, you or the White Warrior and so on, which was also part of the game to keep me hidden in here. Everything, *everything* was done to get you and me, right here. Oh," he said as if just remembering something, "and if you're wondering about her magical ability to teleport," he grinned, "all me. I saw in her mind where she wanted to go and moved her with my own magic." His smile made me want to claw his eyeballs out of his skull. "A woman like that, a stranger, could never love you, or know you, or want to protect you the way Rabryn does."

Did, I thought sadly. I meant it as a private thought, but here Hathum heard everything.

Hathum hummed softly and leaned down again, resting his arm across my chest, and propped his head up with his other hand. The point of his elbow dug into my bones as he put weight behind it. "Yes, I see that you and Rabryn are on the outs since that incident in the woods." He clenched his teeth and leaned down towards my face again. "And I'm really, *really* going to enjoy driving the wedge tighter between you two until I drive him off completely."

I couldn't help the tiny smirk that came to my face in this small victory. Hathum noticed it, and his brows dropped in confusion. *You don't know my brother*, I told him matter-of-factly.

"Oh, I know it will be tough to drive him off," he said casually and then smiled again, which made my minute bit of confidence drain away. "But it'll happen. Especially when he finds out what I have in store for all your friends once I take control of your body. Speaking of which," he said sitting up, "they're going to be expecting you to wake up soon. Well," he said with an evil glint in his eyes, "they're going to be expecting *me* to wake up soon."

My heart jumped up into my throat, which was the only sign of life in me, as weak as it was. *So what happens now?* I asked.

"Well," he said with a heavy sigh, "I'm going to go out there and be you, and you're going to die in here." He gave me another horrible grin. "At which point I will then fully take you over and take hold of your Sword." He bared his teeth in an arrogant, animalistic grin. "And then I win."

My brows dropped in confusion. *Why don't you just take it as soon as you get out of here?*

He rolled his eyes. "While you, the White Warrior, is still

alive, I can't. I'm not pure Shadow in here with you. I have your Light to deal with," he said, annoyed. "But you'll die here soon enough."

Why don't you just kill me now? I asked, actually curious.

He looked down at me again like I was an imbecile. "Because your Light Gods will feel an act of evil like that and retaliate." He shrugged again. "Elral isn't strong enough to take them yet, but he will be. And if you're not dead by then, I'll be back to make sure you are." He stood up and started to walk away. "I'm keeping you alive as a distraction for your Gods until Elral is ready."

I actually managed a small smirk. *So you don't know how long you're going to have to pretend to be me out there?*

He looked over his shoulder at me curiously. "No. Why?"

With what miniscule strength I could, I strained slightly against the force that was pinning me to the floor. *My brother and Ortheldo will know it's not me. They'll find out it's you,* I said slowly and dangerously.

Hathum just smiled at me. "We'll see," he said, and then continued walking until he faded from sight.

I allowed myself to go limp once that invisible pressure was lifted off of me. Then all I could do was clutch my stomach and curl up into a tight ball on my side while I sobbed uncontrollably. I shook violently as I cried every ounce of everything I ever held back. I'd failed. I'd completely and utterly failed my father. I'd failed at being the White Warrior. I'd failed the world. The Shadow Gods were going to rule again, and I was stuck here, a prisoner in my own mind.

Rabryn, I sobbed in thought. *Ortheldo. Don't make me a liar. Please, please know it's not me out there.* My entire body shook with my sobs. *Please know it's not me and come get me. Please. Please.* I curled up into a tighter ball as I sunk into a sea of despair. *Please.*

SIXTEEN

HATHUM

My eyes opened and I looked around at a bedroom full of people. Azrel's friends. Most of them were talking quietly among themselves and hadn't noticed I was awake. I closed my eyes once more and tried to put myself in the mindset of where I had left Azrel before taking over her body.

My God, Elral, had just left Acalith. No, we were further than that. Azrel had just used the Anarran Gem to heal her army. That's right. The Red Flower, Addredoc, had brought her army to Spar Ridges and a battle had happened. Oh yes, and Addredoc had no more magic. I had to tighten my jaw to keep from laughing out loud at that. Okay, so that would probably be everyone's first concern; Addredoc dying from magic loss. I had to be prepared to handle that as Azrel would. What else?

Rabryn hated her. I had to remember to keep him at distance. He would really create problems for me if he stuck around too long. She and Ortheldo were patching things up since she killed Rabryn in the woods, so I would have to be affectionate toward him. But Ortheldo was going to cause problems for me, too, if he stuck around. I had to figure out a way inconspicuously to get rid of him.

She had just reunited with her original crew after nearly a month—Lisswilla, Reese, and my idiot twin brother, Yarin. It would be interesting interacting with him again as Azrel. I resisted the urge to sneer as I thought about him. I might have to get rid of him, too. He might not know Azrel that well, but he knew me damn well. He could cause problems.

I sighed softly. Life would just be easier if I could get rid of them all, really. But how could I do that without being obvious about it and blowing my cover? Natural causes would work—and by natural, I meant killed in battle. They were all resilient and fiercely strong warriors, though and, as my own past attempts had proven, extremely hard to kill. So how could I overwhelm them quickly and efficiently, while still sticking to Azrel's original mission of fighting my God? I felt my mouth working slightly as I thought about it and had to bite the inside of my cheek so they wouldn't know I was awake yet.

Well, Azrel had lost a lot of soldiers in that battle. She'd likely want to replenish her ranks. My eyes snapped wide open as it dawned on me. I knew what to do.

"Azrel," I heard someone say in a breath of relief.

I looked to my right and saw Ortheldo coming toward the bed. He leaned over me and rested his lips on my—or what he thought were Azrel's—lips. I immediately tensed up since I'd never been kissed tenderly like this before, but quickly realized Azrel wouldn't do that. I forced myself to relax and brought my hand up to his cheek.

He pulled away and looked down at me lovingly as he took my hand into his. "How are you feeling?"

What would Azrel say? "I'm fine," I replied and repressed a flinch at hearing her voice when I spoke. Ortheldo waited expectantly. There was more. What else?

I scanned her memories of similar situations and tried to figure something out she would say. "My army," I said, remembering that it was her healing of them that had caused her to pass out. "Are they okay? How many survived?"

Ortheldo smiled down at me. "All of them," he said tenderly. "Thanks to you."

I nodded. This was going to be more difficult than I'd thought. I had to get these people who knew Azrel so well away from me, and I needed to do it now—but I had to be gentle so I didn't raise suspicion.

"Listen," I said. I sat up, swinging my legs over the edge of the bed, and looked at all of them in turn except Rabryn, whom I didn't suffer a glance at. "I still lost a lot of soldiers in that battle, so I think we need to keep recruiting."

"But Azrel," Reese said, stepping forward. "We just reunited. We have five and a half million strong!" He gave me a sad look that reminded me of a wounded animal. "Can we just stay together for a few days before we separate again?"

Azrel smiled a lot. I knew that from her memories. "No, no," I said lightly with a smile. "I meant all of us should head out to recruit together."

"What do you mean?" Acalith asked, sitting on the edge of the bed near me.

I felt the hairs on my arms stand up and looked to where I felt eyes on me. It was Rabryn. He was glaring hard at me with his arms crossed. I returned the glare, but it didn't even faze him. That had better not be suspicion in his eyes already.

"Can I help you with something," I asked snidely, "or is there some other reason you're staring at me like that?"

He didn't even flinch. "I'm wondering why you haven't asked about Addredoc yet."

Damn it! My eyes went wide and I quickly looked at Ortheldo with the best pleading eyes I could muster. "What is it? He's okay, isn't he?"

Damn! Now Ortheldo looked at me with suspicion—well-hidden suspicion, but suspicion nonetheless. "He's *dying*, Azrel."

"Azrel," someone else said, saving me from trying to come up with something. I looked over and Lisswilla stepped forward, looking agonized. What a bunch of pansy-ass, overemotional whiners this lot was! "I was thinking. Do you remember how I told you about how your father saved me when I lost my magic? How he returned my life force without returning my Sallybreath Flowers or my magic?"

I searched Azrel's memories and nodded when it popped up. "Yes, I remember."

"Maybe you could do the same thing to save Addredoc."

I sighed and bowed my head. I knew Azrel's answer to this one; it was a common excuse for her. "I don't think I can," I said feigning regret. "I'm not crowned, Lisswilla. I don't have the kind of power my father had. Not yet."

Lisswilla started wringing his hands. "We have to do something."

For some reason, as I scanned some of Azrel's memories, I felt the need to make a joke here. Azrel joked around sometimes. "Since when do you give a rat's ass about Addredoc dying?" I said lightly. "If I recall, you threatened to kill him yourself not long ago."

The strange, awkward hush that came over the room in that moment made me think the joke may have been ill-timed or that I'd underestimated how much Addredoc meant to these people. I dared a glance at Rabryn and saw his eyes were narrowed into slits.

That either meant he was really pissed at Azrel or he was already picking up on the fact I was not her.

"Look!" I said, raising my hands and standing. "I can't help Addredoc in the condition I'm in." I sighed and then softened my tone. "But there might be someone who can." They glanced around at each other curiously.

This was perfect. Yes. This would fit in nicely with my plan. People of Light were always itching to throw themselves into the paths of arrows for each other. Addredoc's condition was exactly how I was going to get them in the paths of my proverbial arrows right now.

I sighed with feigned regret and glanced at the floor before looking at them all again. "But it won't be easy, and you won't like it."

"I don't care," Reese said with gentle confidence and stepped up next to Lisswilla.

Lisswilla was already nodding. "We'll do it. Whatever it takes."

Most of the others nodded along with them. I looked at Ortheldo, whose word carried about as much weight as Azrel's did in this tiny company. He looked up at me and nodded as well.

I sighed and tried to hide my glee. "A person who might be able to save Addredoc will likely be found in the same place I want to try to recruit from."

"Where?" Rabryn barked from the corner.

I gave the bedroom a final once over. "We can go to Tribletwel."

It was deathly quiet for a few moments. I wasn't even sure anyone was breathing. It got very uncomfortable very quickly. I squirmed a little. I wondered for an instant if all of them could see right through me now. Would Azrel do something this crazy to save someone she loved? I thought so. But now I wasn't so sure. Not with the way her crew was looking at me.

"What the hell is wrong with you?" Rabryn suddenly shouted and stormed toward me so forcefully that Reese and Lisswilla had to hold him back. "Are you trying to kill us all?"

"Look Rabryn," I managed with a little force, "Tribletwel is an incredibly vast, untapped well of ridiculous magical power— some of it *ancient* power. Magic users from every damn century are imprisoned in there. Do I really need to remind you of the massive disadvantage I'm at with a Shadow God on the loose now?"

Yeah! Now I was getting the hang of being Azrel.

"Azrel," Ortheldo said stepping up to my side. "You *know* the kinds of people that are in there!"

I looked around the room again, holding my arms out to my sides. "Do you have any idea how many innocent magic users are in there right now?" I asked. "Magic users that Hathum framed to get them out of the way before I could recruit them. Norka, for one."

Rabryn instantly froze at the mention of his sorcerer friend, whom I'd put in Tribletwel myself.

"Remember him?" I asked, which I quickly realized was a bad move because Rabryn's teeth clenched and his eyebrows drew tightly together. "There are thousands more like him locked up in there." I managed a confident smile. "They see me, and they will come running to my ranks." I looked around the room again. "And one of them just might have the power to save Addredoc's life."

"Rabryn," Reese said softly, stepping in front of him. He and Rabryn looked at each other. "Please? We have to try to save Addredoc and we need you. Please."

Rabryn sighed before looking at me. "Fine. I'll teleport us to the barrier."

I nodded once.

"What about your army?" Acalith asked out of the blue.

I met her eyes. "What about them?"

She looked at me, confused. "Where do you want to send them? We still have a Shadow army to deal with."

I rubbed my forehead roughly with my fingertips, wondering if I could slaughter all of them somehow without it being noticed. *Not yet. Not yet.* Elral was not strong enough yet. Elral would be capturing Godel next, recruiting the millions that refused to join the White Warrior's army. "Where has that army been spotted?"

"Heading toward Godel."

"Well, send the army south to head him off."

"To Godel?" Acalith asked, astonished, as she stood. "It will take them more than half a year to get there from here without Addredoc to teleport them."

"Well," I said shrugging, "they'd better leave quickly then, huh?" They all gave me confused looks. I realized I had to do more backtracking. "My only concern right now," I said forcefully, "is Addredoc." I let that go around the room for a moment. "Now let's go."

With a final glance at each other, all of them headed out of the bedroom to give the orders to the army and take care of their respective duties, whatever they might be. Rabryn was the last to leave, and his narrowed eyes lingered on me a little too long. I felt so uncomfortable that I wondered if being near him for any length of time was wise. I was beginning to doubt it, as he closed the bedroom door behind him.

"Meet back here in four hours!" I called just as it shut.

No, it was not wise to stay near Rabryn too long. I had to think of something else.

———

When I heard the bedroom door open again four hours later, I was ready. Still, I couldn't suppress the cringe that came over me when I felt that blasted Gold Flowers' eyes on me.

"We're waiting for you," Rabryn said flatly.

I took in a deep breath and continued to look out the window. "I'm not going with you."

"Excuse me?"

I turned and saw him flinch when I laid my eyes on him. "I'm not going with you."

"You're not? So what are you doing?"

"Why do you care?" I tinged my voice with annoyance and slightly narrowed my eyes.

Rabryn squirmed a little under that question. He hadn't yet forgiven, or even trusted, Azrel since she'd murdered him. That things were very unsettled between the two worked out perfectly for me because Rabryn, if he looked close enough, would likely be able to detect it was me—not his sister—in Azrel's body. Though he didn't look closely now, I knew if I journeyed with them through Tribletwel, he'd eventually notice.

Rabryn's lip twitched and his eyes narrowed. "Because it's Tribletwel, and we need all the help we can get. Addredoc's life is at stake."

"And I'm sure you'll do a fine job getting someone to help

him."

His eyes went wide before they narrowed again. "What is wrong with you?"

"What's wrong with *me?*" I asked, pretending to be appalled. "Boy, don't even start."

He shook his head with a look of disgust and sadness. "It's like I don't even know you anymore."

I gave him an exaggerated grin. "Welcome to the real world, kid. Where people are awful and everything else is even worse."

His eyes went wide, and I felt something small and invisible penetrate my skull. I realized it was Rabryn, unconsciously acting on his instinct—one of the three ways his magic worked—that Azrel really wasn't herself. A short shake of my head disbursed the queer feeling, and I put a thin shield of my own magic over my mind just in case his instinct became more forceful. He'd get in my head and see Azrel with ease if I wasn't careful. I couldn't risk it, not before Elral was strong enough to defeat the Light Gods.

"Who are you?" he said suddenly.

I nearly blanched, fearing he'd spotted me somehow, but realized he wasn't actually asking who I was. He was just stating that he didn't know who Azrel was anymore.

I took a step toward him, only to see him take a step back. I nearly grinned but had to hold it back because Azrel wouldn't. "I'm the one with a Shadow God on my ass and bigger issues to deal with than one lost soldier."

Rabryn brows drew together and his fists clenched. "Addredoc? Is that all he is to you? Just another soldier? Is that all *any* of us are to you?"

This was going swimmingly! Better than I had hoped. I'd wanted to drive a wedge deeper between Azrel and her brother, and he was just making it too easy!

I looked up at the ceiling, pretending to think about it for an instant. "Um"—I met his eyes—"yeah. Pretty much."

The Salynn was on me lightning fast, with one hand wrapped around my throat. He pushed me backwards so forcefully that I heard the glass break in the window I'd been looking out a moment ago.

"Who are you?!" he screamed in my face. His blue eyes burned into me like a flame. I could have sworn I saw them even flicker, like blue fire, as he looked down at me.

I felt what could have been a pang of glee come from Azrel in that moment, like she knew what was happening out here, and was silently taunting me with "I told you so."

How had I screwed up? How? No. This had to be salvageable. It had to be! I couldn't fail my God. I couldn't!

"Answer me!" he screamed slapping his palm against the glass causing it to spider web under his hand.

An idea came. Yes! The same cover that had fooled Azrel for months would certainly fool him, and my life would get about a thousand times easier.

"All right. All right!" I cried out, knocking his hand away me. He wasn't holding too tightly, I guessed, because it was still his sister's throat. I rested my hand over where he'd held me and glared up at him. "I'm The White Warrior."

He froze, astonished, for a moment. "You bitch!" he screamed. "Let me talk to Azrel!"

"I can't."

"Right now!"

"I can't!"

"*Now!*"

"She's dead!" I yelled, and instantly the air was sucked out of the room.

It was so quiet that I could hear Rabryn's heart thumping. I'd never seen anyone's face drain of so much color so fast. He became a ghost in front of me. I half expected him to vanish before my eyes.

"I'm sorry," I said more softly, trying to mimic compassion. "But it's true."

Rabryn stumbled backwards a few steps. He turned away, presumably to leave, but his legs buckled. He caught himself on the corner of the bed as his knees hit the floor. I watched his back rise and fall with deep, deliberate breaths, as if he were forcing his body to recall the process of air.

This had worked like a charm.

"Humans can't tangle with Gods and survive," I explained gently, though I couldn't keep from smirking a little at his back. "And Azrel was just a human." Rabryn's breathing sped up. "She used too much power in a short amount of time—she just had nothing left, and her life force slipped away."

Rabryn began to breathe strangely, the sound a mix between a sob and a groan, and his entire body shook worse than a leaf in a windstorm.

"I'm truly sorry."

I felt Azrel's despair thicken until I could barely sense her at all, and I grinned broadly. *I told you, Azrel,* I said to her softly. *You are defeated.*

Don't miss the next adventure

EMBERS
UNDER
THE ASH
the white warrior series: book five

Nichelle Rae

Coming soon...

Find me online!

Facebook: www.facebook.com/NichelleRaeAuthor

Twitter: @Nichelle_Writes

Web: www.nichellewrites.com

Email: Nichelle_Rae@yahoo.com

www.ingramcontent.com/pod-product-compliance
Lightning Source LLC
Chambersburg PA
CBHW031316120626
46554CB00001BA/433